Whew! what a ride!

I've enjoyed all of the books in this series and this one was no different. You're quickly pulled in to not only see if they finish this crazy race, but also to see how they're going to overcome what put them at odds in the first place. A bit more suspense woven through from a crazy ex, and you've got a great story you won't want to put down.

I'm so excited about the next story in this series too. Valiant, Texas, is a place you'll want to visit again and again.

AMY ANGUISH

I read this book through Kindle Unlimited and I love it. It's written in perfect deep Point of view so that I could picture everything happening. The characters are well-rounded and bicker while secretly infatuated with each other as they attempt to win a Texas canoe race to save their jobs. And it's filled with plenty of tension that kept me turning pages as the two characters fall in love. A wonderful romance read.

DEBRA ALLARD

This novella entertained from page one! A prank gone awry hilariously lands the two main characters in a grueling canoe race down an unpredictable river. Their opposite personalities in close proximity create humorous situations that are relatable and entertaining. I loved how the author masterfully developed and matured the two opposing characters thru a difficult 4 day race. The bulk of the novella centers around the Texas Water Safari, an annual race occurring on the Guadalupe River, where people across the nation compete. I would very much recommend this adventurous, sweetly romantic book!

NANCY ROBISON

What a treat to read this book! I really enjoyed the dynamic between the two main characters, Nat and Sy, as they figured out how to survive the Texas Water Safari. They don't call it the world's toughest canoe race for nothing! Mary Pat Johns brings the events of the race to life - sometimes humorous, sometimes hair-raising - so that you feel you're right there alongside Nat and Sy as they fight both the river trying to beat them and the love blooming between them. It kept me turning the pages because I wanted to know what would happen next!

C. L. KESS

Published by Scrivenings Press LLC
15 Lucky Lane
Morrilton, Arkansas 72110
https://ScriveningsPress.com

Printed in the United States of America

Paperback ISBN 978-1-64917-482-6
eBook ISBN 978-1-64917-483-3

Editors: Regina Rudd Merrick and Heidi Glick

Cover by Linda Fulkerson, www.bookmarketinggraphics.com

All characters are fictional, and any resemblance to real people, either factual or historical, is purely coincidental.

For Nancy and Phillip. Do you remember the year I gave each of you a T-shirt with the phrase, "Mom's Favorite"? It's still true. You've grown into such lovely adults, I'm doubly blessed to be the one you call Mama.

ROMANCE IN VALIANT BOOK FOUR

WAITIN'
ON
PAIGE

Enjoy!
Rescue
+ Redemption

Mary Pat Johns

MARY PAT JOHNS

Scrivenings
PRESS
Quench your thirst for story.
www.ScriveningsPress.com

"I know that my Redeemer lives, and that in the end he will stand upon the earth. And after my skin has been destroyed, yet in my flesh I will see God; I myself will see him with my own eyes—I, and not another. How my heart yearns within me!" Job 19: 25-27

CHAPTER ONE

"Jesse won't miss his wedding day, Brenna." Of all the things that concerned Paige Munoz about this wedding, a no-show groom wasn't one of them. At least until a few minutes ago, but she dared not let it show. Her job was to convince the bride her wedding would be perfect.

Standing behind the bride, Paige gazed into the mirror and addressed the panic in Brenna's eyes. "Jesse's crazy about you. He wanted to get married six months ago."

The renovated space they were in served as the prep room for the bridal wedding party. It adjoined the barn, and despite the copious amounts of flowers everywhere, Paige still detected a faint horse smell. She stifled a grimace. This was Texas. Rural odors abounded.

She spared a critical look at her dress, adjusting the tiny spaghetti straps on each shoulder.

"Does the dress fit?" Brenna stopped dabbing at her face to cast Paige another anxious look. "Are those spaghetti straps comfortable? They make me feel like I'm wearing a nightgown." She fanned her cheeks with the program. "Are you sure the AC is working? It's hot in here." She swiveled around on the bench, green eyes darting to the vent.

"I checked. The AC is going full-blast. Nice and cool in the main area. As far as my dress goes, you were smart to let the bridesmaids choose their design—I adore mine. The aquamarine color is stunning. Perfect for all the bridesmaids." She leaned down with her face next to Brenna's. "But you, my dear, are exquisite." Paige meant every word. Her friend was beautiful on any given day, but today, she was radiant.

A tiny moan emitted from Brenna's throat. She hugged Paige tightly. "Thank you. Guess I've got a case of pre-wedding jitters."

Careful not to crinkle Brenna's wedding gown, Paige untangled from the hug, keeping a hand on her friend's shoulder. "I've got this. We've done our due diligence with every aspect of your wedding. Your job is to enjoy it."

"Yep. You need to chill, baby girl. It's your day. Cain't shine like the sun if you're upset."

Spiky heels stabbed the floor as a mountain of aquamarine blue ventured into the room. Paige thought Dicey, the other bridesmaid besides Vi, was intent on making herself a spectacle. She'd chosen the most voluminous dress, swishing her skirts around like a dark, fluffy bird. Already tall, she'd insisted on a beehive updo. Brenna and Paige exchanged a knowing look as Dicey joined Brenna on the bench.

Dicey looked dubiously at the neat row of makeup lined across the small table. Organization was part of Brenna's DNA. "Ain't none of that gonna work for me."

"Well, not the foundation, silly. Here, try some eye shadow." Brenna handed her a peacock blue shade, absorbed in the moment.

A relieved sigh gently swooshed out of Paige's lips as she

watched the two women. How they had forged a solid friendship with such drastically different personalities remained an ongoing miracle.

Vi entered the room. Her normally vibrant coloring had a greenish cast. She tilted her head toward the door as her eyes bored into Paige. Without a word, Paige followed her out.

In the hall, Vi faced her. "Update on the groomsmen. Nothing to be concerned about, I'm sure. Except we've momentarily lost track of Jesse."

"How?" The word squeaked past Paige's fast-closing throat.

"He didn't show up when he was supposed to, and he's not answering his phone. Rory's gone to find him."

The breath Paige swallowed hurt going down. "Don't tell Brenna—her chief worry today is he will freak out at the last minute and not want to marry her."

Vi snorted indelicately. "As if. She's been the one with cold feet—not him."

"I know, right? Now she's here and ..." She couldn't bring herself to finish the thought. "He's just running late"—Jesse never ran late—"or something has happened ..." Not a good thought either.

"I'm sure Rory will find him. Or he'll turn up all apologetic, sidetracked by some minor detail." The reassuring words didn't match Vi's drawn expression.

"Okay. They're doing makeup now. We'll just wait in here until Jesse and Rory arrive. It's just them, right? The others are here?"

"Yes." Vi's terse answer left plenty unsaid.

Jesse, where are you?

Twenty-eight endless minutes later, they sat in the makeshift dressing room with no update. Paige was doing her best to appear calm, as if a wedding on hold was a normal occurrence. Dicey had given Paige a scathing look when she came back into the room. As if it were her fault Jesse was running late. Bless her big heart, though, Dicey had speedily changed gears and wheedled Brenna into helping her apply a pair of audacious fake eyelashes. The woman deserved a trophy for the longest-running eyelash application. Brenna's hands and mind had stayed busy the entire time. Still, the pressure in the room persisted. Alive. Breathing. Rising to combustion.

A flurry of knocking sounded at the door. A small man wearing a royal blue hoodie and jeans burst in. Not exactly wedding attire, but the hoodie looked new. Paige gaped as he brushed aside her objection, then loped over to where Brenna and Dicey sat.

"What are you doing here, Emilio?" Brenna's question could have chipped glass.

Emilio panted, hands on his knees, then looked up. "I'm sure Jesse's on his way. Boss wouldn't miss this for nothin', you know ... everybody's cool with it."

Brenna's face blanched. She dropped the tiny tube of eyelash glue she'd been holding and shot a look of betrayal at Paige. "He's not here? What time is it?" She reached for her phone, but Dicey snatched it away.

Paige fumed over Emilio's unwelcome news, then interjected in what she hoped was a calm voice. "There's plenty of time."

Brenna saw through her indirect answer. Fists clenched, she turned away from Paige and snapped, "What time is it, *Dice*?"

Dicey was waggling a finger at Emilio, who managed to appear angelically sorry. "Get out of here, fool."

Emilio did a double take, then backed away with caution, not taking his eyes off Dicey's bristling form.

When the door shut behind him, Paige watched helplessly as two huge tears rolled down Brenna's cheeks. "Why isn't Jesse here?" The hurt unfurling across her face was too much to bear.

Paige's eyes filled. She opened her mouth, then closed it again. Her normal self-possession had deserted her. She had no clue how to address this catastrophe. Through the roar in her ears, she heard or felt her phone ring. She turned away from Brenna to fish it out of her pocket. Rory's name flashed across the screen.

Thick-fingered with fear, she clicked it on. "Give me good news, boss."

"It's Jesse. We're on our way. Let me talk to Brenna."

She felt faint, but motioned to Brenna and mouthed *Jesse*.

Brenna took the phone. "Jesse?" The hesitancy in her voice had Paige sniffing back more tears. *God, get them through this.*

She couldn't hear Jesse's end of the conversation, but Brenna's body language morphed from stiff to relaxed as she listened to what had to be the mother of all apologies. She even giggled at one point. Paige wanted to cry with relief.

The conversation wasn't long, but Brenna gave Paige a trembly thumbs up when she clicked off. "They'll be here in ten minutes."

Vi had slipped back into the room, looking paler than ever. Her eyes brimmed with the question they all wanted to ask. Why was Jesse late for his wedding?

Lips sealed tight, Brenna swung around to the mirror, frowned at her face, and declared to Dicey. "I'm getting married today. Help me repair this teary mess."

Elation filled Paige where fear and sadness had reigned only moments before. Now that the groom was on his way, it would be smooth sailing.

"AND NOW, you may kiss the bride," Pastor Mike announced, his eyes gentle, a smile tugging his lips sideways. Jesse leaned toward Brenna, anticipation lighting his eyes.

Tavo Morales was happy for them, especially now that the inauspicious start to the wedding seemed smoothed over. However, a deep disquiet had lodged in his heart, and he couldn't seem to jar it loose. His close-up view as a groomsman wasn't helping. Once upon a time, he thought marriage would be his ticket, too. But that was back in high school, for pity's sake. Before the only girl he'd ever loved up and left him.

The expected kiss was over, but Jess leaned in for another one. *Oh, here we go.* Tavo's stomach clenched. He wasn't sure how much more he could take. When Brenna shifted closer to Jesse, the space she'd vacated filled with Paige. The tiny crease between her brows assured Tavo she was as jangled as him, though she'd never admit it. She gazed at him for a moment before looking elsewhere.

Tavo, Rory, and Jesse had remained close since high school, and the girls were best friends as well. He didn't know the other bridesmaid, a tall dark woman, but Rafe, the third groomsman, was Jesse's cousin. They weren't a couple outside of the wedding, so he didn't feel like the odd man out. Until he remembered Rory and Vi had tied the knot a few months ago. Today, Jesse and Brenna were following the same path. Happily ever after. Tavo's jaw ached from grinding his molars.

After living in San Antonio, then Frisco, he'd moved back to take care of unfinished business, the first being his relationship with Paige. But it had been twelve years. Since he'd returned, he'd not made one stitch of progress. It had stayed the old proverbial one step forward dance. Only for every tiny step forward, there had been multiple steps back. Tavo couldn't crack the just-friends veneer Paige wore twenty-four/seven, but there had to be a way. Even though he hadn't maintained a close relationship with God, he knew—he just knew—this was the right step. Somehow, he would reclaim her love. *Please, Lord. Let it be sooner rather than later.*

CHAPTER TWO

R elieved when Jesse finally ended the extra smooch, Tavo and everyone else looked at the preacher. Pastor Mike's smile burst into a grin. "And now, ladies and gentlemen—"

Tavo had noticed Vi sway slightly during the ceremony. Probably wasn't feeling too good, hot as it was. He tugged at the stiff tux collar. That little bump of hers was cute, not that he knew much about pregnant women. Beside him, Rory jerked to attention, hyper-focused on Vi. Yeah, his wife didn't look so great. And now she was floating downward into a puddle of blue dress. Rory dashed around the preacher, but it was the tall dark gal who caught her under the arms and kept her from face-planting on the rustic floor.

Tavo's feet seemed stuck, but Paige had turned at the commotion. Now *she* looked ill. Her hands crept up and cradled her jaws as if they hurt. Her look of shock loosened his feet. He strode over to her, his boots thumping an erratic rhythm on the straw-covered floor. The tall woman had gently lowered Vi to the ground. She came to quickly, looking dazed and irritated. Rory stroked her arm, murmuring things nobody else could hear. Brenna covered her mouth and started for Vi, but Jesse gently pulled her back. The wedding seemed forgotten.

Pastor Mike moved around the podium. Squatting next to Vi, he calmly asked a couple of questions, as if a bridesmaid fainting at a wedding was no big deal. Rory helped her up and kept his arm around her. At Rory's nod, Pastor Mike said something that made the audience laugh, then he motioned everyone back into their places.

"Where were we? Oh, the most important part," he announced to more laughter. "Ladies and gentlemen, I present to you, Mr. and Mrs. Jesse Jacobs." Tavo's frozen lips thawed into a reluctant smile. He clapped and hooted along with everyone else. Louder.

With a quick backward look, as if to make sure everything was all right, Jesse jaunted down the petal-laden aisle with Brenna possessively tucked into his side. Rory whispered into Vi's ear, then swung her into his arms and carried her down the aisle. The audience tittered, but Rory's face was bent toward his wife in their private world.

Tavo swallowed hard as the woman he'd never stopped loving glided toward him. Paige took his elbow with firmness, and they walked in sync down the aisle. Her familiar scent and the rustle of her shimmery blue gown stopped his breath. He blinked, desperate to stay in the present. Walking down a wedding aisle together wasn't helping. They were only part of Jesse and Brenna's special day. It meant nothing.

"We can do this, Gus," Paige murmured softly. Surprised, Tavo glanced at her. No one called him Gus anymore. Rick, his younger brother, had shortened Gustavo to Tavo years ago, and it stuck. Paige belonged to a small handful who knew. She smiled at him. For a second, it almost seemed as if she needed his support. Then her gaze broadened to include the wedding guests, a clear signal the intimate moment was over.

A spark of hope surged. Just as quickly, he slammed it down with a hard dose of reality. She had only offered a crumb.

Much to his chagrin, his mind insisted on a replay. There was something in her tone. Longing? More likely, she was encouraging him through this juggernaut of emotions. Like game days back in high school. She always sensed when he was wound up.

However, one thought lodged and refused to leave. Between his old name and the just-for-him smile, something happened. And Paige had initiated it.

PAIGE TOOK a deep breath and curled her toes in the tall heels. She stood at the back of the large room, her feet aching abominably. On a bright note, they had segued into the reception without drama. The buffet was a hit. The music was exactly right—a blend of classic love songs. Many couples were taking advantage of the dance floor. Paige exhaled a sigh of relief. The hours of prep work and detailed planning had paid off.

Her first paid event planning gig.

She'd offered her services free of charge, but Jesse and Brenna wouldn't hear of it. In the end, she'd given them a steep discount, but fair was fair, she reasoned. They were allowing her to practice her event-planning skills with their reception. She was born for this. Elation filled her, and she couldn't stop smiling. Until a fine black ribbon tunneled her vision. The room swayed. She blinked, then blinked again.

"You okay, Paige?" Rory, her boss and friend, had appeared. Concern filled his gaze.

"Fine. Just famished." She covered the lingering dizziness with a laugh, hoping it was nothing. "So tell me—it's the million-dollar question today—why was the groom late?"

A deep chuckle rumbled around Rory's throat. "If I told you, you wouldn't believe it"—he pulled out his phone—"but here's proof. Here's the text he sent to Brenna after they talked." He thumbed down, then handed the phone to her.

As she read the text, a warm, contented feeling enveloped her.

> I wanted you to have this because I know how fond you are of hard copies. Please forgive me for being late. It had nothing, and everything, to do with you. I was at a favorite boyhood haunt, saying goodbye to childish things. Thanking God for the honor of getting to be your husband. But I got so focused on writing you the perfect letter, I lost track of time. And had no phone. What can I say? Woman, you've addled my brain! I'm coming, love. As long as there's breath in my body, I won't miss our wedding day. No reason to be afraid. I'm on my way.

Paige blinked away happy tears. "Aww. What a sweetheart. He has a knack for saying the right thing."

"Well, it sure saved his bacon this time." Rory's gruff tone belied the sparkle in his eyes.

"But why do *you* have the text?" Paige still found it confusing.

"He'd forgotten his phone. When I found him, I already had you on the line." Rory ran a hand down his beard, his lips stretched in a grin. "You should have seen him. When he realized he was late to his wedding, he got that determined look in his eyes—like the day he informed me I would walk again. No way he'd let Brenna think he wouldn't follow through. After sending her the text, he broke every speed law on the books driving to the church."

Paige loved happy endings. "Well, that's adorable."

Rory rolled his eyes. He glanced around the room, taking it in. "You've outdone yourself. This is outstanding." Twinkling lights gave the remodeled event center a warm ethereal glow. Soothing music played softly in the background.

"Well, pat yourself on the back, boss. You're the one who gave me the time off to make it happen." She looked to where a noisy group of young men egged Jesse on as he proudly displayed a garter. A deep pink blush wreathed Brenna's face. Her husky laugh echoed in the large space.

From long-standing habit, Paige's eyes found Gus. Head and shoulders above most men in the room, he stood on the periphery of the group, hands in his pockets. Wearing his cop expression. Stoic. Patient. Emotionless when he was nothing of the sort. An undignified noise bubbled in her throat.

Rory had followed her gaze. A tiny corner of his mouth turned up, though he resumed their conversation as if he hadn't noticed. "You only took your accrued vacation time." He gestured to the refashioned barn. "This is magnificent." His expression grew serious. "Did it provide enough opportunity to consider doing it full-time?"

"Yes," she said carefully, knowing where his question was going.

He studied her for a moment. When she didn't volunteer more, a roguish grin peeked out from under his mustache. "And?"

"I love it."

He leaned forward and hugged her. "Stinks for me, but I'm happy for you. Vi and I have been praying you'd know."

She stepped back. "But I don't have enough bookings yet to leave my day job."

"No hurry on my end." Sincerity shone in his slate-gray eyes. "When your bookings increase—and they will—we'll talk about finding you a replacement then."

"Thank you. I'm grateful you're willing to work with me on this—" A shout rose from the group of rowdy young men as her twin brothers fought over the coveted garter. A huff swooshed between Paige's lips. Rory lifted a brow and gave her a knowing look. The twins needed no encouragement. Despite their age, Carlos and Miguel weren't mature enough to date, much less entertain thoughts about getting married.

When Vi and Dicey headed their way, Paige leaned toward Rory with a grin. "Vi looks recovered."

"So far, so good," Rory said dryly. "She doesn't eat often enough, but if I mention it, she says I'm crowding her space. These fainting spells she refers to as a few lightheaded moments are anything but. I have to watch her like a hawk— which I love." The stern edge softened into pure sweetness.

Paige suppressed a smile. She could well imagine Rory hovering, even if he came by it honestly. Before they were married or even an item, Vi had tumbled into an old cistern, and Rory saved her life.

His mustache curved upward. "Yeah, okay. I get a little protective, but Dicey said she'd keep an eye on her."

Laughing, Paige laid her hand on his arm. "Rest easy, boss. That gal will make sure they visit the buffet."

Rory joined in with a deep chuckle. "I'm counting on it."

Vi strode up to them, motioning to Paige. "You need to come. Brenna is waiting on you so she can throw her bouquet."

Catching the bouquet was the last thing Paige wanted to

do, but duty called. Especially if Gus was going to stand in the back row and shirk *his* duty. She would set a good example even if he chose not to. Vi and Dicey steered her toward a loose circle of women.

She gave Rory her best stink eye, but he only responded with a playful shrug.

They were all in cahoots to throw her under the bus.

CHAPTER THREE

Tavo slipped a finger into the tight collar to breathe easier. He'd had about all the wedding atmosphere he could handle. As soon as he could escape, he planned to lift some serious weight to drain off the excess energy pulsing through his veins. Before a case of the wedding day blues overwhelmed him.

Maybe he'd ask Rory to join him. Making his way over to the punch bowl, he stopped at the buffet, picked up a delectable-looking cheesy appetizer, and popped it into his mouth. Paige would have a fit. No plate. No napkin. But Jesse, the man of the hour, wouldn't give a flying fig about Tavo's manners.

Idly, he watched as Paige caught Brenna's bouquet. No way she could have missed it. Brenna had aimed it at her as if she was the bullseye. Her being next in line to get married exposed the wishful thinking on the bride's part. He'd have known if Paige was dating someone.

Renewing their relationship prevailed as the main reason he'd returned to Valiant, but they weren't anywhere near closing the gap. He didn't deserve her, not with the mistakes he'd made, but he couldn't seem to let go either.

The twinkle lights cast a golden glow over the large reception area. Gauzy white fabric wound its way around the rafters. White tablecloths adorned each round table set with an arrangement of pink and white flowers. As usual, Paige had nailed it. Her knack for making things pretty kept her in demand. He'd heard she was considering event planning as a career.

"Gus." He stiffened at Paige's hint of reproach, then moved toward the punch bowl. Did the woman have eyes in the back of her head? She'd just been in that gaggle of girls doing the bouquet thing. He wasn't up for a scold, no matter how sweet the delivery.

"Can you help with the tables?" Paige came toward him, still wearing her gown, but barefooted.

"Sure thing, darlin'." He forgot he committed to help with the breakdown. "Feet hurt?" He gave her an indulgent smile, even as a poignant memory rose to the surface. The one where she'd let him rub her feet after a long evening of cheerleading. She had massaged his shoulders in return. His gut twisted again.

"Yes. No shoes should be okay this late in the game," she said uncomfortably. Paige, with her penchant for making things pretty, had always been appearance-focused.

He forced his thoughts back to the present. "Someone might report you to the shoe-police." He chuckled when she stuck her tongue out at him. Perfect. If he couldn't have her, then aggravation was the next best thing. "What's left before the breakdown?"

"The girls are passing out the bags of birdseed, then the sendoff."

The great grand sendoff. Where everybody threw birdseed,

of all things, at the departing couple. Nutty way to end a momentous occasion to Tavo's way of thinking, but no matter. This ordeal was almost over.

"I'll round up the twins to help." Paige's eyes drifted to the buffet.

"Have you eaten?" When she shook her head, he said, "Let me round up your brothers." She could do it, but he didn't want her to. Wrangling the twins proved an onerous task on the best of days. "You stay here. Check out what's left of your marvelous food bar and see if something meets your fancy."

"Thanks. It is almost over, right?" Relief mingled with insecurity in her almond-shaped eyes.

"Jesse and Brenna want you to have fun, Paige." Funny how they both fell into their former roles of reassuring each other. "You outdid yourself. The decorations. The food. Everything is stunning."

She flashed him a smile, only it was the merest shadow of previous times. His vague feeling of unease grew. He couldn't seem to bridge the emotional distance she'd put between them. Polite but chilly. Much too reserved, as if they had no history.

As if they'd never loved each other.

Tavo forced the traitorous thoughts away. Round up the boys. Break down the tables. Shoving his hands in his pockets, he crossed the wide area to the place where he'd last seen Carlos. He nodded to Rick at the deejay station. His brother loved these gigs, and the extra money he earned doing them. Said it helped balance the hours behind a computer screen. He'd worked as a company analyst right out of college. After a couple of years, he'd struck out on his own, preferring to contract his services. Tavo suspected some of his jobs involved hacking, but he didn't lose any sleep over it. Rick was a white hat at heart despite the long hair and worn jeans.

Over the years, he'd built up a reputation for providing the perfect music for any event. He'd also amassed an impressive collection of equipment to do the job. Tavo glanced at the massive speakers that resembled giant warfare robots, then sneezed. Another excellent reason to wrap this up. The frou-frou smell from the multitude of candles was tickling his nose.

PAIGE'S TASTEBUDS salivated as she popped a wedding-sized chunk of watermelon in her mouth. Standing behind the buffet, she viewed the room. Vi and Dicey had disappeared with Brenna to help her out of her gown and into travel clothes. The short honeymoon they'd planned in San Antonio was by design. They were saving every penny for the house Rory was building for them. Between wedding plans and their new home, Brenna had talked of little else the last couple of months. Paige had worked hard not to turn into a green blob of envy.

It had happened so fast. Her two best friends were married with dreamy places to live. A far cry from her cottage-like house. Paige loved Brenna and Vi like sisters, but she didn't quite fit in with their married status.

Oh, well. If her plan to become Valiant's go-to event planner gained momentum, she'd be much too busy to develop a serious relationship, which suited her just fine. She was quite aware Gus would be thrilled to pick up where they left off, but she couldn't do that. What they'd had in high school had been idyllic. But he'd been too serious, and Paige had a different mission. She had to attend college because she couldn't bear the thought of ending up like her mother. Her father stayed gone far more than he was home. Paige had vowed early on that would never happen to her.

Except the college scene had included a bad relationship. Once that had fizzled, her interest in the dating/relationship scene tanked right along with it. Now she only cared about preserving the memories she'd had with Gus. Her one good relationship. If they dated again and it didn't work out, she'd lose the lovely, tender moments they'd shared.

Her eyes strayed to him. At six feet, six inches, she'd had to special-order his tux. Oh, but he looked good. The powerlifting, his latest sports interest, had only accentuated his already large stature. Short-cropped dark hair, craggy features, and the warm smile that made her knees melt—*back to business, girl.*

Miguel and Carlos scampered off when Gus moved in their direction. Did they honestly think they'd be a match for him? His size, along with the "I'm-in-charge" police officer air, commanded attention. She shook her head. At eighteen, the twins were wiry as electrical cords, unpredictable as lightning, and half again as wild. They'd been running over Mama for years.

Now they raced around the deejay station, acting like ten-year-olds. Miguel had snatched the garter. Carlos stayed in hot pursuit. She stiffened. A wedding reception was no place for their shenanigans. Gus called out for them to stop. Miguel slowed, and Carlos spied the chance to catch his brother. One ferocious tackle later, they rolled into a heavy speaker held up by a giant tripod.

The cumbersome piece of equipment wobbled. Then everything happened too fast. "Gus, no!" she screamed, but he darted into the falling object's path. For a big man, he moved swiftly as he shoved a young girl out of the way. The tray of birdseed packets she held popped into the air. Amid the chaos, the tiny, sparkly bags fell like water drops to the floor.

The monstrous speaker continued its descent, but Gus

couldn't outrun it. It struck him on the shoulder. He slammed onto the floor. The speaker landed next to him with a dull thud, inches from his head. Only then did Paige realize she was screaming again.

This couldn't be happening. Not Gus. Heedless of her long gown, she ran over to where he lay motionless, but Rory beat her there. He stuck his fingers under his jaw. Paige wrung her hands. The twins, their eyes huge and scared, stood motionless.

Rory gave her a grim nod. "His pulse is strong, but he's not in good shape. His face smacked the ground. Don't know about the rest, but no one can withstand a hit like that—not even *El Jefe.*"

Paige whipped her phone from her pocket, but her hands were shaking so badly she couldn't punch the keys. Panic-stricken, she gazed at Rory. He snatched the phone from her and punched in the emergency numbers.

Gus moaned and stirred. Rory stopped communicating with the person on the other end long enough to say, "Get in his ear, Paige. He shouldn't be moving right now. Not until the EMT checks him out."

Tears streaming down her face like ribbons, Paige dropped to the ground and grabbed his hand. She leaned in and whispered, "Gus. Don't move." His body stilled. Heartened, she continued to patter about help, the reception, anything to keep him still.

The minutes seemed like hours before men in uniform stood at her side. "Ma'am, you need to step back if you want us to help your friend."

She stared at them without comprehension until Rory pulled her away. Noooooooo, she wanted to shout. Her feet and legs were prickly from the straw on the floor. She could barely stand.

Jesse sprinted through the warm haze from the twinkling lights. Where was his wedding attire? Then Brenna showed up, wearing the cute outfit Paige had helped her pick out. They looked stricken. What a way to end their special day. They should be leaving for their honeymoon. When Vi appeared, the last vestige of Paige's emotional strength fled. Sobbing, she crumpled into her friend's arms.

How could this lovely event have gone so wrong? But that wasn't the worst of it. Her body thrummed with chaotic tension. She needed Gus's quiet, steady presence. Her throat was raw. Involuntary sobs kept making their way up her throat. Vi rubbed gentle circles on her back. One thought kept her from completely losing it.

Gus would be all right. No other option existed.

CHAPTER FOUR

"**D**id Jesse and Brenna leave on their honeymoon?" Tavo asked irritably. That much he remembered. The reception had been drawing to a close, but everything else was a blur. His body ached like he'd careened into a mountain. Still, a hospital was the last place he wanted to be. He glanced around at the sterile surroundings. White bedding. Silver machines. The only color in the room was Paige's gown. Her disheveled look delivered a wallop to his painful haze. At the wedding, her hair had been up, but now stray locks straggled around her face and neck. Tavo's fingers itched to brush the strands back. She would hate the untidiness of her appearance.

"Yes. Once they heard you were awake and"—One of Paige's black eyebrows arched—"your usual grumpy self. You gave us quite a scare." Another pang struck Tavo at her puffy, red-rimmed eyes. Had she been crying on his account?

"I'm fine." The words ended with an explosive snort. He shifted, sucking in a sharp breath at the jolt to his shoulder. "What does the doctor say?"

"They've taken X-rays, but we know nothing. Yet."

Tavo's nostrils flared. He opened his mouth to speak, but Paige cut him off. "Patience, Big Guy. The doctor will tell us what we need to know. The pain meds will kick in any second now."

A worried look crossed her face. She leaned in and touched his cheeks. "Mm. Your hands are cool," he said.

"You're going to have some bruises. Does it hurt?" Her fingers traced over his forehead.

"No." Drowsiness was creeping in. Bruises? Why was his face bruised? Before he could ask or form a coherent answer, heavy footsteps clomped his way.

"Why are you here, Paige?" The words brimmed with impatience.

Tavo fought to surface against the marshmallow-y tug of the pain meds. "Dad?"

"What happened to you?" Tavo saw, or rather sensed, the accusatory glare Dad shot at Paige before looking back at him. His breath hissed at the hurt darting across her face. The events that led him here were slowly coming back. The twins acting rowdy. A gigantic speaker toppling off the tripod. Pushing the little girl out of its path. None of that was Paige's fault, but Dad had never cared for Paige, even back in high school. When she'd left him for bigger, better things, Dad's I-told-you-so had added another layer of pain.

Unable to work through his broken-heartedness about Paige, and his ongoing disagreement with Dad about career choices, Tavo had taken the easy route. He'd just left. Gone to San Antonio and completely lost his way.

Now he was back to mend fences—take care of unfinished business. With his father. With the woman he loved. And with God.

How's that working out for you? An inner voice taunted.

He'd been dancing around the God issue for months. Small

wonder he'd made little progress with his dad or Paige. *Just take the first step.* Except he was rapidly losing the ability to stay awake. He grasped Paige's small hand and held it tight. "Paige stays." The hard lines of his father's face faded as Tavo drifted into sleep.

PAIGE STOOD at the front door of Gus's house, a bouquet of daisies in one hand, and a sack of trail mix in the other. At one time, his favorite snack. The daisies were over the top. Who brought a man flowers? Still, she couldn't resist their perky cheerfulness.

When no one answered the door, she sent a text. Seconds later, footsteps came. Gus appeared, wrestling one arm into a shirt. A navy sling held the other arm. Surprise and pleasure creased the corners of his eyes. Paige's lungs went on life support. This would never do. She was merely visiting an old friend.

"Thought these might cheer you up." She thrust the daisies at him. "And your snack of choice—or used to be. When the doctor said the accident dislocated your shoulder, I knew you'd be bummed, so—"

Eyes the color of her favorite black tea twinkled with amusement at her rambling. Warm, rich tones swirled with darker brown. Oh, this was going badly. Her chin dropped onto her chest.

"Come in, Paige. I'd love for you to cheer me up." Teasing underscored the authority ringing in his voice. And he'd deliberately misconstrued the reason for the daisies.

He held the door wide so she could enter the living area. She hadn't been here in years, but the masculine décor hadn't changed. Bereft of any female presence, the walls held no pictures. The heavy wooden table and chairs seemed more suited to a sailing vessel. Saggy furniture shouted comfort. But then, any sofa or recliner belonging to Gus or his dad would lose support sooner rather than later. Their size guaranteed it.

An arm still out of the sleeve, Gus crossed to the kitchen, pulled a pitcher out of a cabinet, and filled it with water. A slightly musty odor hung around the sink. Paige arranged the daisies in it while he attempted to put on the shirt. Only it wasn't working.

"Sit." She directed. He sat in a kitchen chair and let her remove the sling. Her eyes widened at the black shoulder brace as she wrapped the shirt around his back and guided his arm into the sleeve. "Better?" She thought about buttoning the shirt, then decided against it. His nearness, once such a comfort, proved unsettling. She quickly sat in the other chair.

He didn't answer, but watched her, not missing a thing. He never had. Gus always knew when she was nervous. Why couldn't they just be friends? She could use a friend. He could too, she'd bet. Except the current flowing between them these days didn't lend itself to mere friendship.

She marshaled her thoughts back to the present. "How long with the sling?"

"About two weeks. Then I can start PT." His lips puckered into a frown. "Whatever needs to happen so I can get back to normal."

"As in back on duty, right? What about powerlifting?"

"Both, though the doc doesn't seem too keen on the powerlifting." Gus reached for the bag of trail mix.

Paige chose her words carefully. "It'd be scary easy to overdo with the amount of weight you lift." Strangely enough, sleep had eluded her last night because she'd been thinking about this very thing. "You're competitive as they come, Gus. It goes against your nature to take it easy." *Cluck. Cluck.* An old mother hen had nothing on her.

"You worried about me, Paige?" A corner of his lips tweaked. His eyes searched hers, then he took a handful of the mix and popped it into his mouth.

"No, I'm not worried about you," she said tartly. "I want you to ... be careful, that's all."

"I know how to be careful, Pep." He'd used her old nickname. Paige the Ultimate Pepster, they called her in high school. Ugh. It was the teenage take on her role as head cheerleader. She hadn't much cared for it then, but thirteen years later, it was downright embarrassing.

He offered her the bag, but she shook her head. They sat in silence, but Paige had never felt a need for ongoing conversation with her living version of "still waters run deep." She always breathed a little easier when he was in the vicinity, even if he was in slow-motion, like today.

"You know the weight-bearing issue with PT goes away with aquatics. Swimming. Pool exercises."

He gave her a dubious look. "You love the water. I don't."

Her shrug might have been on the elaborate side. "Just sayin' ..."

"I know what you're sayin', Paige." A slight edge had entered his voice, a signal he knew where she was going with this. "You tried to get me in the water for years. It rarely happened then. Not happening now." When her mouth opened in protest, he said, "End of discussion."

A musical tone filled the air. Her phone. Gus's dislike of the water was a battle for another day. She dug it out of her purse. Out-of-state number. She clicked on and greeted the caller. "Spence Enterprises."

She listened, growing more curious by the second. Her glance at Gus revealed droopy eyes. Part of her brain registered that he was still on pain meds. He motioned down the hallway. She nodded. He was allowing her privacy, but she'd check on him after the call.

"Yes, Spence Enterprises can handle a large remodel." A smile tipped Paige's lips. "Yes, I understand the term overhaul. That's well within the range of what we do if everything else lines up." Such as the finances and what the client wanted. Rory wouldn't take a job if it didn't meet certain criteria.

The front door creaked loudly, and Rick walked in. Paige motioned toward the hallway, assuming he'd come to see Gus. Rick nodded, heading that way, a shabby cap covering a mass of curls any woman would die for.

Paige called on a patience she didn't feel and finished with the questions. Self-serving as the caller seemed, Paige secured an appointment. If this guy was for real, it sounded like a lot of money could be involved. The caller said he was Ed Clarkston's assistant. Why did the name sound so familiar? It almost sounded like the guy expected her to recognize it. Still pondering his attitude, she stood as Rick reentered the room.

"Tavo wants to say goodbye." Rick's expression was carefully bland.

What did she do with that? "Okay." She paused, uncertain as to her next move. Was she supposed to sashay down the hall to his room?

"Better hurry. He fades pretty fast on those meds." He peered at her, picking up on her confusion, answering her unspoken question. "Same room as always."

She hastened down the hall and peeked into the bedroom. He lay on his uninjured side, eyes closed. "Gus?" When he didn't answer, she moved closer. His massive chest rose with even breaths. Good. He needed the rest.

Saved from the awkwardness of further conversation, she gazed around his room. In a corner, his guitar stood in its stand. Sheets of music lay in a messy pile on the floor. A wave of nostalgia crashed into her as a sharp memory of him playing the guitar during study breaks surfaced. He'd warble off key, then settle into one of those wonderful love songs. His mouth stretched into mild contortions with the high notes. An unnamed ache needled her. *You can't go back.*

All she could do was keep the memories safe. Resigned, Paige turned to leave, then paused at the framed picture of them on his desk. Homecoming King and Queen. The photo appeared a tad grainy after all these years, but there was no mistaking their jubilant expressions. A tiny smile curved her lips. They had just shared their first kiss. In the center of the football field at halftime, the stadium filled with hundreds of people.

She rushed from the room as if she were being chased.

CHAPTER FIVE

Tavo's shoulder didn't appreciate the pace or the exercises Silas, his physical therapist, was administering, though he'd expected no less. He grunted through a set of pulls as sweat broke out on his forehead. *Thirteen. Fourteen. Fifteen.* He blew out a choppy exhale and began again.

The large therapy room at Peeps was almost devoid of people. A lady on a stationary bike pedaled while gazing at her phone. Through an office window, Tavo could see Silas focused on his computer. Thinking up new methods of torture, no doubt. The guy's crisp instructions left no wiggle room. Not that Tavo wanted any. Not really. But this hard-core military style left him parched for ... what? A timeout? *Four. Five.* Ugh. His shoulder ached like a giant bee sting. Str-r-r-e-e-etch. *Six. Seven.* Tavo panted, stopping the pull midway. Easier wasn't happening. He huffed a noisy breath. *Finish the set, dude. Eight. Nine.*

"How many?" Silas had slipped up beside him ninja-style, resting his hands on slim hips.

"Ten," Tavo grunted. He slung his arm out for another rep.

"Don't slop through it. Nice and slow."

Did the man miss anything? Tavo gritted his teeth as he ground out the last five reps. His body trembled with the effort.

"Good work. You're getting there."

"How ... how can I help this process along?" Tavo worked to appear as if the pain wasn't making him sing soprano.

"It takes time. Aquatics would help with the weight-bearing aspect of it. Lessens the pain." At Tavo's grimace, Silas gave a short, humorless bark. "You asked."

First Paige. Now Silas. But Silas was a professional, Tavo's mind argued. And Paige was part fish. Swimming was her exercise of choice since they were kids. Didn't mean he had to do it.

Silas's eyes bored into him. "Never too young or too old to change. If you want to help that shoulder outside of here, aquatics is a great way to go about it."

An image of his brother surfaced. Rick splashing about in the pool. Choking. Gasping for air. Spluttering for help. Tavo savagely knocked the thought away. *Help me, Lord.* Where had that come from? Tavo hadn't been on speaking terms with God since Paige had ended their relationship. During the intervening years, nothing had changed because he hadn't dealt with any of it. But the pressure to return to Valiant had been unbearable. Here he was, no more equipped to deal with Paige or his dad than when he was eighteen.

Help me, Lord. This time, he meant it.

An idea began to form.

―――――――――

PAIGE STARED, caught herself, and then stared again at the man climbing out of the white convertible. Oooh, la, but he was gorgeous. The white convertible was the highest-priced rental available. She angled in for a closer look, dangerously close to ogling—something she didn't do. He didn't come near Gus's size, but his face, hair, and—mercy—that self-effacing demeanor put him in a different class. Another car drove up and parked behind the convertible. Two muscular men lazily climbed out but made no move to join them. Their eyes scanned the property. In a rural community outside Valiant, Rodeo Drive was a throwback to an area that once boasted horse farms.

Paige and Rory stood under a huge, shady oak tree to ward off the heat. A sticky humidity cloyed the air. She dodged a gauzy spider web languishing from a thick limb and glanced down. It took a few seconds to realize what she was looking at. She'd assumed it was some kind of hardy grass that didn't mind shade, but no. Hundreds of fallen acorns had sprouted. Tiny seedlings that would never become trees covered the dry ground. She tried to move her sandaled feet so she wouldn't crush them, but it proved impossible. The sheer waste pressed on her soul.

A geeky guy wearing glasses with overlarge frames and coal-black hair stepped toward her and Rory. "I assume you're who I talked to on the phone." Ah. Mr. Self-Important. He consulted his phone, then said, "Paige?" He turned to Rory. "And you are ..."

"Rory Spence. Spence Enterprises." Courteous, but Rory's jaw tightened. No impression like a first. These two were blowing it.

"Right. I'm Corona. Like the beer. Enough about me, though. Let me introduce you to the man. This is Ed Clarkston." He paused as if expecting a drumroll. Paige's lips curled inward. Was this guy for real?

Her face must have appeared as blank as Rory's because a

slight crease appeared between Corona's brows. "Ed Clarkston from Hollywood."

Oh! Paige wasn't into the celebrity scene, but she knew the name. Now it made perfect sense. The guy was gorgeous. The muscle men must be his security detail.

"That's enough, Cory." A rueful look passed over Ed's face. He extended a hand to Rory first, then to her. A chill zipped up her spine when he held it longer than necessary. Those eyes. Soft and dreamy like a blue jay's feather. Highlighted blond hair parted down the middle with a cut that enhanced his pretty features. Her nose twitched at the exotic fragrance that clung to him.

"I'm guessing these people have better things to do than read *People* magazine." A perfectly modulated chuckle rumbled up his throat. "Cory may have explained what I'm looking for." He swept an arm around the area/land where they stood. "This one intrigued me enough for a look-see. I'm up close and personal when it comes to where I live. And I adore remakes." Paige felt like a germ under a microscope as his eyes lingered on her. What was that about?

"What brings you to Texas, Ed?" Rory sounded cordial enough, but Paige heard the minuscule edge in his tone.

"Well, you might say I'm looking for a place away from the bright lights. The artificiality of Hollywood wears thin after a while." He gestured again around the area. "I need space to think. Refine the creative juices. I'm a cowboy at heart." He cast a wistful eye around the scrubby land.

Charming words, even if they sounded scripted. The twins had taught Paige not to swallow every sweet thing she heard, but this guy could convince the hardest heart. No wonder he made millions. Getting acquainted with him would be a unique experience. She'd never met a famous person.

"Well, daylight's burnin'. We'd best see if restoring this

place is what you want to do." Hands in his pockets, Rory strolled toward the sprawling estate once owned by an uber-wealthy eccentric. Empty for years, it was a derelict mess. The falling-down barn and overgrown corral didn't help the appeal factor.

Paige's optimism about this job took a nosedive. Rory's normal enthusiasm had waned, but maybe he was just tired. Mercy, the man was only human. Between building houses for the new subdivision and Vi being pregnant with twins, the timing wasn't best for a custom remodel—especially one of this magnitude.

They slowly followed. Rory fiddled with the lockbox. By the front door, dead fronds shagged the trunk of a tall palm like an old graybeard. Ancient. Abandoned.

Ed deserved kudos for even thinking of bringing this old wreck back to life.

Her practical side wondered why he would bother with such a ginormous undertaking. It spelled p-r-o-b-l-e-m from the get-go. One had to have the heart for these kinds of undertakings. The ability to envision the end result beyond the mess. Ed was fun to look at, but restoring this place would take serious chops.

Rory said once he had remodeled the home he and Vi lived in because he couldn't *not* do it. Paige remembered his energy level during the project. How excited and alive he'd been. Restoring the house had been a pure labor of love. The remodel had also cemented he and Vi's relationship during a turbulent courtship.

Once in the house, they walked around large broken pieces of cement blocks and other debris into a sunken living room. No one talked as each person seemed to take in the overwhelming neglect. The dwelling had an unfriendly feel that set Paige on edge. Chilled, she wrapped her arms around her waist. Strolling over to a huge partition of glass that seemed to serve as a wall of sorts, she peered through it. Her mind slowly adjusted to what she was seeing.

A large pool sprawled in the middle of the house showed evidence of vandalism. Someone, or several someones, had tossed cement blocks, bricks, and palm fronds into the brackish-green water. She backed away as the others joined her.

Ed talked excitedly, asking Rory questions but not paying attention to his obvious skepticism. Ed seemed more interested in throwing out one eloquent suggestion after another about how he would bring this place back to life.

A shudder rolled across Paige's shoulders. The TLC this place would require would drain them dry. No invigorating energy here. If it were up to her, she'd bring in a big bulldozer and level the place. Some jobs simply weren't worth it.

Later, they dined in a spacious corner booth at Hugo's, a popular restaurant in downtown Valiant. The two men who drove the other vehicle were also there. She'd concluded they were an odd mix of bodyguard and PR because they ran interference between Ed and the fans who wanted to have their pictures taken with him. Paige found herself in awe. She'd never met anyone who required bodyguards. But her jaws hurt. She was grateful they were taking care of security issues, even if they were a tad on the creepy side.

Rory sat on one side of her, Ed on the other. Corona perched on the outer edge, which was fine with Paige. From the moment they'd entered the building, nothing had met with his approval. He'd complained about the slow service, declared the menu was sparse, and turned his nose up at the appetizers. Finally, Ed shut him down. To his credit, he did it quietly, though it was hard to miss the harshly whispered expletives. Or the entertainment it provided for the bodyguard who overheard. After that, Corona said little, but frequently signaled for more beer.

Strangely enough, Ed grew more animated, though he'd consumed very little alcohol. He gushed about the restaurant décor, which was a fairly standard version of Texas chic. Corrugated tin for paneling, Lone Star State memorabilia adorning the walls, and rustic furniture. When Ed's knee brushed hers for the second time, out of habit, she scooted closer to Rory. Too late, she realized that option was no longer viable. Before Rory was married, they would pretend to be a couple at the many networking functions they attended, especially if either of the opposite sex came on too strong. But their pretending abruptly ended when their closest friends assumed they were a couple too. Once Rory married, they set healthy boundaries for both their sakes.

"I'm guessing you two are a thing, right?" Ed grinned easily.

A thin smile poked between Rory's mustache and beard as he motioned to himself and Paige. "That would be a no. I am hopelessly devoted to my wife." A hint of steel entered his voice. "But I've worked with Paige for years. She's like a sister to me."

"I see."

Paige didn't think so. It sounded like Rory's veiled warning went in Ed's ear, picked up speed, and flew out the other. Aside from Ed's short attention span, she found him fascinating. However, she wasn't interested in more than a get-to-know-you conversation. Her abysmal record with men precluded anything deeper.

CHAPTER SIX

"So, considering the changes we talked about during the walk-through, how many millions is this going to run me?" Ed's well-manicured hands drummed the tabletop. He flitted from subject to subject like a hummingbird around a feeder.

Rory gazed at him. Paige knew exactly what he was thinking. Did A-lister Ed Clarkston have the money for a project of this magnitude? "Upwards of five million, and that's a conservative estimate." His fingers creased another pleat in his napkin, but he didn't break eye contact. "By far, the better deal would be for you to let me demolish the existing structures, then build it new from the ground up. There won't be near the problems, and you'll get exactly what you want."

Ed's well-shaped lips flattened as he digested the information. "But what I *want* is for you to restore the place we saw this afternoon. I can already see it right here." He tapped his temple. "I don't expect you to understand. You're not a creative." He used the word like it was an elite category of people. "You're the foreman. The one who makes my ideas happen."

Paige shifted uncomfortably. Rory wasn't a foreman, and Ed's vision had no actual substance. Pinning him down with practicalities would be an ongoing nightmare.

"I'll pay you double." Petulance marred his perfectly modulated voice. Corona, who up to this point, had only seemed interested in getting another beer, put his mug down and gave Ed a stare that could have gored a bull.

Rory's back stiffened. Uh-oh. Her boss's feathers didn't ruffle easily, but when they did ...

He surprised her with an almost cheery expression. "Why don't we all sleep on it? It's been a long day. I'll talk it over with my wife and get back to you." Paige mashed her lips together to keep from smiling. Rory only wanted to go home and see Vi.

Ed's almost imperceptible snort communicated weird vibes. Like he was used to getting his way immediately. With no interference. He hadn't liked the wife-reference either.

But chasing a dream could make a person unreasonable. Hadn't Gus said the same thing about her? Single-minded to a fault was the phrase he used. If so, she and Ed had one thing in common.

Despite Ed's fixation, Paige shared Rory's professional opinion of the restoration. New construction made far more sense from a contractor's point of view. Drat! She slid out of the booth. Ed was a bona fide celebrity. You didn't meet one of those often. Certainly not in Valiant.

After Ed insisted on paying and left the server an exorbitant tip, the small group made their way outside. To Paige's surprise, a gaggle of women instantly came forward, clamoring to have their pictures taken with Ed. The muscle guys stepped in and brought order to chaos. Wow. She'd had no idea. But Ed seemed used to it as he posed with the different women and said just the right things. He seemed larger than life.

Corona had traipsed off, supposedly to bring the car around. Ed had lifted a brow but let him go. The muggy evening made Paige want to hurry into cold AC, but politeness required they not leave before Ed and his entourage. She stood close to Rory while he texted Vi. A soft sigh escaped. Must be nice to brush aside a multi-million-dollar project for a higher priority.

Rory put away his phone, shook hands with Ed, then looked at her. "Hang tight, Paige. I'll get the car."

As he strode off, Corona drove into the portico. Ed signaled him around to the passenger side. The sheepish smile he directed at her melted her insides. "Guess I'm the designated driver tonight." He seemed to pause, then leaned toward her and bussed her cheek. "What I'm looking forward to most is working with you." His eyes held hers. Then he straightened and headed for the driver's side of the rental. Corona slumped on the passenger's side, eyes closed. Ed didn't look back as they drove away.

Paige gazed at the sky. Her eyes adjusted to the glow of orange lanterns that lit up the portico, and the stars came into focus. Millions of them. She touched her cheek where Ed— Hollywood actor—had kissed it. Through her pleasant haze, an ancient cliche intruded.

Did she have stars in her eyes about Ed? The man was a mystery. Gorgeous for sure, but he possessed some unflattering traits. His stubbornness about that old wreck of a house for starters ... and the way he'd treated Rory and Corona smacked of condescension. She supposed people with money were used to getting their way. An unfortunate learned behavior—but all learned behavior could be unlearned. A peek inside the man enticed her most.

Stars in her eyes? She shook off the idea as Rory's white Lexus came through the portico drive. Years of raising her brothers had provided lifelong inoculation against charmers. All she wanted was to know—really know—the real person behind the celebrity-slash-moody artist façade.

***

"WHAT ARE YOU DOING HERE, *JITA*?" Paige's mother, a diminutive woman with lively eyes and hair streaked with gray, quickly folded the letter she held.

"Do I need a reason to visit my *mamacita*?" Paige squeezed Mom's shoulders, not missing the way she stuck the letter into a pile of other correspondence.

"Absolutely not, but you're a busy woman these days. Want some lunch?" She rose from a long dining table covered with a lacy tablecloth. Paige reached toward the pile, but Mom brushed her hand away. "These are not your problem."

Problem? Paige followed her into an immaculate kitchen with an island. Fresh flowers in a vase acted as a centerpiece. "What's the letter about?" She pulled the vase closer and inhaled the sweet scent of roses. Mom loved roses. Must be why Paige loved them too.

"Sandwiches or lemon chicken soup? The soup has a kick to it."

"I'll try the soup." Soup rarely made the menu growing up, much less a spicy one with lemons. Mystified, Paige stroked a showy orange rose, enjoying the velvet softness of the petals.

Mom moved to the stove with the container. As she spooned soup into bowls and warmed them in the microwave, Paige repeated her earlier question. "What's in the letter?"

Her mother's brow furrowed, and she sagged against the counter, fussing with a pair of mitts. "The doctor wants to prescribe medicine to stave off future heart issues, but it's a name brand, and our insurance doesn't want to cover it."

Paige studied her. "I imagine it's super-expensive to pay out of pocket." Mom remained mute, busying herself with testing the soup. "Have you talked to Dad about it?" It was worth asking, even though Paige had little faith her father would come through. The nature of his work took him everywhere but home.

"I'll mention it when he calls." Using the mitts, she placed the steaming bowls on the table. Motioning to Paige to sit, she plucked two spoons from a drawer and lowered herself into a chair.

Waiting for her soup to cool, Paige glanced around the kitchen. Her parents, or Mom, rather, had moved a few years ago into a newer home than the one she'd grown up in. "Do you even know when he'll be home next?"

Her mom shrugged. "Soon, I hope, but Paige"—A pleading note entered her voice—"I doubt he knows either. There's a lot you don't understand about his work."

"So tell me." Paige worked to stay reasonable, but she had zero confidence Mom would enlighten her. Paige had asked since she was old enough to realize her father wasn't home like other dads. The vague answers Mom provided weren't enough, but she always said it was for Paige's protection.

The nature of his work was covert. Just like him. Detached. As if he could not form deep relationships. Her mother dealt with Paige and her siblings as if she were a single parent. Through the years, it had left a sour taste in Paige's mouth.

"Someday," firmness underscored the word.

Sighing, Paige reached for her mom's hand. "Let's bless the soup." The knot between Mom's brows loosened, and she squeezed Paige's hand. They ate and chatted about Paige's siblings. Then Paige told her about meeting Ed Clarkston.

"He's a real looker, Mom. Easy enough to see why all the women swoon."

Mom's expression was mischievous. "Is my level-headed daughter swooning too? Just a little?"

Paige shook her head vigorously. "You know me better than that, Mom. If anything, I'm more interested in getting to know the man behind the acting façade."

Mom's mouth sobered into a line. "Careful what you wish for, *jita*."

"Mo-m," Paige protested. Looking at her phone, she rose. "I'm late." Rounding the table, she hugged her mother. Though they were the same height, Mom seemed smaller today. Not the robust woman who had raised her. Was her heart already failing?

Mom needed the medicine. Paige could make that happen.

CHAPTER SEVEN

The patrol car purred as Tavo cruised down Old Main. This road led straight to downtown, but the city had grown east. No longer the main drag, it served as an alternative route with four expansive lanes and a middle turn lane. His presence *should*—operative word there—help other motorists stay closer to the speed limit.

Empty fields lay on the west side, enclosed by sun-rotted gray posts. A few businesses brave enough to stay when the town moved east stood by the road. An auto shop with weathered buildings. A Mexican restaurant with a daily buffet. An ancient sno-cone stand. *Raspas, Daddy! We want raspas.* When his mom had been around, she could coax Dad into stopping. Tavo had always chosen strawberry. Green apple was his brother's favorite. Back when life was easy.

The familiar white Jetta streaking past his patrol car interrupted his musings. What—no! Sucking in air, he blew out a frustrated sigh. He snatched the radar gun out of the dash mount and clocked the car's speed. "Good night, Paige. What are you thinking?" He pulled into her lane, accelerated, and hit the siren. A loud whoop blazed into the scorching afternoon. Her vehicle immediately slowed as she pulled over on the road's shoulder. Good sign. Not so distracted, she didn't hear or see his lights.

A traffic stop wasn't how he'd wanted to see Paige again. *Okay, bud. You've done this dozens of times. Friendly, but in control.*

Even when he felt anything but.

He took his time getting out of his vehicle. Paige leaned over to the passenger seat to get her purse. Yeah, well, she ought to know the drill. She racked up warnings like an NBA player shot baskets. Every so often, an on-target patrol officer would count the warnings and issue her a ticket. She'd slow down until the next big hurry. He rubbed a hand over his damp upper lip. Paige's normal responses signified a healthy measure of self-control. Behind the wheel of a car, however, an inner wild child took over.

From long habit, he touched the trunk of her car, peered into the backseat, then stood next to the driver's window. She'd already rolled it down. "You know why I pulled you over?" he adopted a conversational tone. This awkward situation could at least begin on a pleasant note.

"Cause we're old friends and you want to say hi?" The mega-watt smile that had ensured her homecoming queen status three years in a row was on full display.

Despite the circumstances, the corners of his mouth tweaked upward. She had that effect on him. "Hi, old friend," he said, matching her playful tone. "What's the other reason I'm standing here sweating bullets?"

"Mm. It's your job, I suppose." Her lips turned down. "And I was probably speeding." She looked away.

"Yep. Why the hurry?" She seemed skittish, but Paige knew better than to be afraid of him—didn't she?

"I was at Mom's for lunch. We got to gabbing. I didn't notice the time. Rory and I have work to do, so I was—"

"Getting from Point A to Point B like a supersonic jet," he finished for her. She didn't deny it. "I need your license, registration, and insurance."

She held a dainty crimson billfold in her lap. Feminine and classy. Just like her. Man, he had to quit obsessing over these details. She thumbed through several cards and pieces of folded paper, then handed him the items. Her fingers brushed his, making him highly aware this was more than a routine traffic stop. For him, anyway.

"I'll be right back," he managed.

She inclined her head a fraction, clearly dejected he was following through.

His inner self launched into an argument as he walked to the patrol car. *What do you expect me to do here, doll? Overlook the last three warnings?* Paige drove too fast. It scared him. He'd seen enough crashes, pileups, and mangled bodies to never want that for anyone. Paige in an auto wreck? He couldn't bear to finish the thought.

He wrote out the citation with a tight hand. Maybe ... just maybe, the consequences of her actions would take hold this time—help her make slowing down a habit. Heels dragging, he covered the distance between their vehicles again.

"Need you to sign here." He set the pad on the car window, hating the way her eyes rounded and filled. What was going on here? Paige's composure was legendary, but her stiff jaw told a different story.

"Gus, please. You don't have to do this."

This new behavior stymied him, but he'd have to process it later. "Paige, you were driving sixty-eight in a forty-five."

A wince deepened the crease in her forehead. "I'm sorry. I

had no idea—" She stopped. Yeah, that explanation wouldn't help.

As he steeled himself to finish, exasperation crept into his words. "You need to slow down—people love you. Please respect that." He nudged the pad toward her.

The breath she blew upward ruffled one side of her ebony hair. The hair he longed to touch. *Down, boy.* A desperate idea popped into his mind. He couldn't take back the ticket, but ...

"I've been thinking about the pool, and your offer to help get my shoulder back on par." Not exactly her phrasing, but he hoped she would overlook that part.

She gave him an interested look, took the pad, and scribbled her name at the bottom of the citation, much to his relief. "What did you have in mind?"

He shrugged, but the ache in his shoulder made him wish he hadn't. "I dunno." Inspired she'd taken the bait, he flashed his dimples at her—she used to love them. "You're the mermaid. I figure you know plenty about aquatic exercises."

Her eyes narrowed as if she suspected his ploy. Paige had tried to get him in the water the whole time they dated, but he'd been too proud and stubborn to do much besides watch her. "I'm going to the gym today after work. If you're serious, meet me there."

No backing down now. Tavo strolled back to the patrol car with a lighter step. It wasn't a date. But if they could find some type of rhythm, it would establish the foothold he'd been looking for.

Now to conquer his fear of the water.

———

PAIGE SAT on the pool ledge of a swim lane, breathing hard. She slicked back her wet hair, completing the motion down her arms. Ten laps already and she'd yet to find her breathing rhythm. The anticipation of Gus meeting her here was making her antsy.

A relentless inner voice ticked off the reasons she couldn't get involved with him again. She needed the independence of her own business. Gus would disapprove of her goal since he'd often stated a woman's place was in the home. Therefore, she had to keep him and his Neanderthal attitude in the friend zone. Deep down, however, she knew it was more than that. If they got close again and things didn't work out, it would decimate her. She savagely kicked the water, creating a frothy pattern.

The wall of windows showed the late afternoon stealing into dusk. She had the pool to herself since most folks were already home or on their way. Orangish rays of sun, striated streaks of pink and lavender. Her lips lifted at the dramatic show. Footsteps slapped the rough tile.

Gus. Clad only in black swim trunks and flip-flops. *Oh, boy.* The snug shoulder support brace with a short arm sleeve stretched across his back and chest. Powerlifting had trimmed his bulk into pure muscle. Already tall, the overall effect could be intimidating. Not that he'd ever acted that way with her, but people on the wrong side of the law probably had a different perception.

She scooted over. He kicked the flip-flops off, joined her on the ledge in one fluid movement, and dangled his feet in the pool water. In high school, he'd had gawky moments, as if he didn't know how to manage his size, but that stage was past. He grinned. Her perusal hadn't gone unnoticed. Warmth crept into her cheeks. She ran a hand through the water and splashed him. He jerked with a bark of laughter.

Wiping a hand down his wet face, he said playfully, "I came to exercise but—" He scooped a handful of water and flung it back. An involuntary squeal burst from her lips. Too late, she covered her eyes. Laughing, she rubbed water from her brows. "Good thing I was already wet."

Still smiling, Gus flexed his elbow and rotated the braced arm carefully. The only sign of pain was a slight hitch in his breathing. Ever the stoic one.

Paige's jaw clenched. The memory of the giant speaker careening into him remained vivid. She shook her head to clear it, showering tiny drops of water into the air. Replays of "How are the mighty fallen" would not help his shoulder heal. She clambered up and stood on the tile. "I did a bit of research, so I'll walk you through a handful of exercises. Fifteen to twenty minutes ought to be enough for today."

Slanting a look at her, Gus rose from his sitting position. His height dwarfed her, but she found it comforting. At one time, she'd considered him her safety net. Before he became too serious. Even then, she could count on him to be there for her. Until he wasn't. Unfair since she'd been the first to leave, but it still gnawed at her.

They stood on the tile as she instructed him on underwater punches and how to create resistance with a noodle. Then she demonstrated the crazy arms exercise. He mimicked her movements carefully. Why was he so set on doing something he hated? Maybe he was ready to get past the incident when his brother almost drowned. Or was he simply ignoring his fear? That sounded more like him.

At any rate, previous sports training made him a quick study. His excellent form was a delight to watch. Hm. She averted her eyes. "Good. Now that you've got those down, move to an empty lane and get in the water. Walk the pool length, up and back, doing each exercise."

He jumped into the water with only the slightest hesitation. She slipped into the next lane. Unable to touch the pool bottom, she kept a hand on the lane marker, but Gus could handle the depth. The water barely covered his shoulders. Perfect.

"What are you going to do?" He ran a hand down his face, sluicing the water away.

"Ten more laps—if I can get my breathing right. Then I'll show you how to spider crawl on the side of the pool. If your shoulder cooperates." She shot him an impish look.

"It will."

Or die trying. Still macho to the bone. Avoiding another peek at the support brace on his muscled chest, she pushed away from the wall with her foot.

They had history, but that was where their relationship needed to stay—in the past. No crushing over his filled-out physique. No delving into the new level of maturity. No wishing for something she couldn't have.

She dragged in another breath between arm strokes. Ten laps might not be enough to get her mind back to where it belonged.

CHAPTER EIGHT

Now that the water wasn't there to provide buoyancy, Tavo's shoulder throbbed like a you-done-me-wrong song. It was crying for ice, but relief would have to wait. Paige emerged from the women's dressing room, looking impossibly fresh and ready for another round. Exactly what he'd hoped.

Surprise lit her eyes. "I thought you'd be long gone. Your shoulder has to hurt after what we put it through."

"Got my second wind," he fibbed. "I'm going to Jeremy's for a burger. Wanna meet me there?" He knew a hamburger wouldn't be her first choice, but she had once loved their sweet potato fries.

A glimmer of something flashed across her face but dimmed just as quickly. "I have some work—"

"You still need to eat." He'd make one more play, then let it go. "Seems I heard something about you starting a business. Have to admit, I'm curious. But, hey. It can wait."

He made the first move toward the double doors, then remembered it was dark outside. The creeping hour. If nothing else, he'd provide an escort to her car. When he turned, she'd caught up to him.

"I'll come. But just friends, right?" She looked as if she might change her mind in a nanosecond.

A hammer thudded into his heart, but he managed a smile. "Just friends."

The décor of Jeremy's hadn't changed in years. Plastic red and yellow tables. Same colored booths. But the burgers were great, and the place was always busy. When Paige showed up, still skittish, he confirmed what she wanted to eat, then ordered while she grabbed a corner table.

Once the server brought their food, he wasted no time getting to a subject that would make her more comfortable. "Rory mentioned you're starting an event business." Safe enough. There weren't a lot of secrets within their close-knit group. A pang of guilt coursed through Tavo. *Except for the ones he kept.* Things had happened when he lived in San Antonio that he preferred not to talk about. He hurried past the depressing thought. "Since it's general knowledge, I'm looking forward to a firsthand account."

He wouldn't mention an arrow had flown into his heart the day he'd heard. Not that he should be the first to know anything these days about the lovely woman sitting across from him. Good night, she worked for Rory. By rights, he was several notches ahead of Tavo in the need-to-know realm. It ached, nonetheless.

Paige dipped a crispy orange fry into a small cup of ranch dressing and popped it into her mouth. At least he'd remembered right on that score. "It's still a fairly new gig. Jesse and Brenna's wedding was the first big event." A grimace pulled her lips down. "You know how that went."

"Jesse being late to his wedding wasn't your fault, doll. All was forgiven by the time he arrived." If only Tavo had Jesse's gift for wiggling out of tight spots. The guy had always performed admirably under pressure. As it was, Tavo's responses in his personal life ranged from erratic to falling apart. Suddenly famished, he took another bite of his cheeseburger.

"I know. But between Jesse forgetting his phone, Vi fainting, and you getting hurt because the twins were acting stupid ..." Regret filled her eyes, and she pushed aside the carton of fries. "It was all a bit much, don't you think? Who will want to hire me now?"

Out of former habit, Tavo placed his hand on hers, remembered he was a "friend," and dragged it away. "Again, none of that was your fault. If this business is the direction you're supposed to go, you'll get the jobs you need to make it happen. Hold on to your faith." Self-conscious over his last words, he picked up one of her abandoned fries and ate it. Where did the faith-bit come from? It had been years since he'd encouraged anyone about their spiritual walk. Judging from Paige's rounded eyes, she was wondering too.

The awkward moment passed. With little effort, they segued into chit-chatty small-group news, and Tavo shared work highlights. By unspoken agreement, they steered clear of their shared past or sensitive subjects like his dad, but the conversation flowed easily. He found it heartening. This was the most progress they'd made since he'd moved back home.

When Paige looked at her phone for the second time, he took the initiative. "Guess we'd better wind this down." Paige nodded, but her eyes said something else. What if she checked her phone out of habit, rather than a desire to cut her time short with him? Time to step up. "I've enjoyed this, Paige. I've missed our friendship."

She looked everywhere but at him. "Me too ..."

Certain a "but" was coming, Tavo jumped in again. "How

about we stick to being friends?" *For now.* "My shoulder still needs water therapy, and it's easier with a pal. You up for that?"

A flash of something he couldn't identify streaked across her features. "It depends on my schedule, but ... yes. A partner helps with the accountability factor." She looked as if she would say more but pressed her lips together. Already thinking around the corners of his proposal.

Tavo knew when a subject was closed. They left the restaurant and walked to her car. He kept the conversation light, but an element of stiffness had intruded. He hoped he wasn't setting himself up for disappointment. If she didn't want to be around him, it'd be stinkin' easy not to be available. Even if she showed, he didn't know how long he could keep up the friend ruse.

As he walked to his car, his phone rang. Unknown number. He stuffed it back into his pocket.

ED CLARKSTON'S appointment was an hour ago. Paige sat behind the desk in Rory's office at Spence Enterprises, alternating between fuming and berating herself. She could well understand a little tardiness—but an hour? Then the berating would kick in. This meeting was important to her, but it was a small cog in a celebrity's wheel. She had little to no understanding of the demands of fame. What she needed was more patience. Yeah, right. The mental cycle repeated ... over and over.

When an emergency at his new subdivision cropped up, Rory had wanted to postpone the meeting with Ed, but Paige had insisted she could handle it. In truth, there wasn't much to say. No way on this side of heaven would Spence Enterprises undertake a remodel of the existing structure on Rodeo Drive. Rory had called in subcontractors to check the foundation and structural damage. Their vigorous thumbs down had sealed Rory's initial opinion.

Of course, she'd broach the subject with more diplomacy, but no matter how delicately worded, it wouldn't alter the end result. Spence Enterprises would not make Ed's dream come true. Not unless the dream changed to a more realistic project.

Now it looked as if the meeting might not happen at all. Despite Ed's spirited defense of artistic vision, surely, he suspected a negative answer. Rory had outlined the problems and made his unwillingness to tackle them clear. Ed's offer of more money only aggravated him. Paige excelled at giving people the benefit of the doubt, but even she could see Ed's stubbornness wasn't serving any legitimate purpose.

She hoped to soften the blow. She glanced at her phone again. If Ed didn't call or walk through the door in a few minutes, that would not happen either. When did fashionably late become just plain rude?

Becca, the office receptionist who worked for Rory and his dad, entered the room. Rory had insisted Paige conduct the meeting in his office instead of her smaller one. *"Ed is all about appearances, P. The more clout, the better. And he's used to getting what he wants. He'll want you to promise things we can't deliver, so don't let him,"* he'd cautioned.

"There's a man here. Says he has an appointment," Becca drawled. "If this 'un's the one you've been waitin' for, he's late."

Paige suppressed a chuckle. Leave it to Becca not to mince words. "I'm aware. But this will be a short meeting."

"I'll be glad to sit in with you. Purty as he is, I bet he's used to getting his way." The older woman cackled.

It was impossible to predict how Becca would act. She

might fawn all over him or glower at his tardiness. Either way, this meeting needed to be handled with finesse. "I got this, Beck. You can show him in."

"I hope so," she muttered.

In short order, she ushered Ed in. The moment Paige made eye contact, her resolve wavered. Mercy, those blue eyes were stunning. Soft and deep. An infinite well of compassion.

He sat with a look of chagrin. "I'm abominably late. No excuse."

He acts for a living. She added an edge of steel to her voice, usually reserved for her brothers. "You're lucky I had work to do. But this won't take long." His hopeful look yanked at her emotions. "Mr. Clarkston, Spence Enterprises won't be able to take on your remodel."

"As in now? Or ever?" The words sharpened to a fine point.

She clasped her hands together on the desk. "I'm sorry we can't do it. I know you had a, uh, vision for it. But Rory—Mr. Spence performed due diligence with foundation and structural experts." She let that sink in. "They all reached the same conclusion. The cracked foundation makes it untenable. No good remodel happens on a faulty slab. Extensive termite damage riddles the existing walls. Even the building permits would be iffy."

The tantrum she'd been halfway expecting never came. Ed sat as if carved from stone for several seconds, then gave an offhand shrug. "It doesn't matter. There's always a way." When he rose, Paige did too. "I wanted you guys to do it, but there are other contractors. Someone else won't be afraid to take on a project of this status."

Afraid? Fear had nothing to do with Rory's decision, though it was best not to say that. She forced a smile. "Sorry we couldn't do business." Ed had his head in the clouds about the estate. Even so, she'd been looking forward to working with him. There had to be more to him than this obstinate side. The guy was a mega-star, even if he didn't know beans about the building industry.

He turned to leave, then swiveled back as if an idea had occurred to him. Her pulse marched double time at his knockout grin. "Well, you've made your, or rather *Spence's,* position clear about the house. But that's cool." Those startling eyes bored into her. "I heard you're an event planner."

Paige's jaw sagged. "How do you know that?" The question popped out before she could think better of it.

A charming smirk tweaked his mouth to one side. "Your boss isn't the only one who does 'due diligence.' I'm impressed with you, and I'd like to procure your services. How about you arrange a meet and greet, then a party or two, so I can get to know the movers and shakers in this town?"

Paige was speechless. Her confidence had flagged after Jesse and Brenna's wedding. Ed's proposal would allow her to meet people beyond her small circle. But could she work with Ed? Granted, he hadn't made the best first impression, but if she planned events for him, she could get to know the man behind his fabulous looks. Imagine the work that would flow in if she added a Hollywood A-lister to her portfolio. It would provide the money for Mom's medicine. Thank goodness, he didn't seem to notice her distraction and kept talking. "I'll enjoy working with *you*, and"—One eye closed in a sly wink— "I pay quite well."

Now he looked at her as if he was perfectly aware of the effect he was having. Drat! She'd learn to ignore those hypnotic eyes. Paige cleared her throat. "I'll, uh, put some ideas together and get back to you."

"Great." He leaned in. When Paige realized he planned to kiss her, she stepped back. Surprise lifted his brows, then his lips parted in an amused smile. "Oh, this is going to be fun."

CHAPTER NINE

Tavo punched beneath the water, keeping his head above the splashy churn. The shoulder still ached, but the muscles seemed stronger. Silas said the aquatics were helping. They'd better. A low growl rose in his throat. The exercises Paige prescribed were boring and painful, but they'd met three times now. He'd keep doing them no matter what.

Paige swam up to him in the next lane after a few laps of the butterfly stroke. The way her upper body arced out of the water in a repetitive movement made his shoulder hurt. "Looking good, Paige." So good his conscience would prick if he looked too long. Her one-piece bathing suits were modest, but he still needed to keep his imagination in check.

Droplets flew everywhere as she shook her head. "Hardly. But it's a fun stroke to play with."

"I've been thinking about this Hollywood dude." When Tavo asked what she'd been up to, she had bent his ear about the guy. Now Tavo had questions. "Why do you suppose he picked Valiant as his 'home away from home'? I'd think a rich guy would be more interested in Dallas or Houston—he's used to a glitzy lifestyle, right? Not going to find that in Valiant."

Paige jerked her head sideways to dislodge the water. "He says he's tired of the bright lights, so I guess we'll find out." She paused long enough to give him a heart-stopping smile, then tilted her head the other way. "I'm just excited he's giving me the type of work I want to do."

"You think he'll be easy to work for?"

Teeth nibbling her lip, Paige pondered the question. "I think so. He knows more about parties than remodeling, that's for sure."

Tavo didn't share her optimism. From what she'd told him, the guy's love for parties probably included things that wouldn't fly on her radar. Illegal things.

"The first event is a simple meet and greet. Everyone will want to see him, so it will be easy to put together. Ed says he wants it casual, but I'm holding out for something formal. First impressions run both ways. If he's serious about living here, even on a part-time basis, it would go a long way if he put his best foot forward."

Tavo held in a smile. She was clueless. "As much attention as he's used to, he probably won't see it that way. Famous people are used to being catered to, not the other way around."

"I hear you. And I'm not saying he's different. I'm just hoping he'll go for an invitation-only event to kick things off. You ready for another round of exercises?" She reached for a noodle.

He grabbed the elastic bands from the tile by the pool ledge and tossed her one. "How about spider crawls, and you do them with me?"

Paige dropped the noodle to catch the elastic band. "Why do I need to build up *my* shoulders?"

"It's good overall health." He grinned. "And I'll do more if you're close by." He made fists and flexed his arms in a pose. "So I can impress you with my muscles."

A blush stole over her cheeks, even as her eyes rolled skyward. "Oh, that. Well then, let's get to it, Big Guy." She moved to the side of the pool, put the band around her forearms, and scaled the wall with her fingertips.

Big Guy? In school, she'd called him that because he rescued her from a couple of hoodlums. He liked her current use of the old nickname. His lips curved as he followed her actions. Stretching the band taut, his fingers crawled up and down the pool wall. The water equalized the pressure. It would hurt later, but for now, his shoulder moved like oil on the barrel of his Glock.

They worked through three sets, stretching the bands and moving their fingertips in sync, not speaking. When they completed the last set, they were both taking deep, measured breaths. Paige wrapped her arms around her shoulders. "Oh, wow. My delts are going to fuss about this tomorrow."

Tavo's shoulder was already singing a noisy complaint. "Enough for today." He hauled himself out of the water and sat on the pool ledge. The slight chlorine smell permeated the area. Paige made use of the stairs at the shallow end and sat on a bench next to a painted blue wall. She picked up a towel and mopped her face. He grabbed his towel and joined her.

"You hungry?" he asked.

"Yes, but I'm meeting Ed for dinner."

Reality washed over Tavo, colder than the pool water. "Where are y'all going?"

"Someplace private. He'll text me where." Paige giggled softly. "This is all new to me. Apparently, A-listers keep their whereabouts on the down-low to avoid creating a scene."

"But you and Rory met with him in public, right?"

"We did. Ed was getting a feel for the town—catching the

Valiant vibe, I believe were his words." A smile hitched the lips he still longed to kiss.

Tavo grappled for patience. "Paige, I'm not sure you know what you're getting into. You hardly know this guy—"

"We're not in high school anymore, Gus. I can handle myself." Her almond-brown eyes turned flinty.

"I know you can." He knew no such thing. Paige wouldn't know how to interpret a man who was selfish to the core and played dirty.

"This job will jump-start my event-planning business … and something else. I have to make it work, but you know I'm careful."

"You have a great job with Rory." He ran a hand over his short hair, at a loss for what was driving her.

She snatched up her bag and stuffed the damp towel into it. Brushing past him, she shot him a glare. "Don't get me wrong. Rory's a good boss, but I'll never be more than his personal assistant … and I refuse to be my mother."

He stared after her retreating figure. What on earth did that mean?

After a shower, Tavo drove by an Asian fast-food place and picked up egg rolls and various fried rice options. His appetite had waned after the exchange with Paige, but now his stomach was yowling. Too bad he wasn't any closer to understanding what had set her off.

Well, no. He had figured out one thing. She'd misinterpreted his be-careful warning as too much machismo. As if he was beating his chest or something equally ridiculous. Not true. He made a mental note not to ruffle that particular feather in the future. But what her mother had to do with anything remained a mystery. His face scrunched with bemusement. From what he remembered, her mom had been a sweet woman who always looked overwhelmed.

He pulled into the driveway. Dad's white pickup was parked in the garage. Unusual. It was almost 7:30. Good thing Tavo had picked up extra food. The pantry didn't hold more than a few cans of strange-sounding soup and dry crackers. Carrying the takeout, he used the garage entrance to the kitchen.

After his youthful attempt to take charge of his life, i.e., the dreadful stints in San Antonio and Frisco, he'd moved back home for two reasons. He'd matured enough through the school of hard knocks to understand if he didn't at least attempt to reconcile with his dad, it would haunt him for the rest of his life.

Then there was Paige, but the Texas Two Step had nothing on their back-and-forth relationship. He sighed ruefully. Best clear his head of Paige for now. Dad was plenty enough to deal with at the moment.

He'd no sooner set the bags on the table than his father walked in barefooted, wearing jeans and a T-shirt. Shorter than Tavo by a couple of inches, his size and air of authority still made bad guys go the other direction. He eyed the bags and sniffed appreciatively. "Enough for both of us?"

"Yep. Leftovers too." Cooking wasn't high on their list of priorities unless it involved grilling, but that was rare with just the two of them. Tavo's stomach growled again. He opened a white bag and offered it to his father. "Might as well start with these." Dad loved egg rolls.

When a car door slammed, they paused. A minute later, the back door opened, and Rick sauntered in. Dad looked at Tavo with a deadpan expression. "There go the leftovers."

Tavo eyed his brother. "Did you smell the food?"

Rick intercepted the bag Tavo still held and helped himself. "Timing is everything." He took a huge bite of egg roll. Tavo's mouth watered.

Dad set plates on the table and snatched the bag away from Rick. "Best meal I've seen all week."

Tavo filled his plate, ignoring the desire to fork food straight out of the carton. They ate in companionable silence. Finally, his dad pushed away his plate. "That was exceptional."

Still working on the chicken fried rice, Tavo nodded.

Dad sipped his longneck. "I hoped you'd be home. A situation came up today that needs addressing. Are you aware Ed Clarkston, the famous movie actor, is in town?" His voice held curiosity, along with a faint thread of irritation. Unfazed, Rick's head stayed buried in the chicken fried rice carton. He was used to police talk.

"Yep." Tavo suspected he was being buttered up, but for what?

"His presence will have every weirdo in the county crawling out of the woodwork. Houston, too. I don't want anything happening to him on my watch—the guy needs a tail." He leveled his Chief of Police gaze at Tavo.

"He's already got security. They're doing their job, from what I hear."

Dad's gaze sharpened. "What have you heard?"

"When he conducted business with Rory Spence at Hugo's, the inevitable fans appeared. Ed's personal security had it well under control." Tavo would keep Paige out of it for as long as possible.

But when it came to omissions, Dad had the nose of a bird dog. "According to Paige, I assume. She's still Spence's PS ... PA or whatever you call secretaries these days?"

So much for keeping Paige out of it. Rick pulled up from the carton, a pained expression crossing his face. "What's your beef with Paige?"

Tavo gritted his teeth but said nothing. Dad didn't even look Rick's way.

"Even if it's under control, I need our department on it. Surveillance and security. You up for a moonlighting stint?"

"Would it do any good to say no?" A rough edge of sarcasm laced Tavo's response.

The older man regarded him steadily. "You're on light duty. This will help with the boredom. Give the shoulder a better chance to heal. Besides, I trust you. You'll get the job done and not blab it around the office."

His fork stopped mid-way to his mouth. A rare compliment wrapped around a job he would otherwise spit out of his mouth. Dad must really want this.

"I'll make sure it's worth the aggravation." The older man said.

Tavo had no worries on that score. Dad held the record for the longest Chief of Police in Valiant for excellent reasons. The man had a gift for getting the best out of his employees. Tavo had idolized him growing up. Still wanted to follow in his footsteps, but Dad doused cold water on that dream at every opportunity. It had been at the root of Tavo's decision to strike out on his own. "I'll do it," he said in a low voice.

The deep crease in Dad's forehead disappeared. "Thanks, son."

Tavo blew out a long sigh. "I love you, Dad." Funny how the more he said it, the easier the words came, but he couldn't resist a tweak. "But I'm not doing it for you."

CHAPTER TEN

Dad's brow arched, and he opened his mouth. Fortunately, at that moment, his phone buzzed. Probably a good thing for all their sakes. They'd get an earful if Dad interpreted Tavo's remark as disrespect. Instead, he picked up the phone and headed into the other room. Tavo had seen the screen, knew as Chief of Police, his dad didn't have a choice.

He turned to Rick. "As long as I'm doing a *favor* for Dad, I'm gonna need one from you." Rick snickered at Tavo's heavy emphasis on favor.

"Sure, bro. Whatcha need?" As brothers, they'd had their share of squabbles, but when it involved Dad, their solid front was born out of necessity. And now Tavo needed his brother's cyber skills.

"I need a full rundown on Ed Clarkston."

The easy shrug of Rick's shoulders said it'd be no problem. "I need to tell you something too. Before Dad gets off the phone."

Tavo's last bite of pork dumpling lodged on the way down. "Shoot."

"Mom and I are communicating." The words carried a nonchalant vibe that came with practice.

"O-kay." Tavo blew out a breath. "What's that got to do with me?"

Rick stared at him, then snorted. "She's trying. You need to forgive her."

An unwelcome ache bloomed in Tavo's chest. "I've tried, and nothing seems to change. You were younger, Rick. Around her more. You don't remember what it was like."

"I know she's sorry."

"If you want to believe that, go ahead. The truth is, she left us to pursue her goals. We weren't enough."

"She wants to talk to you, bro. It'd be good if you would open up enough to hear what she has to say." He spoke again through a clenched jaw. "Just giving you a heads up, big brother. You need to figure a few things out before it happens."

Tavo threw his hands in the air, barely missing the ceiling fan. Figure a few things out? He had no clue where to start with his absentee mother. All he knew was she'd left when he needed her.

PAIGE PUSHED BACK from her small kitchen table, stretched her arms over her head, and looked out the tiny window. A mellow orange sky settled into grayish blue as twilight stole the day. She squinted at her computer screen, which displayed a Pinterest board of color schemes and various décor for Ed's meet and greet. A yellow pad lay to one side, full of notes and sketches inked in black. Gus should be here by now. Her jaw twinged when she swallowed. No sore throat, but the slight pain persisted. Must be why her concentration was off.

The doorbell chimed. Finally. Her bare feet slapped the floor as she hurried to answer it, more relieved than she should be. The more she saw of Gus, the harder it was to keep him in the friend zone. Surprisingly, renewed determination to keep him at arm's length didn't follow. She swung open the door. A ripple skittered up her spine. Her greeting came out breathier than she would have liked. "Hi, Gus."

His expression morphed from stern to resigned. "You need to use the peephole, Paige. What if it had been some smarmy sales guy instead of me?"

"I knew it was you." Her jaw pinged as if to commiserate with the lame excuse.

His deep brown eyes gazed at her. "Make sure, please."

"I will." She stepped back and waved him in, then shut the door. His fresh shower smell and solid presence were making her jitters dissipate. Well, aside from minor irritation over his tendency to fuss when she wasn't careful. She could handle that. What she couldn't manage was letting her heart get too close. Even if the rest of her wanted to lean in and soak up his strength.

His boots clomped in a steady rhythm as he followed her into the kitchen. "Hungry?"

"I'm always hungry, Paige. Nothing's changed on that score." A grin spread across his face, making her smile too.

"Okay. Do you want a sandwich or leftover taco casserole?"

"Yes."

His eyes caught hers. And just like that, they'd fallen right back into their high school routine when he'd show up after football practice, weary and famished.

Dimples dented his cheeks. "I'll fix a sandwich for me. Want one?"

"Yes. But make mine half." Warmth crept up the back of her neck as she turned to the fridge to pull out sandwich ingredients and the casserole dish. She motioned to a drawer where Gus found a knife. He assembled sandwiches while she dished up bowls of the casserole. His ringtone played. He glanced at the phone screen. "Same strange number."

"I get those too."

"If it's important—" Tavo recited. She joined him. "They'll leave a text or a message." They exchanged another grin. Another blast from the past worming its way into the present.

Once the food was prepared, they sat at the small table for two. "Would you like to say grace?" She extended her hand across the table.

His jaw set like giving thanks was the absolute last thing on earth he wanted to do, but she bowed her head. *Please do this, bud. It'll help you return to your faith.*

An exasperated huff filled the air between them, and then warm fingers wrapped around her hand. He tentatively began, "Umm. Lord, thank you for today. For keeping our city safe. I, uh, we thank you for this meal, and uh, for the time together. In Jesus's name, Amen." When he gave her hand a soft squeeze, she snatched it away and shook her head more to herself than to him.

"What? You started it."

The lower part of Paige's face throbbed like someone had placed a hot coal on each jaw. To her utter dismay, her eyes filled, tears threatening to spill down her cheeks. "Sorry," she choked out. "Don't know what's wrong with me today." Her conscience protested. No way she would admit how Gus's prayer and holding his hand had orbited her back to their happy place.

The microwave dinged, and she sniffed back the tears. "Eat. I'll be fine." She motioned to his plate.

He hesitated, then took a bite of the sandwich. Then another. The pain radiating from her jaws settled, and she swallowed a bite or two of her sandwich. When he'd eaten the sandwich and polished off the bowl of casserole, Gus set his plate in the sink. "You done?" He looked askance at her barely touched plate. She handed it to him. He took it, scraped the remains into the disposal, and filled the dishwasher while she pulled out the sketches she'd made for the meet and greet.

He sat back down. "For both our sakes, let's make the Ed stuff short. I saw where he'd chartered a plane to Houston."

"Yeah, he flew in to watch a rodeo. Said he'd never seen one live. I was glad for the opportunity to work on the meet and greet. It's going to be like pulling a rabbit out of a hat, getting it done on time." She blew out a frustrated breath. "An outstanding event doesn't just happen."

"I did security for several celebrity gigs in San Antonio. Show me what you've got."

Tavo helped her work up a security-minded room arrangement at the Country Club and shared a few tips, but by the time they'd tweaked it to both their satisfaction, her energy was at a low ebb.

He held out a hand. "Let's go to the living room. I'm thinking you need to take it easy." She allowed him to help her up. A strange weariness was invading her body. Her muscles felt like jelly.

TAVO PULLED the big sofa chair close to the couch where Paige sat and settled into it. She was definitely not her spunky self. Her eyes had lost their sparkle, and she seemed bone-tired. Had she wanted to accompany Ed to Houston, or was something going on with her physically?

As he puzzled over the change, she asked, "Why did you leave Valiant?"

He gazed at her in confusion. "What?"

Her shoulder lifted a notch as if her question were no big deal, but her eyes looked haunted. He rubbed a hand down his face. "You know why."

"Your dad? He was pretty vocal about not wanting you to go into law enforcement, if I remember right."

Her memory was correct as far as it went. "He was part of the reason."

"Why else?"

He stared at her, unable to comprehend this ... unwarranted curiosity after all these years. Like their relationship had been a trophy she'd placed on a shelf and suddenly wanted to relive. "What's with these brutal questions, Paige? Asking a little late, don't you think?"

"Not if we're going to be real friends." The sincerity in her eyes made his heart speed up. "What else made you leave?"

"It was lonely because you weren't here anymore." The words jarred like a chisel hitting a rock. Oh, brother. Since he was spilling his guts ... "Why did *you* leave?"

She looked away. "You know I had to."

The old anger flared to the surface, and he stretched to find a reasonable tone. "Forgive me, doll, and I mean that. But I knew no such thing. I thought we were in love, then you decided whatever you wanted to do with your life didn't include me."

"Is that what you think?"

"What was I supposed to think? You were hell-bent on getting out of Dodge—"

"It wasn't either/or. I was immature—"

"We both were." At least they could agree on one thing.

Paige nodded her head. "We were so young, and you were

so serious. I cared about you—only I wasn't ready to settle down yet."

"I get that now." He understood all too well. "But I couldn't wrap my brain around it then. After graduation, the friction with Dad about me following my heart into law enforcement, and you not being around anymore … I had to get away. At least that's what I told myself." A bitter note entered his voice.

"So you moved to San Antonio."

The hurt flickering in the depth of her eyes bewildered Tavo. As if his leaving Valiant broke her heart the way she'd broken his. "Yes. I had some savings. Got a part-time singing gig to help make ends meet while I attended the police academy there. It was a good call despite the mistakes I made along the way."

"We both made mistakes, Gus." Sadness filled her expression.

Yeah, but if she knew the lines he'd crossed, any second chance would be over before it started. He changed the subject. "I have a question, but it's not about us. What did you mean when you said you refused to be like your mama?"

She seemed to think about it. "You know Dad wasn't around much." Gus nodded. He'd only seen the man twice in all the years they'd dated.

"Mom raised us by herself." Her look was intense. "I don't want that. I don't want a bunch of kids—or any kids—if that's the case." She shrugged. "If that means I stay single, then I need a good job to support myself."

Paige didn't want kids? He gazed at her warily. "You won't stay single, Pep. You're way too pretty. And I'm still not sure what we've accomplished by crawling under every old rock in our past."

Paige rose and moved closer to where he was sitting. "A good airing out of our relationship was long overdue."

"Did we resolve anything?" Skepticism filled his words.

"What do you think?" Her face was void of emotion.

"You want to be friends." Dare he say that would never be enough for him? "I want ... that too." *And so much more.*

She held out a hand. "Let's shake on that."

In one fluid motion, Tavo rose. When he took her hand, the connection blazed. He pulled her into his arms. She trembled but didn't resist. His hands cradled her jaws, and her eyes closed with a moan. Oh, how he had missed this. Determined not to rush the moment, he angled his head and slowly lowered his mouth toward hers. As he brushed her lips, an insistent buzzing came between them.

She stiffened. Not wanting it to end, Tavo hugged her, then reluctantly shifted his arms to her shoulders. Paige fumbled in her pocket and pulled out her phone. "Ed?" She shot him a guilty look. Shrugging out of his arms, she walked away.

CHAPTER ELEVEN

G ood thing Paige had ordered enough appetizers to feed a hometown football crowd. Tavo shifted his feet as he stood by the massive entrance doors. Not that Ed's goons had approved of his presence. They'd made it clear he was a pain in their collective rears, but Tavo wouldn't budge. Too many things could go wrong with the light security they provided, but convincing them of that? He'd have to draw it in crayon.

The clock hand was moving toward nine o'clock, and Ed had yet to make an appearance. The small band that had played through their repertoire of his movie theme songs twice was now taking a break. Lines to the complimentary bar snaked through the tables. Everyone still seemed in good spirits despite the guest of honor's slow roll. Almost like they expected this behavior. Tavo gazed at his favorite person in the room. Paige was breathtakingly beautiful tonight. The black gown accentuated her petite figure. Hair all swept up. Long, dangly earrings. Beneath the façade of calm, however, she was in pain. He'd first noticed it at her place. Now here.

They hadn't really spoken since that almost-kiss. The wall

that had gone up afterward was agonizingly familiar. Her focus had narrowed to this blasted meet and greet, but he would ask about her physical pain. How he longed to wrap her in his arms and make it go away.

His feet moved as if to jar his thoughts back to his job. Food deliveries were complete, but he doubted anyone bothered to lock the door. Too many times, an unlocked door was how uninvited guests gained entrance. Ed's security wouldn't like it, but that was too bad. He hastened through the busy kitchen. Sure enough, the delivery door was open. Ed's personal assistant stood just outside, his fingers wrapped around an electronic device. Tavo hated vaping. Before he could say anything, a flash of something disappeared around the corner of the building. His professional instincts flared. Making a split-second decision, he stayed put. His primary job was to secure the premises.

"Are you in or out? This door needs to be secured."

The guy didn't budge from his spot. He ignored Tavo and the question. *Jerk.* Tavo didn't feel like cutting him slack, but his father's voice rang in his ear. He'd heard it a thousand times growing up. *For the greater good, let the anger go.*

Finally, the guy spoke. "I'll lock it when I'm done."

Tavo gave him a firm "hold-you-to-it" nod, but he'd shadow the guy right along with Ed. As Tavo made his way back to the dining room, he passed by the bar. The head of Ed's security brought the rest of the team around with a flick of his fingers. Tavo stood behind a large potted plant and listened. Pointing to his earpiece, the man said, "Here's the message. Light duty tonight. Guests are a bunch of townies and do-gooders."

Another guy piped up, already sounding as if he'd had one too many. "Well, what do you expect? This is Podunkville."

Tavo's irritation lodged like a shard of glass. He sucked in a deep breath. Their opinions carried no weight. He'd stay alert because they surely wouldn't.

At that moment, Ed finally arrived, flanked by the mayor and his wife. Paige had pre-arranged an early meeting with them so they could help Ed with introductions. The band leader launched into a lively rendition of the celebrity's latest box-office theme song. A kaleidoscope of color flashed around the room. A bright white light trained on Ed.

Paige had taken his suggestions to heart and tweaked them with her trademark elegance. She had worried about the money, but he assured her most celebrities were used to, and even expected, such treatment. As he glanced around the room, their eyes found each other, and Paige gave him a playful wink. *Oh, mercy.* Ed could lap up all the attention he wanted. Tavo had won the real prize.

Once they finished the first round of photos—Tavo knew photo opportunities would compose much of the evening—Ed sat down amid much ado and fawning. Tavo grudgingly gave him points. The guy knew how to work a crowd. He said all the right things and acted completely sincere. If Tavo hadn't experienced the private lives of other celebrities, he might have swallowed it. Even Paige, who invariably thought the best of everyone, mentioned Ed could be cantankerous—her word—when he didn't get his way. That sounded far more like the famous people Tavo had encountered.

Once Paige took her chair next to Ed, he leaned over, presumably to tell her something, when a shriek came from the kitchen. As Tavo headed toward the noise, another shriek split the air and turned into boisterous crying.

Tavo's teeth ground as a large, unkempt woman barreled her way past startled guests, yowling at the top of her lungs.

Oh, no. Homeless Sue was on the loose.

Ed had half-risen out of his chair, curious about the

commotion. Sue hurtled toward him, her long blondish-gray hair flying about her shoulders. Seemingly unaware of her audience, she wrapped her body around Ed. "I'm supposed to have your baby."

Ed froze. His security team came running with blood in their eyes. Tavo picked up speed and planted himself between the woman and Ed's angry team.

He wouldn't allow Ed's bullies to hurt a mentally ill woman. They only wanted to save face in front of their boss. *Help me here, Lord.* Homeless Sue needed compassion. Good grief, the woman suffered enough pain from her condition. Podunkville or not, Valiant was his town, and this calamity happened on his watch.

"Let me handle this, fellas." He'd try a reasonable approach first. Glowering, Ed's musclemen didn't back off, but no one attempted to pull Sue off Ed either. Hard to blame them. She smelled like week-old garbage. Then the photos started. Individuals crowded in, angling for shots of her draped over the celebrity. Great. Nice way to put Valiant on the map.

The rustle of skirts caught his attention. Paige leaned over, whispering into Sue's ear. The entire room seemed to hold its breath as she gently unwrapped Sue's arms from around Ed. He stepped out of Sue's range quickly, composing his features into a mega-star grin.

Tavo wanted to tear Sue away from Paige. *Stat.* The woman had already proved her unpredictability. Ignoring his feelings, he gently took her elbow. "C'mon, Sue. Let's get you a plate of dinner." Her nonsensical jabber didn't let up, but she allowed him to lead her into the kitchen.

STROKE. Breathe. Stroke. Breathe. Paige sliced through the clear pool water with a vengeance. As she had feared, news of Ed's meet and greet had splashed across the front page with a photo of Valiant's infamous bag lady clinging to Ed. A decent shot of him, anyway. Did the man ever take a bad picture? The headline, "Homeless Sue Finally Nabs Her Man," canceled any positives about the event. And, of course, the story had gone viral. She plowed through the water, pushing herself beyond her normal stopping point.

When every muscle screamed for a break, she swam to the side, placing her arms on the pool ledge. She gasped for air, her lower body still in the water.

"Hey, *chica.*" Gus's face appeared above her. A gentle smile tugged at his lips, creasing his cheeks. Those dimples made her heart race. And the uniform—he came to see her on his break? She hid her head. "Go away."

His knees popped as he squatted closer to her level. "Your meet and greet was a roaring success, Paige."

She raised her head in disbelief. "You were there, Gus. Since when is an event deemed a success when a homeless woman yells obscene things at the guest of honor?"

His shrug suggested Sue's actions were of no consequence. How dare he? "Gus, everything I touch is a disaster. First, the wedding—"

"There were glitches, but Jesse and Brenna are quite happy. That's what matters."

Paige shook her head so hard, drops of water landed everywhere. "How can you say nothing bad happened? Your dislocated shoulder was more than a glitch."

"Expecting perfection all the time is a recipe for frustration. Hitches, glitches, and weird twists are going to happen, but you need to roll with it. You can't get uptight over every little thing." His steady smile removed any sting from the words.

Still. His insistence on a different perspective aggravated her. "Jesse being late to his wedding doesn't count as a little thing. Brenna was crying, for heaven's sake."

"Yeah, okay. Big fishtail at the beginning, but everything turned out fine. Better than fine if you listen to them talk. The groom being late was one thing that made their special day unique."

Despite her ire, Paige suppressed a chuckle. That sounded almost romantic. Especially since she knew weddings weren't his thing. Tired of staring at the blue tiles lining the pool ledge, she hoisted herself out of the water. When Gus reached for her, she backed away. "I'm wet."

She tip-toed gingerly across the wet tile to the bench. Gus beat her there. "Sit down and talk for a bit? You need to hear me out."

She fished a towel out of her bag and sat far enough away so as not to drip on his work clothes.

"I had a feeling you'd be beating yourself up this morning. Paige, your perception is skewed. Life happens. Bad things happen. Sue crashing the party last night wasn't your fault. It was unexpected and surprised Ed along with everybody else, but he also made sure nobody forgot about it."

Snuggling deeper into her towel, she secretly agreed with his assessment. She couldn't let him know that though—he'd be insufferable. She scratched around for more ammunition. He refused to believe her problems were serious. "What about your shoulder? You must admit it's a setback."

"If I had to do it all over again, I'd still push that little girl out of the way. It's how I'm wired. Yeah, I miss powerlifting and hope I can get back to it, but it's not the end." He gave her a sly look. "The silver lining is water therapy with you."

CHAPTER TWELVE

W as that really how Gus felt? She'd suspected, but that comment left no wiggle room for her just-friends theory.

Trouble was, she also looked forward to their pool sessions. But it couldn't last. She had a career to plan. "Speaking of that, I'm getting busier and busier. Chances are, I won't be as regular from here on out." Seeing his face fall, she rushed on, "You know the exercises now. No reason you can't do them without me."

He ran his fingers down a strand of her wet hair. "What happened to us being partners?"

Why did he have to do this? She rose, snugging the towel around her torso. "We'll always be friends, Gus."

"Paige." Longing wrapped around her name. It messed with her decision not to get involved with him again. He didn't rise, as if he knew she'd stick around until he did. She wanted to dive into the pool and stay there until she remembered why she couldn't do this. His deep gaze pierced her defenses. "You're not yourself. What's going on, Pep? You're in pain."

Her eyes filled. She'd forgotten how observant he could be. "Sometimes, my jaws ache, but it's not a big deal." As if to contradict the lie, her fingers massaged the tender spot beneath her earlobe.

"Mm-hmm. As a friend, how about I take you to get it checked out?"

Even as she shook her head, she knew perfectly well why he volunteered. She still carried the mentality that going to the doctor was a last resort. When she and her siblings were growing up, it was an extra Mom couldn't afford. In high school, Paige had put off going to the doctor until a mild case of bronchitis turned serious. Gus took her to the clinic when she couldn't breathe. Warmth crept up her damp neck at the memory.

"You don't need to take care of me, Gus." Ouch. He was just being his sweet, generous self.

"What if I want to?"

She had no response to that.

He unfolded from the bench and stood. She stayed close, not wanting to leave things on a sad note, but it would be wrong for her to encourage anything more than friendship.

"Friends?" Her question squeaked with nervousness.

"Of course." His lips pressed together tightly.

She didn't quite reach his shoulder. It shouldn't have bothered her, but it did. He'd always topped her by several inches. Back when they'd hung out, she'd worn the highest heels she could find, but it never made a smidge of difference.

He'd always been out of her reach.

MINUTES BEFORE MIDNIGHT, Tavo stood in the locker room at the police station again. The ceiling fan wafted the ever-present odor of human perspiration around the room. Ochoa had called earlier, asking if Tavo would take his shift. He'd said yes. Never hurt to have a favor to call in. Two shifts in twenty-four hours were no piece of cake, especially since he'd pulled security duty last night at the event for Ed, but it wouldn't matter if he slept through his day off. Since Paige had redefined their "friend" status, he had no plans.

When she let him hold her the other night, he'd hoped they were finally getting past the friend zone but apparently, he was wrong. Again. Her words at the pool this morning had made her stance crystal-clear, but her body language conveyed something different. Like she wouldn't object if he massaged her hurting face. Or kissed her. She'd seemed pretty torn up about it. He stuffed his duffle bag back into the locker and slammed it shut.

This just-friends deal hogtied any forward movement. Nothing he could do if she wasn't on board. He'd just have to bide his time. Surely her infatuation with Ed Clarkston, mega-celebrity, would run its course. She'd deny it, but Tavo had seen the stars in her eyes when she sat by him during dinner. The photographer had seen it too, thus, the *other* picture on the front page. Ed had looked interested, but Tavo doubted there was an inch of commitment on his part. Oh, sure, he had the looks females seemed to like. A sigh puffed through Tavo's lips. He'd never been in the class of men who drew women's attention—more like they saw him coming and lit out the other way. He was too tall, his features too large to win any poster boy contest.

His phone chimed. He froze when he saw the screen and struggled to get past his hesitancy. "Sharla?"

Her familiar voice washed over him, bringing an ache of guilt so deep he nearly doubled over. He listened. Regret tore through him. A longing to change what had happened. The certain knowledge he couldn't fix what went wrong.

She seemed nervous, but he detected something else in her voice as well. "We need to talk."

"Sure." He wasn't sure at all. "What's this about?" A dozen other questions came to mind, especially why she'd call when normal people slept.

"I need to say it in person." A strained chuckle filled her end. "No worries, Tavo. This isn't a plea for reconciliation. Name a day. I'll come to you."

He heard it again. Sadness, but the ever-present sarcasm was gone. An uncomfortable minute passed as they firmed up a date. She clicked off first. An uneasy feeling swirled in his gut. After no communication for years, what could Sharla possibly want?

Picking up the pace, his boots thudded on the linoleum in the hallway. He stopped at the door and faced the sergeant on duty. He looked straight ahead and drew his hand to his brow in a crisp salute. "Evenin' Sarge."

"Weren't you just here?" A map of lines etched the older man's forehead. A toothpick dangled from one side of his mouth.

"Yes, sir. Taking Ochoa's shift, sir." The musty smell of the old building filled his nostrils.

"Okay. Stay alert out there, Morales."

"Yes, sir." Tavo entered the room for assembly. The few faces he recognized weren't friendly. Most assumed he was a conduit for relaying information, i.e., gossip, to his dad. Ochoa remained the ongoing exception. Mostly because he and Tavo shared a similar mindset about not socializing with the people they worked with. Sharla, the one exception he'd made early in his career, had nuked any desire for closeness with other coworkers. The ultimate cautionary tale.

Once the sergeant barked through the memos: a minor change in a local ordinance, a birth announcement for an officer he'd met only once, a retirement party, and a new safety tip, Tavo fell in with the other officers for inspection. Dad remained a stickler about officers being prepared. After checking pistols and the body-worn cameras, they received the "Fall Out" command. He turned on his radio and listened to squad assignments. Feeling older than his years, he was relieved his assignment included the same sector and squad car from his previous shift. Between Paige's "friendship" and the upcoming meeting with Sharla, he craved stability in one area of his life.

Once he logged in the 10-08 code on the squad car computer, letting others know he was available for assignments, he pulled out of the parking lot. Streetlights lit the black sky with an artificial haze. Red taillights from other vehicles winked in and out of diminished traffic flow. The night shift had never been Tavo's preference. He missed the daytime sounds of increased traffic, construction noise, and the bustle of people going about their business. The absence of the sun seemed to bring desolation. Loneliness. He welcomed the chatter of dispatch that broke into his musings.

Tavo responded, accepting the assignment. He drew a long breath. Family troubles were disheartening, but that didn't negate the need for a mediator. He glanced at the address on the computer and pressed the accelerator. The sharp scent of the antiseptic wipe he'd previously used on the backseats clung to the car's interior. Whenever he pulled the night shift, he always hoped for a quiet night, but if not, a backseat occupant might appreciate Tavo's desire for a clean-smelling vehicle.

Outside a stately red brick apartment complex within a residential area, a young mother cried, "You have to do something." She gripped her phone with white knuckles. "He was supposed to bring her back hours ago."

Tavo shook his head regretfully. "It's not a police matter, ma'am—"

"He doesn't have the stuff to take care of her. No food … diapers. She's only nine months old." Fear poked its ugly head through the words. Tears streaked her face, and she seemed on the verge of falling apart.

"You said he's the baby's father?" At her nod, he continued. "It's a custody issue, ma'am. That jurisdiction belongs to the courts. I can't interfere." Tavo wanted to kick some sense into the guy. Who knew what the real story was, but the lack of communication only made it worse.

The mother shifted a diaper bag over one shoulder, still sobbing.

Tavo hated to leave it this way, but he had no other option. "I'm sorry. Go back inside, please. Waiting out here isn't a good idea."

She sniffed and turned to go. Her shoulders slumped in defeat. Tavo acted as if he would get in his car but watched until the door shut. If police work had given him anything, it was the ever-growing conviction to be a good dad. A prospect looking more unlikely by the minute.

Three hours later, Tavo pulled in at a convenience store on the corner of a busy intersection during daylight hours. Now there was hardly any traffic. The store owner had his act together—meaning no illegal stuff on the side—and he sold excellent coffee.

He stretched his legs, glad to be out of the patrol car for a bit. The radio chatter wasn't much company tonight. At least not the kind he needed. He cleared his throat. He'd put this off way too long. "Um, Lord? You already know how sorry I am about … well, a lot of things … but especially the way things ended with Sharla." He let loose an extended sigh. "I've messed up with the people I love most. You brought me back ... so help me with this reconciliation business." He huffed and looked skyward. "Cause you know I don't have a clue about what I'm doing."

As he continued in the same vein, divine forgiveness seeped through the dry, hard ground of his heart. He soaked it in like moisture to parched ground. Breathing lighter than he had in months, he stepped out of the patrol car and into the convenience store.

"Sup?" He greeted the lone woman behind the counter. She didn't look thrilled to see him—many folks weren't happy to see the uniform, but he'd learned it wasn't personal. He filled a cup with Colombian roast and perused the shelves for trail mix, still flattered Paige remembered his favorite. Peanuts, raisins, and M&M's. No need for weird nuts or any of that yogurt-flavored stuff.

He paid, attempting another conversation with the check-out gal, but she wasn't having it. Mm. Highly allergic to the uniform.

Walking out, he took a sip of brew and observed the intersection. Dispatch crackled in his ear. Taking care with the steaming cup of coffee, he hurried to the patrol car and eased into the light traffic.

DOWN THE ROAD from the corner he'd just left, Tavo zipped around slow-moving cars. Lights flashing red and blue, he parked beside a dark sedan stopped in the middle of the intersection. As he approached the vehicle, the driver's head lay against the steering wheel. Another man riding shotgun was asleep or passed out. The car wasn't running.

Peering into the car, he knocked on the glass window. The driver stirred. The car keys in his hand slid to the floorboard. A female patrol officer who Tavo recognized jogged over. Cupping her hands, Bianca looked into the passenger window. She backed out and said, "No blood that I can see. I'm going to open the door."

Tavo nodded and opened the driver's door. The distinctive odor of alcohol assailed his nostrils. "Hey, wake up." He'd long since mastered the unique law enforcement blend of authority and how-can-I-help-you.

"Are you okay?" On the passenger side, Bianca's face twisted into a grimace at the smell.

The passenger stirred. When she asked again, the driver lifted his head and looked around.

Aww. No! Tavo stared at the occupants of the car. Dark mops of hair and faces too similar for anything except a familial bond. Oh, man. Tavo wished he was anywhere but here. He swallowed hard and echoed Bianca's words, "Are you all right? Can you tell me your names?"

Tough break. He already knew them. Carlos and Miguel, Paige's twin brothers had been drunk enough to pass out in a busy intersection.

Tavo's protective side kicked into high gear. Paige would be livid.

PAIGE HAD NEVER BEEN in the presidential suite of a hotel before. Sitting at an elegant table for two, she had a spectacular view of Valiant through the wide wall of windows. Bright sunshine streamed in, helping to curb the cold temperature of the room. A vase of large white roses adorned the small area. She sniffed appreciatively, then sipped her coffee to steady her nerves. Ed had invited her for a late brunch, but when she arrived, a PR guy answered the door. He ushered her in, telling her Ed would be out shortly. Sounds of water came from a bathroom. She guessed Ed had just rolled out of bed and was taking a shower.

She'd been up for hours already, juggling her workload for Rory and brainstorming fresh ideas for another event. If Ed still wanted her services after the debacle with Homeless Sue.

Her phone chimed with a text. She glanced at it. Gus.

Need to talk. Where are you?

Hm. He wasn't one for drama.

What's this about?

Will tell you in person. Where are you?

She hesitated, then typed her location and pushed SEND. As she did, the door of the master suite opened. Ed strolled out, looking far more handsome than any man had a right to. He slid into the chair across from her with a crooked smile. Barefooted, jeans and a T-shirt. Even his soap smelled exotic, though expensive might be a better word. The made-to-look-natural streaks in his damp hair were more pronounced. Somewhere in her perusal, her jaw had slipped open. She closed it with chagrin, wishing she could wire it shut.

A smile played about Ed's lips as he poured himself a cup of coffee and stirred in creamer. Taking a sip, he looked into her eyes and winked. Oh, boy. She probably came across as a naïve country girl. Desperate not to appear so, Paige blurted out the first thing that came to mind. "Gus is going to stop by."

Ed's eyes narrowed, but he responded easily enough. "Who's Gus?"

Oh. "Gus is the police officer who intervened with the ... uh ... homeless woman at the meet and greet."

"What does he want?"

"I doubt it has anything to do with the meet and greet. He only said it's important, and we need to talk now."

The thundercloud that had appeared on Ed's face somewhat lessened. "So this has nothing to do with me." He made it sound like it should. "He's coming here to talk about the two of you? And you're okay with that?"

"I ... it's not about us." Great. Now she was stammering.

Ed leaned forward so suddenly, she felt his breath on her face. "Should I be worried about him, love?"

CHAPTER THIRTEEN

P aige didn't care for the way Ed made it sound. "It's not like that. Gus and I are friends."

A sharp rap sounded on the door. The same PR guy who ushered her in answered. Ed never took his eyes off her, but called out, "It's okay, Bruce."

Gus strode into the room and made a beeline for her. Something melted in Paige's heart as she took in the deep creases in his cheeks and forehead. His eyes drooped with ... fatigue?

She immediately rose and met him halfway. "Did you pull an all-nighter?"

He gave a curt nod, then glanced at Ed. "Is there somewhere Paige and I can talk privately?"

Paige's stomach flipped. What on earth was this about?

Ed answered in a sullen tone. "Cory's room." He motioned to the room on the other side of the living area, opposite the master suite. Paige followed Gus there. Yikes. Clothes, towels, and food trash littered the floor and every available surface.

Forcing her attention back to Gus, she asked, "What's so

important you needed to interrupt my ... meeting with Ed?" Her ire faded at his somber expression. "Wha ... what's happened?"

"Nobody's hurt." He blew out a long breath. "Carlos and Miguel are drying out in the drunk tank downtown. I had to issue Carlos a DUI."

Her knees turned to butter. She should have expected something like this. Gus took her arm. "Nobody's hurt. Carlos shut off the ignition before he passed out. He must have realized he wasn't lucid enough to drive. That will help. I didn't want you to hear it on the news or from anyone else."

Suddenly, her jaws were ablaze. "What am I going to do with them?"

His grip on her arm tightened, even as he sighed. "You're not responsible for them. They are grown men, whether they act like it or not."

"I failed them, Gus. I wasn't strong enough to rein them in." Paige fought the tears spilling over her lashes. For heaven's sake, she couldn't have a meltdown with Ed in the next room.

"Praying for them will do a lot of good." Gus's expression was a blend of pity, sorrow, and a shred of optimism. She struggled to believe something good would come out of this.

"Look, I'm sorry I crashed your meeting ... or date ... whatever it is, but I knew you'd want to know." A half smile tugged at his lips. "Even if you would prefer not to claim your brothers right this minute."

At a loss for how to process the twins' latest catastrophe, Paige changed the subject. "It's not a date." Did she know that for sure? Ed hadn't quite specified.

Concern shone from the depths of Gus's dark eyes. "Be careful, Pep."

TAVO STOOD IN THE NEWEST PEEPS' workout room as his teammates worked through various powerlifting drills. He'd quit wearing the sling a week ago, but his shoulder still felt tender enough not to participate. No doctor's release either, something he would have insisted on if it had been another team member.

He walked to where Rory sat as he yelled instructions. The huge fans blew the American flag draped on one side of the gym. The stripes seemed to ripple to the music blasting through the speakers. Tavo could have cared less about the loud music thumping, but the younger members claimed the beat helped them maintain a lifting rhythm. Whatever.

As he drew close, he stuck out his hand. "Thanks again for agreeing to oversee this while I recoup."

The redhead shook his hand firmly. "Glad to see I left it in expert hands. You've taken them to a new level."

Tavo acknowledged the remark with a dip of his chin. The aluminum bleacher squeaked in protest when he sat. Rory eyed him. "I'm ready to hand the reins back to you whenever you're ready, Chief."

Again, Tavo nodded. "I'll let you know. I came to boost morale. Also knew you'd conk me on the head if I tried any lifting."

"Right about that." Rory gave a short blast on the whistle he wore around his neck. Several team members looked his way, but he pointed to a small guy. "Slower reps to build muscle, Curtis." He cast a side-eye at Tavo. "I'm not even going to ask what you were thinking when you allowed him access to practice. The guy spends more time trying to impress the girls than anything else."

Tavo lifted his good shoulder and let it drop. "Curtis is a royal pain-in-the-rear. The upside is he keeps everyone on their toes, including me."

Rory rolled his eyes and blasted the whistle again. He gave instructions to the woman next to Curtis. They adjusted accordingly. "How's it going with Paige these days?"

"You're the one with the inside line on Paige," Tavo snapped.

Rory's lips curved into his mustache. "Have you kissed her yet?"

"Don't pay any attention to him, bro." Jesse appeared and sat on the other side of Rory. "All he thinks about is kissing his wife." Tall and lean with olive skin, the man punched Rory in the arm with a frown.

"And you don't?" Rory shot back.

"Not yours to know." Jesse reclined, putting his hands behind his head. Rory's prying didn't faze him in the least.

Tavo debated. Jesse and Rory were his best friends. If he couldn't confide in these guys … "Paige has made it clear she just wants to be friends."

"Oh, that's the worst." Rory winced. "What are you going to do?"

Tavo's breath hissed. "I don't know. She's all caught up with A-lister Ed. Planning parties for him. Having dinner in the presidential suite …" He stopped to keep the bitterness from taking root. Funny, that. Never before had it concerned him what he allowed into his heart.

"Ed's a jerk. It'd be way better for her if he left Valiant." Rory scowled.

Jesse looked no happier. "Yeah, but that's something Paige needs to figure out. You guys harping about him will only make it worse."

Tavo knew. His veiled "be careful" had riled her enough.

As much as he wanted to share what was bothering him, he sensed it wasn't the time or the place. He needed a fresh approach with Paige, but that wasn't what was bugging him the most. Unfortunately, a tall blonde woman appeared at the double doors. An hour early.

Both Jesse and Rory stared for a moment. Well, why not? Sharla was a stunner in any setting. Jesse slid off the bench, his Director of Operations antenna waving madly.

Before he could head toward Sharla, Tavo rose hastily. "I got this, Jess."

"You know her?" Rory's eyes were still on the woman as she walked their way. She wore soft lavender pants and a matching top that complimented her hair. Glided was a more appropriate way to describe the way she moved. Tavo knew it was unconscious on her part.

That was the trouble. He knew her far better than he'd ever had a right to.

"Sharla. How'd you know where to find me?" Tavo met her with a light hug. For old times' sake? This was unfamiliar territory. When they'd parted, there had been no question of finality.

Her lashes lowered. "When you weren't in the lobby, I made some deductions. Turns out I was right."

Experience had taught him that was all the answer he'd get. Sharla liked to think she was mysterious. Secretive was more like it. "Okay. Where to now? Coffee? Dinner?"

She glanced around the room before answering. As if taking it all in. The giant American flag. The loud music. A few curious powerlifters looked their way, but mostly, they focused on their routines. "You've picked up a new hobby?" She tilted her head toward the practice floor.

"Normally, I coach, but I'm currently taking an enforced break." He flexed his shoulder. Sharla's eyes followed his movement. Awkwardness ensued when neither of them bridged the gap in conversation.

Sharla cleared her throat. "I came early to see where you

played football." A wistful look darted across her face and disappeared so quickly Tavo might have imagined it. Still, she seemed ... lighter ... was that the right word for it? She'd always carried an ethereal, super-model vibe, but this was something new.

"The football field?" Tavo groped for understanding.

"You talked about football a lot when we first met. If you don't mind, I'd like to see your old 'stompin' grounds." Sincerity rang in her words. Maturity? A definite improvement.

Tavo walked her out of the gym and drove her to the stadium. Sharla said little but seemed content to soak in her surroundings. When he parked, they strolled to one end of the field, safely back from the goalposts. A practice was in progress. The clash of shoulder pads. Coaches yelling encouragement. Frequent water breaks because of the heat.

He peeked at her as she watched the players on the field. Platinum blonde hair hanging past her shoulders. Light blue eyes. Long legs. She used to have curves in all the right places, but now she was rail thin. Her striking good looks had been both a blessing and a curse in the SA Police Department. The men either ogled her or assumed she didn't have a brain in her head. Totally wrong on the last charge. Sharla was smarter than most of her male counterparts, including him. They'd been rookies together, but she'd had a much harder time until his protective instincts kicked in. He never had to say much. His size proved enough of a deterrent to keep the disrespect at bay. They became good friends.

Where it should have stayed.

"Let's walk. I want to see it from the fifty-yard line." Sharla strode with grace through the trimmed grass along the sideline and sat on the lowest bleacher. "Front and center. Here's where it all happened?" She looked at him for confirmation.

He inclined his chin, not quite grasping this new side of

Sharla. Her words smacked of nostalgia, though she'd never wanted to visit Valiant back in the day. When she was his girlfriend. Lover. Significant other.

Until she wasn't.

She watched the players on the field for a while. Clasping her hands together, she sighed. "Tavo, I have cancer." Her voice and mannerisms remained careful and controlled.

Tavo's jaw sagged. If she'd sprouted wings and flown away, he wouldn't have been more surprised. She was staring at him as if she expected him to say something. Anything. The manners that Mom drilled into him as a young boy whirred to life. "I'm so sorry."

Her eyes reddened. "Thank you. I knew you wouldn't gush or bother with any weird displays of affection." Her words served as both observation and warning.

His mind scrambled with questions he didn't know how to ask. Nor was he certain she would appreciate them, so he opted for a question that would let him know real fast. "Wanna tell me about it?"

She explained the crushing diagnosis in an unemotional, almost clinical manner. Through a fog, he heard the descriptions. Aggressive. Difficult location. Doesn't respond well to any known treatments. When she had wound down, not that Sharla was ever effusive with words, she sat, her normally tanned skin pale porcelain, letting him digest the news.

"What can I do?" he finally asked.

She studied him for a long moment. "I have some assets I need you to take care of. My family ..."

No need for her to finish. He knew. Sharla's family exhausted every facet of the word "dysfunctional." At first, he'd thought she was exaggerating, but after having met a few of them, he could freely acknowledge she wasn't wrong not to trust them with anything she valued. Any investments or bank accounts would only serve as fresh fodder for more booze and drugs.

"I can do that."

"You're willing?"

It was the least he could do. "I am."

She brushed a lone tear away from her cheek. "There'll be paperwork."

"Just let me know."

She rose in one fluid movement. "Thank you. Now you can take me to dinner. My appetite has been on the lam lately, but I'll enjoy watching you eat." Her mouth upturned the tiniest bit. "I've missed your zest for food. And now that the cancer-downer is out of the way, I have other, much better news."

He reached for her hand, and she let him take it. As the sun sank, leaving the sky a dark gray, they walked to his car.

CHAPTER FOURTEEN

O nce they chose a table at The Water Station, the classiest restaurant in Valiant, and placed their orders, Tavo allowed Sharla plenty of space. Live music floated from the outside patio. Though it was early summer, it was still too hot to sit outside. Sitting by the floor-to-ceiling windows would be warm. Otherwise, AC kept the temps pleasant.

Sharla squeezed a slice of lemon into her tea and swirled the ice in the glass. Her hands were calm and steady. Though he expected her big revelation in increments, she surprised him.

"Do you remember the times you shared something about God and I blew it off?" A half smile curved her cheeks.

Oh, whoa. Another surprise. "I do." She'd turned her nose up at anything having to do with "his religion."

"Well, when you receive a cancer diagnosis, you think about things. I paid very little attention at the time, but you were the only person I ever knew who talked about eternal life." A smile ghosted her lips. "I had nothing to lose, so I told God if He was real, I wanted to know."

"One night I was cleaning out drawers, and I found your Bible. All those years ago, you once told me to start with the Book of John ... so I did."

Tavo's scattered thoughts reined to attention.

Her eyes welled with unshed tears. "I'd never read anything like it before, but the words made sense. My favorite story ... what brought me to Christ, was the passage about Nicodemus." Her misty eyes held an unmistakable light. "Jesus told him he needed to be born again. And just like this"—She snapped her thumb and middle finger—"I knew that's what I needed too. He came to live inside me. Tavo—" She leaned forward and gripped his hand. "I'm alive now and forgiven. We've both been forgiven for all the mistakes we made—together for the wrong reasons, the guilt, the bitterness—all of it!"

He squeezed her hand, hardly able to believe the words pouring from her. She stopped talking, only because the server brought their meals. His pecan-encrusted chicken smelled wonderful, but his emotions were so chaotic, his appetite had fled. Sharla sniffed her cup of Manhattan chowder and set her spoon down.

Tavo's eyes moistened. His agonized prayers for her salvation hadn't gone unheeded. The questions rolled out of him. As her answers affirmed her new life, his appetite returned. They talked long after the server took their plates. Sharla giggled at his clean dish, but she only managed a bite or two of her soup.

"Thank you for telling me this, Shar. I'd say it means a lot, but that seems inadequate."

"Thank *you* for leading me in the right direction, even though I'm a hardhead. It took a few years—and cancer—for me to listen." A sad expression momentarily etched her features.

"I'm so sorry."

"Oh, don't be." She waved him off. "I've had time to work through it. Yeah, I wish things were different, but for the first time in my life, I have the security of knowing Someone who will never leave me." Her eyes widened. "I didn't mean that as a dig. I want everyone to experience what I have, but I especially wanted to tell you." She paused, biting her lip. "Just so you know ... there are no hard feelings on my part for the way things ended with us." She made a face. "Well, not anymore. Friends who I respect helped me see I was as much at fault as you."

Tavo scrubbed his lower face with a hand. "I was wrong, Shar. It wasn't right to leave without a word. I'm sorry for that."

"I knew from the beginning we weren't really in love." She shrugged as if their relationship hadn't shattered them. "I want you to find your way again." Her eyes studied him cautiously. "Have you made amends with the girl you loved in high school? The one you never got over?"

If only. "I moved back to reconcile, but it's been slow going. Things are better with Dad, though we've still got a long way to go. As for Paige ..." He peered at her to make sure she was onboard with him talking about another woman. Despite her new relationship with Christ, their past was still a vulnerable topic. He didn't want to hurt her.

Sympathy streaked across her features. "I'm guessing that relationship isn't there yet either."

He shook his head. "Nope. Can't seem to get past the friend zone."

"At long last, it's my turn to say, 'I'll be praying for you.'" Her eyes held compassion and a hint of mischief. "But I mean it sincerely. I'm past the point of wanting someone. My interest is friendship-based. I'd like to think we still have that. Most of all, I want you to be happy."

"That works for me. Sounds like you've found true happiness."

"I have." It looked as if she wanted to say more, then decided against it.

Tavo sighed with relief, glad this long overdue conversation had happened. They both needed the closure, though he'd dreaded it. He couldn't deny her forgiveness had loosened a knot on the inside that had bothered him for years.

Her disclosures brought him both joy and heartache, but his instincts were firing one salvo after another. Despite Sharla's revelations, she was still holding something back.

IN RORY'S OFFICE, Paige scrutinized her notes. "The priority is once you finish the custom tweaks on the Dawson plan, get it to me so I can arrange for construction start-up time with Oscar. Don't let yourself get sidetracked, boss. You know his schedule is tight."

Rory gathered files and gave them a "straighten-up-or-else" stack on his desk. "Oscar will make room. He knows how to use bonuses as an incentive for early completion, but he's an absolute ogre about excellence. Perfect combo in a foreman. And your job is the paperwork for the two new homes in the High Meadows subdivision?" White teeth shone between his beard and mustache. "Don't let yourself get sidetracked."

She deserved that. "Scout's honor. How's Vi feeling these days?"

"You mean, has she had any more fainting spells? Which she refers to as 'a bit of lightheadedness.'" Rory snorted, though his eyes shone with joy. "She's fine. Taking it easy is her least favorite thing to do. But she's thrilled about this pregnancy. Worries if everything's all right with the twins. Her doctor dotes on her."

Paige's smile broadened. "A doting doctor seems rare, but the rest sounds normal. I can only hope someday I'll be as lucky." Where had that come from? Paige had never given much thought to having children. Raising her brothers and sisters had been plenty, thank you very much.

Rory's brows climbed so far into his hairline, Paige was certain they'd get lost. "How are things going with Tavo?"

"We're friends. Anything else is ancient history."

Rory's silence was deafening. "I'm too busy to date, boss. Working for you and getting my event business going leaves no time."

"What events are you planning now? Jess and Brenna's wedding was gorgeous. You nailed the details, you know."

She knew no such thing. The falling speaker catastrophe eclipsed her meticulous planning. "So far, a shower next month, but Ed's asked me to plan a couple more events for him."

"As in Ed Clarkston, superstar?" Rory's sharp retort didn't bode well.

Paige couldn't help it if Rory didn't care for the man. Business was business. "He's not savvy about real estate, but he understands public perception. He's willing to put himself out there for our little town because—"

"Because what, Paige? What's his real interest in Valiant? I don't buy the line about getting in touch with his creativity. He's got an agenda, even if it's cloaked in humanitarian jargon." Rory's slate-colored eyes held both fire and pleading.

"He pays well," Paige offered feebly.

"So do I. With no strings attached. I doubt it's the same for him." Rory leaned forward. "Don't rush to do his bidding,

Paige. You're only seeing what he wants you to see. My gut tells me he's not the upfront guy you're hoping he is."

Respect for her boss clamped her mouth shut. Ed wasn't as bad as all that. Sure, the guy had faults. Didn't everyone? Blind spots too. She dared not mention Ed had asked her on a date. Something different from her ordinary existence, he'd promised.

Nor would she say how much she looked forward to it.

PAIGE NEEDED to remember Ed had given her a choice about the date. Now she wanted nothing more than to put her hands over her ears to muffle the trio of men singing—no doubt they could sing, though she preferred something more ... low-key. An unexpected ache rose within her. Gus's love songs were the best, and his vocal range outshined the guys on stage.

Ed stood by her side, totally invigorated by every aspect of the performance. Good grief, could it get any louder? They used their VIP "seats" during breaks, if then. He wore a grungy T-shirt, cap, and granny glasses. He'd been right about one thing. They were safe enough from anyone recognizing him. Between his attire, the bodyguards, and the audience, no one paid them a lick of attention.

Her head hurt as she tried to remember why she chose this event. Oh, yeah. It had been between a popular international comedienne or a one-man parody of nineties flicks. Reviews about the woman promised a sleaze show, and the man ... well, it was no better. So she chose a popular musical trio. It helped that Ed was ecstatic.

Except her vision of watching a touted world-class performance had withered into an endurance contest. The private jet ride to Houston was fun. And she still held out hope for a quiet dinner with yummy food, but *this*? Not her thing, however much Ed enjoyed it.

Phones and cameras constantly clicked. Lots of close-ups. Maybe they weren't as incognito as Ed assumed. Or maybe it was merely part of the concert experience. Camera people were everywhere, not just around the VIP circle. The combined odor of pot and alcohol permeated the theater. Guards stood as sentinels, their eyes roving everywhere.

"C'mon, girl, you need to get with the beat." Ed bumped her hip. She pasted on a smile and lifted her arms to sway with the pounding beat. *When in Rome ...* He clapped his hands enthusiastically. Hard to sing along since the musicians sang in a foreign language. For Paige, it added to the confusion. Ed howled and gyrated like a fan-boy.

She only wanted it to be over.

CHAPTER FIFTEEN

Later, Paige sank into the private dining booth. Ah, this was more to her tastes. A black velvet drape enclosed them in privacy. Taking a sip of the fruity alternative she'd ordered instead of wine, despite Ed's protests, her head and jaws had settled into minor aches instead of the full-on throbs. Ed had wound down on the ride over but was still fairly talkative. At the concert, he acted manic. Nothing like his normal self. Which begged the question. Who was the real Ed?

"So what'll you have, dear? I'm famished." Ed's blue eyes penetrated her post-concert fog. "I'm guessing this quiet spot is far more to your liking. Thank you for putting up with my antics. If I don't let my inner man out of his cage, every so often, the great Ed Clarkston will have a very public meltdown. My agents hate it when that happens."

Paige would hate it too. At least he knew how to handle the pressure. *You call that handling it?* She tucked away that thought for later and turned her attention to the menu. When the server appeared, she opted for the house soup accompanied by an upscale salad. Ed ordered a steak entrée.

The exorbitant prices were shocking, though she was careful not to say anything. Wouldn't want her country mouse roots showing.

"Man, those guys could sing." Ed downed his glass of wine and poured more. Longing etched his features. "I'd give anything to sing like that."

An event idea glimmered in Paige's mind. "So you like music? What if your next event in Valiant had a musical theme?"

"You mean ... I love karaoke. People get the mic and just let loose." For once, his grin seemed purely authentic.

"People letting loose" conjured up negative images for Paige, but she set the impression aside. If Ed was enthusiastic about the idea, she'd pull it off. "Okay. Let me see what I can make happen."

Ed grabbed her hand. "It's a super idea. Informal setting. Plenty of booze. People getting real. I love it!"

Hm. Sounded like a brawl to Paige. But now she had a theme. She'd have the local radio station play Ed's show tunes ahead of time. Prime all the vocalist wannabes. It would require finesse, but that part was easy.

As her brain ticked off specifics, Ed had gone back to his lament. "It'd be so great to sing. I could be a triple threat. The acting part is a snap. I can dance when a role calls for it, but sing? That's beyond my skill set. Listening to it is the next best thing." He swallowed more wine.

His confession surprised her. "I suppose we all want something out of our reach."

"What's out of your reach, Paige?" Was his interest genuine, or were those baby blues doing a number on her overworked state of mind?

She toyed with her glass. The Ed she knew wouldn't appreciate a deep answer. "Oh, the usual. Success. Fame's not on my radar." She nudged him. "My tastes run to simple things. Good food. Good friends. A satisfying job."

"Normal stuff. What's important to you, Paige?" Again, his look penetrated her defenses.

She was still certain he wouldn't want to go there, but he asked twice. "My faith."

Ed blinked. "Faith? Oh, you mean truth. Each person finds their own truth. A personal map to guide them through the universe. Yeah, we're definitely wired for truth." He swallowed more wine and seemed ready to expound.

Oh, dear. "There's only one truth, Ed. It's not a 'to each-his-own' kind of deal."

"So what's *your* truth, Paige?" His insistence on truth being subjective slapped her to attention. His eyes had hardened into azure marbles.

Paige's insides clenched. She wasn't used to frontal assaults on her faith. *Help me, Lord.* "There's only one true God. He's holy and without sin. The rest of us have done things wrong. The penalty for sin is death. So God sent his son, Jesus Christ to take our place. He was the perfect sacrifice because His whole life, he did nothing wrong. Never. Can you imagine?"

She slowed for breath. Ed's eyes were slits, but he seemed to listen. She continued. "When we accept Jesus as our Savior, his spirit comes to live in us and makes us alive. We become a new person."

Ed made a sound between a snort and a scoff. "It's hard to imagine you doing anything worthy of a cosmic death penalty, Paige."

"Human perspective doesn't count. We need to see things from God's perspective." Paige fretted with her napkin. How had this chat become so ... entrenched? Disbelief etched into Ed's features. Uh-oh. She'd been too bold. "Sorry if I came off preachy. But you asked what I consider important ..."

Ed crossed one leg over the other. "Everyone's entitled to their opinion." The snippy undertone belied the light words. "But it sounds so ... rigid. I'm not a good rule-keeper. Too creative, I suppose. A color-outside-the-lines sort of guy. Not perfect, but I haven't murdered anyone. Surely that counts for something."

Paige's hope for a thoughtful response deflated. He seemed very disinclined to believe anything but his opinion. "Any sin counts in God's eyes. He gets the final say, not us."

The whispery swish of black velvet cut off any further discussion. Their food had arrived. Her mouth watered at the sizzle of Ed's steak. A delicious basil-y aroma floated toward her nostrils as the server placed her bowl of soup on the table. Hunger struck with a vengeance.

Ed grabbed his knife and cut his meat as if his life depended on it. Engrossed in the meal, he asked the server for another bottle of wine.

As if the conversation about God had never existed.

***

TAVO NAVIGATED the pool water slowly as he passed a ball in a circle around his body. Hand off in front. Stretch his arms to the back to clasp the ball again. The chlorine smell didn't bother him anymore. It had overwhelmed him on the first day of aquatic therapy. Reminded him too much of Rick's near drowning. Surprisingly enough, the bad memories had faded. He no longer broke out in a sweat at the sight of the pool.

The sound of Paige slicing through the water lap after lap comforted him. She complained about not finding her rhythm, but it seemed steady to him. Outside the glassed wall, the sunset was glorious. Layers of color—several shades of pink, orange, and lavender blended into a soft twilight.

He was thankful she'd showed. Since the day he'd told her about the twins, she'd missed two practices. The first day, grace came easily. Even if she wasn't downright angry, she had to be miffed at him for taking them in. Her second no-show made his heart ache. Today, he'd sent her an "I'm sorry" meme and asked if she was still speaking to him.

Of course, she'd responded positively. She'd brush her feelings aside, because she knew forgiveness was the correct attitude. But if her heart wasn't quite there yet, it'd cause a polite detachment he wanted no part of.

"Hey, are you going to finish with the ball or stare at the sunset?" Paige cautiously navigated the wet tile, wringing out her wet hair.

Wrapped up in his musings, he'd missed her pool exit. "Last one. And I'll still clean up faster." Tavo's legs churned, lessening the gap.

"Maybe not. I brought work home. At least an hour, so I need to scoot." Paige picked up her towel and wrapped it around her waist. Tavo nearly smacked his lips in appreciation of her womanly shape.

"Don't leave without me." His shoulder fussed as he grabbed the bar and climbed the steps out of the pool. "I don't want you in the parking lot by yourself."

Paige slowed enough to look at him. They both remembered the incident that caused his remark. "Got it. I'll be in the lobby."

Not if I'm there first. He was glad Paige had shown for practice, but she'd acted preoccupied as they worked through the exercises.

Darkness had fallen by the time they stepped outside to the parking lot. The lights Jesse had installed shortly after Brenna's abduction rendered the sky more of a hazy gray than black, but shadows abounded.

Paige paused by two decorative benches on either side of the double doors. "I need a favor, Gus."

He cast her a wary look. What was going on in that head of hers? "Do we need to sit?"

Her face gave nothing away, but she rested on the bench, setting her tote on the concrete. He sat, mindful not to get too close. A lone cricket chirruped a whistly note. The humidity of the day had given way to a damp evening.

Paige turned to face him, sliding her leg into a childlike pose. The black yoga pants she wore blended into the bench. "Please hear me out before you decide." Moonlight flickered over her pretty features, creating havoc with his emotions.

Tavo swallowed, settling against the back of the bench. "You've got me curious." Nervous would have been a better word.

She inhaled a deep breath. "The short version is I'm doing an event, and I'd like for you to sing."

That wasn't so bad. He'd sung at weddings and the occasional opry night. Her request wasn't unusual—

"The event is for Ed. He wants karaoke. I get the impression he has this big blow-out in mind, only he's not aware of how many things can go wrong. I'm making sure there will be enough boundaries for the event to be memorable in a good way. Talented singers will help with that." Her words rushed together in a jumble, as if she were ... embarrassed?

Ed not aware? Couldn't be bothered to care was more like it. Paige's attempt to make the event classy ranked with giving perfume to a pig.

His first inclination was to say no, but the plea in her eyes softened his resolve. What better way to keep tabs on the renowned Mr. Clarkston? Tavo would be front and center instead of skulking in the background. Dad was paying him to keep an eye on the guy.

"What do you want me to sing?" The question put a brick in his throat.

"You'll do it?"

"I don't give a hoot about Ed's event, but I'll do it for you."

"Thank you." Paige's delicate brows knit. "It'd be fun to liven things up with a return of the high school trio." He winced. "No? How about a couple of solos? That would be fantastic—you always did a good job with the, um, love songs." Her voice, smooth at first, ended in a whisper.

"Okay."

"You'll do it?" She stared at him.

"Yes." He drew the word out. Love songs were the last thing he wanted to sing. For Pete's sake, the whole town knew he'd loved Paige forever. "But I get a favor too."

He enjoyed her slight squirm. "What do you want?"

"For you to go out with me." The words squeezed past before his lungs shut down.

Paige gave him a stink eye. "You're ... this is blackmail."

He shrugged. "That's harsh. We're trading favors. Your ask was big. I can ask too."

"But ... but ... there's a lot you don't know. I've changed ..." She ended with a sputter.

He reached for her hand, then pulled back. If this was going to work, he couldn't force it. Or use their natural chemistry to gain an advantage. "So tell me what I don't know. Neither of us has changed that much. Tell me you don't care, Paige, and I'll let it go."

To his surprise, tears filled her eyes. Twice in as many weeks. Most unlike her. "You know I care about you. It's just that ..." She shook her head. "I'll go out with you. Satisfied?"

Not if you hate the idea. "I'll sing two songs at your event. Anything related to the high school trio is a firm no. Jess, Rory, and I are still friends. I'd like to keep it that way."

Paige brushed away tears with her forefingers and sniffed. As if her emotions weren't right on the surface. As if their relationship wasn't a mess. "Two love songs. Got it. Nix on the high school trio, even though it'd be an outstanding crowd-pleaser."

"Paige."

She smiled weakly at his warning tone. "I heard you. The trio is a no-go. And I'll go out with you. Once. This is just friends, right?"

"No, Pep."

"No?" Her stunned look emboldened him.

"No." Dare he say it? "Because we've never been just friends."

CHAPTER SIXTEEN

"We need to charge for the event, Ed. Not because you need the money. An admission fee will prevent every troublemaker in the county from showing up. Some people are jealous of your wealth and fame." Paige smiled engagingly. She gazed around the presidential suite, her mind automatically taking in the details. The cleaning crew had cleared the clutter. Yet, even with pristine surroundings, the area still seemed ... impersonal? Too small? Did Ed's magnetism not leave room for anything else, or was Valiant's finest not enough?

"I won't be on stage if that's the issue. And you know I have personal security. They'll protect me, of course, but they also know how to handle crowds." Ed's purple button-down shirt was the perfect complement to his eyes. His hair parted down the middle and lay perfectly.

Easy to see why he usually got whatever he wanted. She tried again. "Ed, Valiant's largest outside venue holds five hundred people. The only other bigger venue is the high school football stadium. My guess is you prefer a cozier setting. Let your team do what they do best—take care of you. I'll handle security." Paige held her breath. *Not the football stadium, please.*

Ed's brow arched slightly as if he knew what she was doing, and then he gave her that heart-stopping grin that made him millions. "Five hundred people is nothing, but whatever. Now that I'm learning what a bulldog you are, I'll sic my publicist on you for future events. She eats nails for breakfast."

Paige's jaw unclenched by degrees but still ached. Ed made it sound as if *she* were the hardnose. ... but the gleam of triumph in his eyes suggested he'd attained what he wanted all along.

Before she could analyze the thought, he said, "Paige, I know the event in Houston wasn't your thing, even if my inner wild child loved it. I need to make up for that because I find myself very drawn to you. What would you say if we went out on an actual date? Not something for me. Tell me where you'd like to go, and I'll make it happen."

Oh, no. When he got all ... gooey, he was hard to resist. He knew it too. It was a sweet thing to say, even if she wasn't buying. Not completely, anyway. But she needed to stay on his good side, so the event planning would go smoothly. If he got prickly and balked, her plans would be toast. Mentally, she pored through her schedule. "When did you have in mind?"

Ed shrugged. "Not much happening on my end these days."

A tiny undercurrent in his voice suggested the sooner the better. "I'll get back to you." She hedged, torn between jetting somewhere she'd never been or staying focused on work.

The hardening of his eyes was so slight she might have imagined it.

TAVO PEERED at his computer screen and inhaled the familiar scents. The building might not stand if not for the layers of gun oil and leather baked into the walls. The smells permeated his earliest memories and were part of what made up his world.

Despite a workout, or maybe because of it, his shoulder twitched. The sole reason he was sitting in the breakroom at the station rather than outside on patrol. It also reminded him of Paige. What little concentration he possessed was fading as visions of her in the pool played through his mind. He shifted in the uncomfortable seat, intent on finishing the report. As it was, he'd typed a word salad rather than anything solid.

A door slammed. Two patrol officers came in and headed for the coffee machine. *Good luck with that.* The dark liquid resembled sludge. Probably tasted worse. The two were new enough, Tavo had no read on them.

"Another boring night," one complained, as he poured himself a cup of brew. He muttered a phrase Tavo chose not to hear.

"Well, what do you expect in a town like Valiant?" the other officer asked. He waited, cup in hand, for his turn at the coffeepot. "I'm ready to sink my teeth into a real problem instead of some idiot on a bicycle riding in the center lane without reflectors. Give me some action!"

The hair on Tavo's neck raised like hackles. If he had to choose the idiot, it wouldn't be the biker. He kept typing, though his focus stayed on the two young men. Work-wise, it took a lot to get him riled up. Their attitudes were quickly becoming the exception.

"He was respectful about being stupid." The first officer lifted his voice to a mocking falsetto. "'I didn't know I needed them, officer.'" He huffed. "Almost had me convinced he didn't know better."

"Easy fix, but he probably couldn't afford it. Gotta love serving the great unwashed." Their sniggers bounced uncomfortably around the room, finding no place to land.

Tavo had heard enough. He rose and stretched his back. They stiffened, surprised by his presence, seeing as how he'd been sitting in a corner, hunched behind the screen. He stared them down, finally putting a name to the first officer.

"What? It's just shop talk. We're not hurtin' anybody." Rojas's bluster dug the hole deeper.

"Nobody but yourselves." Tavo cringed at the nasty edge in his voice. But officers who berated the people and place they'd sworn to serve grew tiresome. He tried a different tack. "Is this your first patrol stint?"

They both nodded warily, as if waiting for the other foot to fall. *Good.*

"I've worked in San Antonio and Frisco." He waited. Sure enough, their attention perked. Probably hometown boys with a strong desire to move to the metroplexes. Most of his fellow officers were in awe because he'd already done it. What they didn't know was why he came back. Now was as good a time as any to enlighten them.

"I can assure you, a guy riding a bike without lights is the kind of problem you want. Valiant is still a safe place to live." Tavo would do everything in his power to keep it that way. "Not so in the bigger cities, depending on where you land. Murder, drugs, and the level of crime are overwhelming. You get paid more, but the headaches, which eventually become heartaches, multiply as well."

"I can handle it," Rojas retorted.

"Easy to say when you haven't tried it." Tavo worked to

soften his response. "I thought that too. You know, ready to take on the entire criminal population."

"You? Who'd mess with you?" the second officer scoffed.

"Anyone with a gun." Tavo shrugged as their eyes widened. "True. There are plenty of scenarios you haven't encountered in Valiant."

"Look, guys," he continued, now that he had their attention. "Bigger cities have bigger problems—like cartels, for one. You don't want that. They raise the crime level exponentially. You know what stands between us and towns riddled with drugs?"

"Geographics?"

"Valiant is on the Highway Fifty-five corridor, but no, geographics aren't as much to blame as you think." He willed them to think deeper, but their blank looks indicated they didn't know.

"It's us." He pointed to them and himself. "We're the reason criminals don't like it here. We stand between the bad guys and decent folks who want to live their lives in peace. As long as we make our town a place powerful criminals don't want to mess with, Valiant will thrive. It's a great place for families to raise kids. Don't you want to keep that?"

Recognition lit their eyes. Maybe he'd imparted a little wisdom too. It didn't keep Rojas from asking another question. "Are you married?"

Tavo's eyes shot upward, but he answered succinctly. "Someday. And yes, I plan to live here. Another nugget of unsolicited advice? Don't knock the minor stuff. Or Valiant. This could be the job and the place where your dreams come true."

His words seemed to stir their curiosity. Not a bad way to start. Chalk one up for keeping his temper and guiding young men. They turned to leave, having given up on a coffee break.

As Tavo brought his computer to life again, he heard one say, "He sounds just like his dad."

"No joke. Think he'll be chief of police someday?" The door shut with far less hubris.

Tavo focused on the neglected report. Chief of police? If only.

CHAPTER SEVENTEEN

Out of habit, Tavo scanned the partially open field. Scores of oak trees surrounded a wooden stage, providing shade and a natural amphitheater. The security seemed adequate. Paige had consulted him, then took his advice about hiring an additional security team from San Antonio. Local units served for traffic control and parking. Clarkston had insisted anyone in a uniform stay on the outskirts, saying he didn't want the crowd inhibited by law enforcement.

Whatever.

The entire event would have been better inside, but that was one thing Clarkston wouldn't budge on, according to Paige. The stage held large industrial fans. Long lines of cable snaked to the nearby barn. People wore cooling neckerchiefs, and hand-held mini-fans abounded. The bar would stay a popular place tonight.

Hot as the temps reached during the day, Paige had been smart to start the event at 9:00 p.m. The fans didn't seem to mind the late hour. Lawn chairs and coolers abounded as people arrived at the freshly mowed field. The grassy fragrance perfumed the air. A few rough-looking characters lurked about, but most people came for the entertainment.

A crew was setting up on stage. Paige, looking cool and lovely despite the heat, wore a red sundress. Tavo's cheeks creased. She'd always loved the color red, the brighter the better. She exchanged comments with Rick, then they both looked toward the stage. Probably making sure every little thing was in place. Tension slipped from Tavo's shoulders when Paige said his brother would be the deejay. Rick was an excellent choice for a family-friendly crowd. The raucous stuff that set people on edge wasn't part of his repertoire.

A small VIP area was front and center of the stage. A lone member of Ed's security team stood within the small area, serving as a deterrent for the overly curious or anyone getting too close to Ed. The star, however, was on stage chatting with Rick as the sound guys set up. Nice to know Ed had a mellow side.

More people trickled through the gates. Paige circled the tables near the VIP section. Once the event got underway, Tavo would join the Peeps' table. He hoped Paige would take time to sit as well. Maybe if he encouraged her. The date he'd insisted on had become worrisome. Still, his gut insisted she'd warm up if they spent enough time together. Even now, her luminous dark eyes found his. Earlier, she'd confided to him her nervousness about kicking off the evening. Most people wouldn't notice, but the slight hesitancy in her movements gave it away. Okay, bud. Enough of the heightened awareness.

She stepped up to the mic and smiled out at the audience. Yep. Ed should take care lest her beauty outshined his stardom. People started clapping. She made a few remarks, then introduced Ed to an enthusiastic crowd. As he explained how he connected with musicians on a deep visceral level, Tavo wanted to spit the taste of him out of his mouth.

He didn't feel an ounce of connection to Ed. He was just a guy blowin' smoke around Paige. But he sure knew how to work a crowd.

As Tavo weaved through people, chairs, and blankets, Paige's twin brothers jogged up to him, blocking his way forward. A sigh escaped. Hard to believe they were eighteen years old. They stayed in perpetual motion, like much younger children.

"Tavo!" They both panted as if they'd run a mile.

"We saw—"

"At the meet and greet. Outside the country club—"

"Something fishy." They rocked back on their heels, satisfied.

"And?" Tavo frowned. Acting friendly would only encourage more blathering. Never mind he'd suspected something was amiss that night at the back door. *If* they were talking about the same place and time.

"Thought you'd want to know." Carlos had always been the braver one. They both rocked on their heels again, hands in back pockets.

"All you've told me is you saw something fishy at the country club. I need more to go on." They stared at him blankly. "Details, guys. Who did you see? Where? What was fishy? Nothing happens without details."

"A guy at the back door. A car drove up. It looked like an exchange," Miguel offered.

Tavo's brow knit. "Would you recognize the guy again?"

"Maybe."

Tavo grabbed hold of his patience. "Listen, dudes, that's not much to go on. Keep your eyes open and pay attention to everything. When you've got more, come talk to me again."

He inwardly cringed at the way their eyes lit up. His very own confidential informants. A cough-snort left his throat. More like the Frito Banditos. If they bragged about it to Paige, she'd demand answers. They shuffled off, heads together in an intense conversation no one else would understand. His hands clenched at his sides. He should have insisted they not tell anyone else.

Soft strains of the first musical number wafted out from the stage. He couldn't wait for this to be over.

———

PAIGE RELEASED a sigh as she joined the Peeps' table. Jesse had his arm casually draped around Brenna's shoulders. His normally intense gaze softened as he chatted with Rory across the table. Vi leaned forward to hear something Brenna said, and they all laughed.

She slid into the empty seat next to Gus. Ed would want her to join him. She would ... eventually. Whenever she was around Ed, her guard went up. Made no difference if he was charming or sulky, Paige never completely relaxed in his presence.

At the end of the table, Natalie sat so close to Silas a paper clip wouldn't fit between them. Once the teen onstage finished a tolerable rendition of "Pretty Woman," Silas pecked Nat on the cheek and whispered something in her ear.

Their "prank gone wrong" was ancient news. Rumor was, when Jesse made it mandatory that his sister and Silas compete in the Texas Water Safari—in the same boat—they'd been furious. The only reason they followed through was to keep their futures intact at Peeps. However, three days in a boat together had caused something no one expected, least of all Jesse.

They'd fallen in love.

Despite her nervousness, amusement lifted Paige's lips. How funny that Jesse's grand idea had backfired.

One of the worship leaders from their church stood on stage. Oh, this would be good. Despite Ed's idea of the karaoke being raw talent, Paige had sprinkled in plenty of genuine talent as well. In her heart, she was proud of Valiant. She'd taken full advantage of the opportunity to let her hometown shine. To make it golden, she'd assigned Gus a prime spot— the last song before intermission. If he still sang as he did in high school, he'd knock their sandals right off.

As a church friend belted out Anne Wilson's "Strong," Gus leaned into her. His warm breath soothed her aching jaw. "Good job, Pep. Everybody, especially Ed, is enjoying this."

She glanced over to where Ed stood on his feet, clapping wildly when the song was over. He was enjoying it. Perhaps she'd read him wrong.

Silas had left the table and made his way to the stage steps, where he waited for Rick's signal. She wasn't aware Silas could sing until Rory assured her the younger crowd would adore him. Sure enough, as he warbled Lifehouse's hit, "You and Me," his coffeehouse vibe radiated through the crowd. Teenage girls started screaming and hugging each other. Fortunately, Silas was oblivious to anyone else in the room but Nat.

Paige's eyes blinked with moisture. Ed hopped up on the stage and extended his hand. Silas shook it with a tight smile and strode off the stage. When he returned to his seat, Nat threw her arms around him and kissed him. His self-consciousness disappeared as he kissed her back.

When Jesse frowned, Brenna elbowed him. "C'mon, Jess. You kissed me before we had permission to date."

He gave her a wry look. "You were irresistible." As the

couple's lip-lock seemed to go on indefinitely, his scowl returned.

Brenna tugged his chin around. "Leave them alone. Or I might leave you alone." Her playful tone conveyed she'd do no such thing.

Jesse started tickling her. His voice muffled as he leaned into her hair, but it sounded like, *You don't play fair, woman.*

The sweet exchange drove an arrow deep into Paige's heart. The part of her that had never healed when she left for college without Gus. She'd missed him terribly. Still did, but it could never work. Aside from not being in their fairy-tale world anymore, she had missions to accomplish. The finances Mom needed for meds would not appear without help. Paige didn't share her mother's faith that Dad would come through. And her event planning business would forever stay grounded without start-up funds. A relationship with Gus would only further complicate things. No matter that her heart begged to differ.

The atmosphere lightened up during the next few songs. As Gus rose to finish the first set, her body tensed. He turned back and winked. "I got this, Paige. It'll be fun."

Her breath stopped as he sauntered onto the stage, oozing confidence. When he took the mic, he asked the audience with more of a drawl than usual, "Y'all havin' fun tonight?" The crowd responded with enthusiasm. "I might need to move on this one, and I hate to dance by myself. Y'all going to join me?"

Oh, goodness. This was going way better than she had expected. "Sing it, bud!" she shouted. Gus pointed to Rick, and the beat started.

As the instrumental lead in began, he boomed through the mic, "Here's how we do it in Texas, Ed." He whirled his finger upward, and the music amplified. Paige watched, spellbound. Gus's size helped him onstage, but this ... this showmanship was so much more than she remembered. He broke into Billy Ray Cyrus's "Achy Breaky Heart." College-age kids formed impromptu line dances and whooped to their heart's content. Gus belted out the song and danced like he'd done it for years.

She clapped along, then caught Ed's reaction. His lips stretched in that gorgeous smile, but something was off. As he gyrated in and out of the lines, it seemed forced. He sang along with the "Achy Breaky" chorus with the crowd, but not with the same zest as the Houston show.

As the song ended, Gus sang the last lines a cappella. Paige joined him to announce the intermission. Taking the mic, she turned aside and whispered to him, "Stay with me." He nodded. Perspiration ran down the sides of his face and trapped inside his dimples. Another memory shook her. After football games, field muck would lodge in the dents. It became a ritual for her to blot the dirt away with a tissue. Afterward, she'd kiss each dimple for good measure.

Forcing her mind back to the present, she explained to the audience where the drinks and snacks were ... all too aware of the man who stood beside her. She scanned the crowd, and her eyes landed on Ed again. He was staring at them, his signature brow arched in a slight question.

What did that mean? Overall, his karaoke idea was proving a colossal hit, though she had tweaked it to more of a concert. Far more popular than she had anticipated.

The second half would be even more fun.

CHAPTER EIGHTEEN

The second half of the program was going off without a hitch. Tavo sat at the end of the Peeps' table, keeping his interactions limited to Jess and Rory. Mostly, though, he stayed tuned to what was happening on the stage. And watching Paige. The atmosphere crackled with excitement as the karaoke revved up.

The music was invigorating, despite the late hour, and nothing awful had happened. For Paige's sake, he hoped it would stay that way. Uh-oh. Lightning flashed in the distance. *Lord, just let us get through this.* Paige had planned a dance after the karaoke portion was done. Tavo wanted to twirl her around the floor at least once.

A couple of professionals were taking pictures. Publicity was inevitable. Perhaps that was why Ed was on good behavior. They wouldn't get close to him, but it wouldn't matter with the right photo lens. His fingers stopped their incessant tapping. He winced as the woman singing attempted to hit a high note beyond her range. The audience chatted among themselves, not paying much attention. When she finished, polite applause followed.

Tavo drained his bottle of water as a guy sang "Amazing Grace." His fingers resumed the tap-tap-tapping. The guy had a decent voice. Next came a group of four teens with a strong Beach Boys vibe. As they attempted to harmonize, it became clear they needed to work on balance—the second was outshining the lead.

In high school, his father had spent a ton of money on vocal lessons with a professional, who'd taught Tavo how to use his ability. Much to his dad's dismay, he couldn't embrace singing as a living. He enjoyed it, but passion? That never happened. His decision not to pursue a musical career had caused a deep rift between him and his father.

The odor of alcohol and cigarette smoke drifted through the air. He was up after the next singer. He'd practiced a medley of Paige's two favorite love songs as a finale. To put it in her words, "So it will end well, Gus. I need you to give everyone something special to walk away with."

Dare he do the medley? It would be perfectly acceptable to do a recap of "Achy Breaky Heart." For the second half, Paige had been sitting with Ed. Tavo found it hard to think of the guy as anything more than a spoiled brat with a moneymaker face. Paige was too savvy to fall for any of his lines. However, she certainly hadn't objected to his hugs or smooches on the cheek. Nope, she'd played right along.

Tavo hoped it was an act. His onstage persona would help him find out.

PAIGE COULD HARDLY WAIT for this to be over. She'd sat by Ed as a deterrent to the amount of alcohol he was consuming. Now she wished she hadn't. He hadn't slowed down a bit. For whatever reason, his mood had plummeted. For the first time, she wondered if drugs played a role in his capricious behavior. One minute, he was Dr. Jekyll, the next, he'd act like Mr. Hyde.

She didn't appreciate the hugs or kisses either. He'd picked up on her negative response, though she'd tried hard not to let it show, and was now more withdrawn than ever. Ed's security guys standing at a discreet distance seemed completely impassive to their little drama. She'd get no help there.

When he gripped her hand, she stood. If he got the message once, he'd get it again. Fortunately, a woman she recognized from high school was up next. She'd often paired with Gus for duets, though she had a strong solo voice. As the music pumped, she broke into an energetic version of Kelly Clarkson's "Stronger."

Heartened by the lyrics, Paige toe-tapped, blossoming into a full-on dance, and others joined her. She stepped lively and pointed to Gus. Her heart ached. Her jaws were killing her. Her feet hurt, but the beat pounded for attention. And she could use a break from Ed. At first, Gus seemed hesitant, but when she whirled back in the other direction, he caught up with her and twirled her under his arm. An overwhelming sense of déjà vu whipped through her. Did he sense it too? They performed the steps together with faultless timing. Finally, she twisted away. He bowed slightly, his eyes piercing hers.

Ed stood by as if waiting for her. He grabbed her hand and twisted it into the air as if it was his turn. Gently, he took her by the waist and swayed with her, weaving in and out, matching his moves to hers. Gus still eclipsed her thoughts. Once upon a time, they'd been good together. If only.

The song went from a mild crescendo to a red-hot gallop. When it ended, she spun into her seat, exhausted. Ed sat down too. He leaned into her and said something. Between the clapping and the shouts, Paige must have misunderstood.

Because it sounded like "I love you."

Through her weary haze, Paige saw Gus onstage fiddling with the mic. Her breath snagged when he looked her way. Ed chose that moment to wrap an arm around her shoulder. Silently, she willed Gus to understand. *This isn't what it looks like.* After this event, she and Ed would talk. Even if her feelings for Gus weren't clear, Ed's PDA was unacceptable.

Gus's face darkened, but he playfully asked the audience, "Isn't this a grand party? Paige knows how to make it happen." He nodded at Rick, then said, "Would y'all believe me if I said I'm going to marry her someday?" He gave her a tight smile. "Yep. I've been waitin' on Paige a long time." As sporadic hoots and hollers rose from the crowd, he continued in the same vein. "Hey, that sounds like a song." The haunting melody of the intro unfurled in a velvety stream through the cloudy night.

Paige froze, a startled deer in his spotlight, heat and ice assaulting her insides. Did he mean those words? Gus chuckled as if he read her mind, "Mm-hm. Just so you know, doll"—he paused for effect—"these songs are for you."

He cleared his throat and boomed out the dramatic opening of "Unchained Melody." He sang with abandon, and the essence of his being called to her. Unbidden, tears flowed down her cheeks. Mesmerized by the lyrics and his voice, she couldn't look anywhere else. Her hands slipped up to cover her open mouth. When he segued into "Can't Help Falling in Love," it was as if there had been no separation between them. No meaningless gap of time. There was only him. And their love.

She was trembling all over. No one else in the entire world existed. As his dreamy voice closed the song, the crowd exploded into applause. Her hands still clasped, she held them toward him. *Thank you.* It was the sweetest, most perfect ending to the singing portion she could imagine. Was he serious about the marriage talk, or was it part of his act? He'd never openly confessed his love before. Did she really know this man?

Before she could think about what needed to happen next, Ed turned her toward him. Eyes glittering, he covered her mouth with his. She stiffened with surprise, but his arms clamped around her in a vise. When she stepped back to break his advance, he stepped forward. His kiss was an onslaught of fury and emotion all twisted together. Shortly, his lips gentled, and he drew away but still retained his hold. Cameras and phones flashed all around them.

He touched her lips. "I'm sorry. I just had to connect with your beauty."

Utterly numb, she had no answer. Her only thought was he wasn't sorry at all.

She looked to the stage. Gus stared at her. She'd glimpsed the hurt before his mask of stoicism slipped into place. He'd made himself vulnerable in the way he sang those songs.

On the stage, Rick held the microphone. Words streamed out of his mouth, but she didn't understand what he was saying. She only knew it wasn't in her notes.

The screens on either side of the stage suddenly went live, and music blared from the speakers. She squinted to see what was going on and gasped.

The high school trio was on the screen.

A younger, full-of-himself, Gus strutted front and center with Rory and Jesse on either side. The three amigos wore fluffy tutus and danced, acting all kinds of ridiculous. Gus sang Diana Ross's hit, "You Can't Hurry Love," in a high falsetto.

Frantically, she searched for him in real time. He was

shuffling down the side stairs, his expression angry and crushed. Rick had disappeared, but the crowd was going berserk. People were mimicking the outrageous actions of the trio, bumping and jiving into each other, singing loud and off-key. Paige barely resisted putting her hands over her ears.

In a daze, she watched volunteers pack away tables and chairs for the after-dance. How had this evening gone so wrong?

OF ALL THE ...

If only Tavo could unsee Paige kissing Ed. After he'd completely poured his heart out to her. A marriage proposal? What on God's green earth had he been thinking, calling her out in front of a crowd? He'd allowed his jealousy of Ed to make him stupid.

He stomped past Rory, who looked at him with something akin to pity. Great. Jess was saying something, but he didn't stop to listen. He had to get out of here. Paige could clean up by herself. He snorted. He'd like to see her get any kind of help out of Ed. The guy was nothing but a sleaze. But if that's what Paige wanted, she could certainly have him. He'd thought they'd connected when he sang. But her response to Ed made it pretty clear who she didn't want. How foolish ... she'd tried to tell him, but he wouldn't listen.

His mind in a complete stew, he headed to his pickup.

"Tavo," a voice called from a distance.

He flinched. The one person he couldn't avoid or ignore.

Slowly, he turned. "Dad." He steeled himself for whatever unhelpful thing his father would contribute to this disaster.

"Enjoyed your songs. Glad to see you've still got it. Come closer."

Resigned, Tavo looked up, only to see his dad standing with a woman Tavo never thought to see again. Ice invaded his body.

Dad drew near. "Son." While it wasn't said as a question, the implication blasted through. *Are you going to do the right thing?*

Tavo crossed his arms. "Hello, Mom." Even from where he stood, she looked nervous. As she should. He'd lost count of how many years ago she'd left.

"Hi, Tavo." Simply dressed in dark jeans, sandals, and a T-shirt with a Valiant logo, her feet shuffled, as if she'd rather be anywhere else but here.

"Your father and I have talked ... you didn't return my calls ... so we, uh, decided a meeting might be best."

Oh, for the love. Why now? Tavo's coping skills had deserted him when Paige kissed Ed instead of him. When he stayed mute, his dad spoke up.

"I thought we could grab a cup of coffee."

When Tavo shook his head, his dad opened his mouth to object, but Mom stopped him. Well, good for her.

"It's late, and I realize we've ... *I've* caught you completely off guard ..." Her words weren't a plea, but not sharp or unyielding.

To Tavo's wide-eyed surprise, she turned into his father. "This was a bad idea. Terrible timing. We should go."

Even more astonishing, Dad put an arm around her shoulders, as if acquiescing to her wishes. Tavo blinked. Back in the day, Dad never backed down. Ever.

But Tavo was done with drama. So done. He had to get out of here. Away from Paige and his happily-ever-after buddies. His dad and a nowhere job. Now Mom appearing on the scene as suddenly as she'd left. It was all too much.

He brushed aside the still small voice singing within.

CHAPTER NINETEEN

P aige hurried to the stage. "Rick, stop the video. Now!"
He gave her a quizzical look and gestured toward the
crowd. "But they're loving it."

"No! Gus didn't want this. Give me the mic." Taking the
mic from him, she waited until the video stopped. She ran
through her spiel with a breezy tone, relieved when no one
seemed to question the abrupt switch. To his credit, Rick
immediately started a popular tune from another of Ed's
movies. A crew had moved the tables to the side. People made
their way to the makeshift dance floor as if nothing had
happened. As if her world hadn't fallen apart.

Rory appeared at her elbow. Jesse wasn't far behind. "You
okay? I take it you didn't plan the last part."

She searched his face and relaxed a fraction. Only concern.
No accusation. "How did you know?"

His shoulders lifted, then dropped. "I know you. That tacky
video wasn't your idea."

"Gus gets the credit, not me. I asked him early on if there
was a possibility the trio might perform. The hometown crowd

would have adored it." She motioned around the field. "But he was adamantly against it, so I dropped the idea."

Vi wore a smirk as she leaned into Rory. "It was hilarious. These guys can handle it."

Rory gently pulled a strand of her waist-length hair. "You weren't the one caught on video acting stupid. Man, we were awful. Good thing people can change."

"Oh, good thing," Vi responded dryly. Rory favored her with an infectious grin and patted her baby bump. She absently placed her hand on his.

The affection they shared only drove the knife deeper. "I need to find Gus. Does anyone know where he went?" Paige craned her neck to check the perimeter.

"Uh, maybe you should text." Jesse's expression conveyed the rest. Had Gus left already? Her mind clicked through what had happened after that beautiful medley. Ed's unwanted kiss. The video. Oh, yeah. He was long gone. Defeat slumped her shoulders. What she'd felt while Gus sang made no difference now.

"Excuse me." Ed moved into view. He took her hand, brought it to his lips, and bowed. "May I have this dance?"

Ed. She'd forgotten all about Valiant's guest of honor. From the set of his jaw, he knew it too. Her fingers itched to text Gus. Or call. He needed to know ASAP that the video wasn't her brainchild. She wouldn't do that. Not after their conversation.

Ed's look of entreaty was also a challenge. For the first time, she wished he hadn't paid so well. The air between them crackled. Something snapped inside of Paige. Stepping away from Ed, she pulled her hand out of his. She couldn't have stopped the kiss, but she was done with his not-so-subtle advances. Fighting for diplomacy, she chose her words carefully. "And cheat other women out of the thrill of dancing with you? I'd hate to disappoint them."

With that, she turned and walked away, praying he wouldn't cause a scene. Judging from the way his eyes hardened, he knew she'd spurned him. Her body trembled with fear and indignation. Ed would either get over it, or he wouldn't.

As she stalked off, Gus's dad stood at the edge of the dance floor. His dark eyes drilled into her. She'd never understood his hostility. If it was because she and Gus broke up, it would make more sense, but he'd acted that way from the day they met. The woman beside him ... no name came to mind. Just a weird feeling Paige knew her. She kept walking.

Nothing mattered, but letting Gus know the video wasn't her idea. Neither was Ed's kiss.

THE INCESSANT HUM of the ceiling fan was cooling down the room. Singing gigs always left Tavo smelling like a bear. He desperately needed a shower, but first things first. Lounging on his bed, he'd scrolled job descriptions for the last hour. As long as recruitment stayed low, he could have his pick.

If he returned to Frisco, they'd make a spot for him. Sarge hadn't wanted him to go. Part of the Dallas-Fort Worth metroplex, it carried the added benefit of being hours away from Valiant. He finished filling out the app and hit SEND, though he had no peace about it. But he had no peace about staying in Valiant either, especially since he sang his heart out to Paige and her response was to kiss Clarkston.

He ought to get serious about studying for the detective exam. The higher-ups had suggested it in both San Antonio and Frisco. With his shoulder on the blink, now was the perfect time. If he could only bring himself to do it. Coming home to make things right had been a huge mistake. If anything, he'd mucked it up worse than ever. He'd lost the progress he'd made with Dad after tonight, but Tavo couldn't deal with his absentee mother right now. And Paige had blasted any hope of reconciliation. She'd made her choice crystal clear.

Tires creased on the pavement, and the quiet growl of an engine sounded in the driveway. His driveway. He glanced at his clock. 12:30 a.m. Who would come at this hour? He rose and slipped on the pair of jeans draped over his desk chair.

His phone chimed as Jesse's name appeared on the blue screen. Mystified, Tavo clicked a button. "Yeah."

"You awake?"

"What do you think?"

"Okay. We didn't want to wake your dad."

Tavo snorted. "The Chief of Police knows when someone's in his driveway. What are you doing here?"

"Rory and I are taking you to coffee."

This just got weirder. "Now?"

"Yeah, now."

What to say? He wasn't up for a chat. And Rory was as nosy as a horse wanting a treat. Still, if he had to talk to anybody, it'd be them. "Be there in a sec."

He slipped on a shirt and slid his feet into sandals. In the living room, Dad was peering out the blinds, a gun shoved into the back of his lounge pants.

"Go back to sleep. It's Jess and Rory." Dad would be curious, but it was enough info to get him out of police mode. Tavo didn't look back as he unbolted the door and slipped out. Inhaling the muggy night air was like breathing through a wet rag. Nocturnal noises scurried through the shrubbery lining the house. Stepping over to the car, he said, "I'm flattered, guys. Hope you don't make a habit of showing up at people's houses after midnight."

"We were quiet," Rory said.

Tavo arched a brow. "As a herd of elephants. Where're we going?" He hadn't been asleep, but the AC blasted away any fuzziness.

No one said much until they sat in the all-night IHOP. Once their coffee arrived, Tavo blew across his cup. Rory tasted his, added more sugar and cream, sipped it again, and made a face. When had Rory become a coffee snob? In high school, his beverages of choice were pop and anything alcoholic. Jess hadn't been into the hard stuff. He was plenty mean enough without it, starting fights over every perceived slight. Back when Tavo knew everything about these guys.

These days, not so much.

Tavo took another sip from his cup. Scalding. Exactly how he liked it. And the only way to survive the horrible coffee at work. Tavo waved to the server. When she came over, he said, "Three orders of fries."

Jesse's lips turned upward. "Best fries in Valiant." That order had been their standby in high school. And all they could afford.

They engaged in small talk until their orders arrived. Tavo's mouth watered at the crispy golden sticks. They ate and continued to chat, mostly catching up on each other's lives. When the conversation rolled around to the karaoke event, Tavo's stomach rebelled. The caffeine and greasy fries didn't help.

"Your singing was outstanding, Chief." Rory squirted a giant glob of ketchup on his remaining fries.

"Sounds like you've gained some experience beyond high school." Jesse reached for the ketchup bottle.

"A few gigs helped get me through the police academy. Nothing fancy, but it helped my confidence level."

"You know Paige had nothing to do with that video of us."

Rory ignored Jesse's scowl. Subtlety had never been Rory's strong point. Tavo picked up a handful of fries and stuffed them in his mouth.

"So have you talked to her?" Rory persisted.

Tavo leveled a look at him. "For what it's worth, she sent a text." Several, but they didn't need to know that. "Said she didn't do it, but how else could it have happened? She left out that part." Tavo's mouth clamped shut. He didn't mention he hadn't answered her calls or texts. The events of tonight were an ever-deepening wound.

"Give her a break. You might try believing her instead of jumping to whatever wrong conclusions you've got going in that stubborn brain of yours." Steel edged Rory's words. "I've worked with her for years. Known her as long as you have. In all that time, she's never lied about anything that I know of."

Tavo viciously stabbed a fry into the red puddle in the basket.

"As long as we're on the subject of Paige, is there a reason you spoke to her—through the audience, no less—the way you did?" The vertical lines between Jesse's brows signaled aggravation.

"Aww, I didn't mean anything by it. When I'm onstage, I sort of say whatever pops into my head."

"Does Paige know that? Dude, you 'sort of' proposed! It was indirect, but she has to be wondering what's going on," Rory snapped.

"The songs. They were the ones you sang in high school when you two were together. It wasn't for old time's sake, either. You were singing your heart out, bud." Jesse shoved his basket away.

Tavo had lost his appetite too. "Yeah, I was singing to her, for all the good it did. Next thing I know, she's laying a big fat kiss on Clarkston." *The kiss he wanted.*

"What I saw was Clarkston acting like a jealous jerk. He initiated the whole thing." Jesse glared at his glass of tea, as if it were to blame.

He did? This was news, but Tavo wasn't ready to let it go. "She played right along."

"For a reason. Paige's MO is to go with the flow, not make a scene." Rory reached for Jesse's basket of fries and helped himself.

"She wouldn't dance with him. I saw him ask. She said something and walked away," Jesse said.

Heads raised when Rory's deep bass guffaw rang through the quiet café. "I'd loved to have heard that one. She puts players in their place so elegantly they don't know they've been insulted."

Well, that was something. But Tavo knew Paige too. She hated being at odds with anyone. She might give in to keep the peace.

CHAPTER TWENTY

Rory paused from polishing off the last of Jesse's fries to hold a finger up in warning. "You don't have to like it, bud, but I've seen Paige roleplay out of necessity. We both did it when we'd attend a big networking event. Those things were akin to swimming in a shark tank. We'd pretend to be together to send a message that we weren't available. But we were so effective, even Jess thought we had something going." He looked exasperated with himself as well as the situation.

"*Jefe*, Paige and I were never a thing ... in a relationship ... or whatever they call it these days. At the time, I was falling hard for Vi, but apparently, it *looked* like Paige and I were together, even to people we were close to. You can't go by how something looks."

Tavo shook his head. "This is incredible. You guys are defending her? Twice now, she's thrown me under the bus."

Jesse's game face was on full display. "Ro's right. You need to listen to what she has to say before you decide that. If you care about her, her version of what happened should count.

And you need to be honest about the things you said on stage. For your sake and for Paige."

He picked one battle to fight out of everything Jesse had thrown at him. "If I care about her?" His outrage was simmering into a boil. "You know that's not the issue."

"Then what is the issue? Faith? Or lack of?" Backing down wasn't Jesse's MO. "You told me you came home to reconnect, but you haven't been back to church. Until you get serious about making things right with God, nothing else is gonna work."

Tavo stared at him. "I don't believe this."

"It's what you used to tell us on a regular basis back in high school." Rory grimaced as if he hadn't meant to dredge up the past. Which he had. "And it was one hundred percent warranted."

"You might say we're just returning the favor. Walking the walk, not just talking the talk." Jesse's mouth slanted at a wry angle.

A stark realization cleared Tavo's confusion. "You're double-timing me?"

"As if that would ever be effective," Rory muttered.

Jesse's noise of agreement had no edge. "Not like that. We're ... helping you think it through."

The fierce words of his friends lodged deep. "I hear you. Anything else you got to say?" The sarcasm was back. Unfazed, Jesse snatched the last fries out of Tavo's basket.

"Who was that woman with your dad?" Rory's countenance was far too alert. Tavo had clung to the vain hope no one else had noticed.

"Ro—" Jesse interjected.

"My mom," Tavo spat out as if it tasted bad.

For once, Rory was speechless. Jesse gazed thoughtfully at

Tavo. "I wondered. There was something about her ... Did you talk to her?"

Tavo's head moved from side to side, as if of its own volition. "Dad acted as if he wanted me to be cool with her suddenly walking back into our lives, but—" He swallowed hard. "I'm not there yet." She'd been a full-time mom, then she just vanished. People talked. He'd hated the hush when he or his brother entered a room.

But nobody explained why she'd gone. He'd asked Dad a time or two. Tavo couldn't remember what he'd said. Only that it hadn't made sense, so Tavo quit asking. Even when the hole in his heart grew so enormous, he thought he'd explode. He hid within the confines of Dad's strict expectations, toeing the line until the inevitable clash of wills. It unleashed years of pent-up emotions. Then he'd left too. It seemed the only logical choice.

"You'll figure it out, Chief." Jesse scrubbed a hand over his face.

"I'd give anything to see my mom again," Rory said wistfully.

Tavo's feelings about his mother were so conflicted, he had no answer.

Raising his arms above his head, he stretched one way, then the other. He felt wounded, but in a good way. His two best friends had cared enough to hold him accountable. They'd certainly mentioned it often enough. A glance showed they were reeling from the tough conversation too. Their grim looks reminded Tavo of their high school playoffs when they had to get it right or die trying.

Rory waved to their server and propped his chin on a fist. "Are we ready to go? I'm missing Vi's arms around me." He yawned, but it didn't hide the glint in his eyes.

Tavo arched a brow. "Thanks for rubbing it in."

A sly grin stole over Jesse's bronze features. "Having someone waiting for you at the end of the day is a wonderful perk. Excellent motivation for *you*"—His gaze left no wiggle room—"to get things back on track."

What track? Tavo didn't know he and Paige had one. A very sore subject. Tavo grabbed the ticket the server placed on the table. "Let's go. I've had all the happily married stuff I can stand." He waited as they slid out of the booth.

No matter how aggravated he was at his friends, their concern for Paige touched him. It was part of their DNA to be ferociously protective of anyone they loved, and Paige was like a sister. They'd gnaw at him for days if necessary. Wear him down. Tavo no longer had the energy or the desire to oppose them.

"I'll talk to her."

STILL DROWSY THE NEXT MORNING, Tavo sent a "we-need-to-talk" text to Paige and sipped more coffee. He'd lain awake for hours after Rory and Jess dropped him off, thinking about his mom and Paige. No splits of thunder or writing in the sky showing him how to proceed. Only he said he'd talk to Paige, and he would. He found the sack of trail mix she'd brought and tipped his mouth to catch the crumbs. She'd remembered his favorite combo. His stomach growled, insisting it wasn't enough.

The front door creaked, and Rick strolled in. "Hey, you're awake."

Tavo shut his eyes and asked the God he wasn't speaking to for patience. "What was your first clue?"

Rick grabbed the empty bag and threw it in the kitchen trash. He peered into the fridge briefly, then gave Tavo the stink eye. "Two of you live here. Both with full-time jobs. What's so hard about going to the grocery store?" He took out a carton of milk and sniffed it. "At least this passes the smell check." He reached for a glass in the cabinet. "Karaoke night was great. Everything Paige wanted and more."

Tavo frowned. "Except for the last part."

Rick held up his hands. "That was supposed to be funny." He drained his glass. A slight milk mustache appeared on his upper lip. Like a five-year-old.

"What was funny about it?" Tavo scratched his head. Paige kissing another man wasn't Tavo's idea of fun. Rick should know that. So why was he rubbing it in?

"Everything was going so well. You brought the house down with those two songs. It was a humorous touch, that's all."

Tavo shot him a quelling look. "Nothing humorous about it."

"You're a stick-in-the-mud. People loved it, but Paige barged over and insisted I shut it down. I still don't know why you two are so uptight. It was just a bit of fun to help people move into the dancing mindset."

"What are you talking about?" Tavo stared at his brother.

Rick stared back. "The trio video. It was the perfect touch, only you and Paige are acting weird about it."

"The video of us acting like dumb butts was your idea?"

Rick rubbed his mouth with his sleeve. "I thought the crowd would love it. And I was right—until Paige got huffy about it."

"I made Paige promise she wouldn't play it." The knowledge Paige had truly known nothing about the video hit Tavo like a discordant note.

"You? Now why would you do something so stingy? Sure, you guys were singing and dancing like total goofballs, but that's why I played it. Because none of you are like that now. You'll have Dad's job someday, mark my word. Rory's gonna be rich as Midas, and everybody does what Jess tells them to. He should run for Congress. What? The three amigos are a bona fide look-at-me-now story."

"And you're a complete bonehead. No wonder Paige was upset. She wrangled a decent event for an arrogant celebrity so he'd look good, and you wreck it with a dumb video." Tavo's teeth hurt. He was wasting his breath.

"Yeah, well." For all Rick's nonchalance, his brows pinched together. "Speaking of said celebrity. I checked into him."

"And?"

"Aside from the usual bad-boy stuff that happened right out of high school—driving too fast, a DUI—there's also a charge for physically abusing a teenage girl, but it was dropped. Recently, there's been speculation and a couple of sealed court records that indicate he may have done it again. It's been swept under the proverbial rug, of course. Probably with a generous pay-off. I had to dig pretty deep. Whoever helps him cover his tracks is good. But the timing of his stint out here, and what I surmise as the last incident, isn't a coincidence. Things got too hot in California. This *finding himself*"—Rick made air quotes—"is more about letting things cool off. Giving people time to forget."

Tavo wanted to hit someone, preferably Ed. "So he's abused one woman and probably more." Men who resorted to violence were usually on a power trip. Ed definitely fit that role.

And Paige was working for him. His fists knotted.

"That about sums it up." Rick eyed him. "What are you going to do?"

What *was* he going to do? If what Jesse saw was accurate, the last time Ed felt challenged, Paige paid the price with that greedy kiss. If the guy sensed Tavo wasn't backing down, he might do more than kiss her. Tavo couldn't take that chance. He'd have to stay in the background. Only Clarkston needed to pay. Feel the weight of his crimes.

It still didn't answer the question of how he would keep the sleazebag away from Paige.

"You going to church this morning?"

"What?"

"Church. It is Sunday. You could benefit. Especially with what I just told you. And maybe get your head in a better place with Mom. She's not going away, you know."

Tavo knew no such thing.

"I saw the shock on your face when you recognized her last night. If you'd answered her calls, it wouldn't have happened like that."

Probably. But he wasn't ready to let his parents off the hook.

Rick kept talking as if Tavo wanted to hear more. "How about you come to church? Hear the truth instead of stewing in your own thoughts."

Good night. His baby brother sounded like Jess and Rory. *Hear the truth.* Was he that far off base? Was there such a vast difference between what God thought and his ideas about things?

The question startled him. And revealed his sorry spiritual state.

Rick had opened the fridge again and scrounged through the drawers as if he hadn't rocked Tavo's complacency. "Nothing in there, bud. Let me change, and I'll take you to breakfast."

"If it's someplace where they serve actual food, I'm in—*if* your offer includes church." Rick's brown eyes flashed with hope.

"It does. Are you going to apologize to Paige for playing the video?" If Tavo hadn't been dead serious, Rick's look of dismay would have been comical.

"So long as you're not breathing down my neck while I do it." Rick shot back.

"Fair enough. First breakfast, then church." Tavo rose, feeling lighter than he had since his return. He was sick of vacillating. He needed answers. About Ed. About his mom. About Paige.

Time to get right with God.

CHAPTER TWENTY-ONE

The church lighting cast a luminous glow over the rows of wooden pews. The sanctuary still maintained a welcoming vibe, despite the exodus that happened after service. Tavo sat in the back row, soaking in the peaceful atmosphere. Rick, sensing Tavo's mood, had nabbed a ride with a buddy. Pastor Mike chatted with a deaconish-looking older man beside the podium. Their voices were so low he couldn't make out any words. It didn't matter. He drank in their soothing presence.

As it was, his rear stayed glued to the seat. He couldn't have left even if he wanted to, so deeply did he feel God's conviction. Similar to the late-night discussion with Jess and Rory. A soul-cleansing ache. The good hurt. Elbows on his knees, he dropped his head, and murmured under his breath, "Why did I wait so long? I'm sorry, Lord." And he was. For all of it. For walking away from his faith when he should have dug in. For Sharla, and for leaving the way he did. Other instances of wrongdoing played through his mind like a video reel. He acknowledged each one. Admitted his guilt.

He'd made plenty of mistakes, but the harshness of the career he loved had eroded his faith. The injustice of the system and the unfairness of life had taken a tremendous toll. He hadn't been strong or wise enough to replenish his ebbing spiritual reserves.

Finally, the reel played out. He took a prolonged breath, knowing there would be more sessions like this one. Humbling as it was, the act of repentance was exactly what he needed. When he looked up, his eyes widened. Pastor Mike sat in front of him with his arm draped over the back of the pew.

"Looks like you and God were tending to housekeeping." The man's smile was gentle.

Tavo cleared his throat, not sure he could talk. He hadn't been this emotional since ... he couldn't remember the last time he'd felt like this. "Long overdue." A frog sounded better than he did. As it was, his eyes were moist. He sniffed, willing them to dry up. A throwing-things meltdown was preferable to weeping in public.

The man must have sensed Tavo's shaky emotional state. "I'm Pastor Mike. You came to the right place, but I think you know that. Let me be the first to say welcome back." He stuck out his hand.

Tavo shook his hand, but words had deserted him. Pastor Mike covered his lack. "I'd like to do coffee sometime if you're up for it. A get-to-know-you chat with no agenda." He grinned engagingly. "Except I heard you sing the other night. Might wanna hear it again someday."

Tavo chuckled. The man's self-deprecating manner was refreshing. But was he easy to offend? Before Tavo opened up, he needed to know. "Coffee first. We need to figure out if we like each other."

Pastor Mike's eyes sparkled with amusement. "Deal."

After a few more minutes of talk, Tavo strolled out between

the two thick wooden doors. It didn't take long to know if someone was trustworthy. Pastor Mike was a safe place. Tavo looked into the endless sapphire sky. His lips tipped toward the heavens with genuine gratefulness.

Though long overdue, he'd finally done his part. And God, ever true to His nature, did the rest. The healing of his heart had begun. His achy breaky heart.

———

PAIGE HAD ARRIVED EARLY at the coffee shop, hoping to claim the two sofa chairs. Best seats in the house. Gus wasn't here yet. She hadn't seen his truck in the parking lot, but his size was hard to miss no matter where he went. Someone else had already grabbed the sofa chairs. Slightly deflated, she sat at a bistro table in an unyielding wooden one. The serene gray and beige decor helped tamp down her nerves.

Planner in hand, she looked up when the door jingled. Gus headed toward her wearing dark denim jeans and a tucked-in navy blue police T-shirt. If anything, the long line of dark color made him look even taller. "Is your order the same as in high school?"

She nodded. "Are you working?"

"Light duty. Riding a desk these days." His grimace communicated more than the brief explanation.

When she reached for her billfold, he shook his head. "I wanted to meet, Pep. You're not paying." His mood wasn't clear, but he got miffed whenever she tried to pay.

"Okay. Yes, the usual is fine." Did he still know how she liked her coffee? She couldn't think of anyone else who cared enough to remember. Her ex-boyfriend had disliked coffee and supposed that excused him from having anything to do with her preferences.

Tavo chatted with the barista as she made their drinks, then carried them over to the condiments counter. She watched in amazement as he added a package of her favorite sweetener and poured in the right amount of creamer. Stirring it, he wiped the rim with a napkin.

He strode over and handed it to her. She took a tentative swallow. The warmth soothed her jaws. "I'm officially impressed. It's been a long time since we've had coffee. It's perfect."

Dimples formed vertical lines on his cheeks. "I make it my business to know your preferences, Paige. And just so you know, this isn't the date you agreed to."

She allowed a small smile. "Thank you for remembering how I like coffee. So, not the date." Her fingers air quoted the last words. "Got it. You said we needed to talk." She mimicked his straightforward approach.

He sipped from his cup, the coffee, no doubt, screeching hot. Small wonder he had a tongue left. The way he studied her made her impatient. "So talk, Big Guy."

His dark eyes brimmed with entreaty. "I'm sorry I didn't answer your texts. I know you didn't plan for the video. Rick told me it was all his idea."

"You had previously made your opinion on the video clear. It bothers me you assumed I did it anyway." Tartness laced her words.

A look of chagrin flit over his face. "Try to see what I saw, Pep. You were the only one I heard talk about it, then ... you and Ed." As if he realized the impact of his words, he held up a hand. "Sorry. I'm mixing things up. A lot happened at once, and ... no, I didn't handle it well."

"I didn't either." Paige kept her voice low. No sense in telling the entire coffee shop their private business. "I was mad at Rick. Then Ed did what he did ..."

"Do you have a thing for him?" Gus asked softly.

She bristled. "Of course not. I work for him. His lifestyle is ... more uninhibited."

"Paige, no matter how charming he *acts,* he's a hundred percent Hollywood. His values will never line up with yours."

His frank words stung her to the core. "I know that. He's asked me to plan one more gig." If only Gus would try to understand. "I understand your concern. Parts of it, anyway." He didn't need to know worries about Ed kept her awake at night. "Except he pays so well, I can't afford not to. It would take a dozen events to make what he's paying me for one." She also left out the part about Mom needing meds. He'd likely have an opinion about that too. Different from hers.

Gus set his coffee on the table and shifted his weight in the small chair. "Please be careful, Paige. I get that women think he's gorgeous, but you can't trust the guy."

She wanted to argue again, this time about him lumping her in with other women. Ed *was* gorgeous. Probably the reason she extended him more grace than he deserved. As they fell silent, the expresso machine whirred loudly.

"Are you trustworthy, Gus?" She desperately needed to know.

Astonishment streaked across his features and settled into confusion. "What? Of course, you can trust me. Why would you even ask?"

"Because you didn't believe me when I said I wasn't behind the video."

His voice rose. "People make mistakes, Paige. I said I'm sorry."

TAVO WOULD HAVE SAID MORE, but caution overrode his desire for the last word. Two phrases rose out of his soul. *Be patient. Be bold.* Conviction swirled like a tornado. Instead of speaking, he took another swallow of his extra-hot coffee. Then another to settle down and redirect his thoughts.

Paige blew on hers, then took another sip of the sweet stuff. "Did you mean what you said onstage?"

He knew what he'd said. But what had she heard? Hard-won experience had taught him they could be two different things. "Refresh my memory. I rattle off a lot of things when I'm onstage."

"You talked about marrying me. Did you mean that?" A note of bitterness crept into her words. "Or was it part of the act?"

Everything inside of him wanted to hide. What if he made himself vulnerable and she rejected him again? *Help me, Lord.* He gazed into her huge, hurting eyes and laid himself bare. "I meant every word."

He didn't look away. She seemed to shrink into the chair. "I'm not ready."

His breath swooshed, mostly in relief she hadn't brought up the just-friends stance. "I know."

"You talked about waiting for me? Did you mean it?"

"Yes."

"But you left after high school."

In what he could only describe as a flash of light, he finally understood why she kept bringing it up. "You came home, and I wasn't here."

Paige bit her lip. "I thought if you loved me, you'd wait."

"And since I wasn't here, you assumed I didn't love you anymore."

She nodded slowly, thinking it through. "Immature reasoning but ... yeah."

He leaned forward and put a finger on her lips. The need to kiss her tormented him. "What you thought wasn't true. It's still not. But if you ever need reminding, I'm here."

"Okay," she whispered. Moisture lit her eyes. Her palms slipped up and cradled her face.

"Your jaws are hurting again."

"Yes, they are." She seemed relieved to admit it. Most likely because she rarely complained about anything.

"You haven't been to the doctor, have you?" When she shook her head, another idea occurred to him. "Why don't you talk to Vi? The pain might be stress-related. If anyone can relieve physical symptoms, it's her." Vi Spence was Peeps' popular massage therapist. When Tavo powerlifted, he signed up regularly. He leaned closer and wiggled his fingers, imitating Vi. "May I?"

She held her cup in her lap primly, then nodded and allowed him to touch her face. He gently caressed her cheekbones with his fingers. Her eyes shut. The quick intake of breath assured him he'd found the tender spots. He massaged and worked his way back to her temples and ears with the slightest tad of pressure.

"Your jaws are warm." Possibly inflamed. Holding her jaws in his palms, he slid his hands down her arms. He'd better quit. They were alone except for the barista, but it was a public place. And he was on duty, though it didn't appear so.

Paige sleepily opened her eyes, then stretched the sides of her mouth. "It's better." She set her cup aside and took his hand. "Thank you."

Tavo held her small hand in his much larger one. "You're welcome." He wasn't sure what just took place, but something had shifted. For both of them, he suspected.

Eventually, she slid her hand out of his, and they chatted about recent happenings at her job with Spence Enterprises.

He was telling her about a funny incident at work when his phone chimed. He stilled. It was Sharla. "I need to take this." He rose and strode the short distance outside.

"Sharla?" His pulse climbed steadily.

"Thank you for answering." Ever polite, her familiar voice washed over him. "I, uh …" She started over. "Tavo, my health is in a rapid decline. Can you come?"

His officer persona took over, even as his emotions bounced around untethered. "You live in the same place?" A pause. "No? Okay. Send me your new address." He listened. "I'll be there." She spoke again.

"Yes, I'll come today."

CHAPTER TWENTY-TWO

Who was Sharla? It wasn't any of Paige's business, except Gus had looked so serious when he'd answered the call. Whoever she was had his full, undivided attention. A worm of jealousy crawled into her heart, curling next to her soul. When he returned, he wasn't brusque, just done with their conversation and ready to move on to whatever this Sharla person wanted.

Paige drained her cup and tried to concentrate on her planner, but the dates and her notations danced all over the page. Now what? She needed to talk to Ed about his next event. Reluctance tainted her usual motivation. All she could think about was Gus's clarification of his remarks on stage.

The timing of Ed's kiss was atrocious—almost like he'd done it on purpose. A way to move the spotlight to himself. That she could believe. The man was remarkably self-absorbed. But jealousy seemed far-fetched. Nor did he come across as vengeful. Ed just craved attention.

A sigh escaped her lips. She put a finger on them, remembering Gus's gentle touch. Surely, Ed had some virtuous trait she could appeal to. Otherwise, this last gig would be a headache.

She shot off a quick text, asking for an appointment. Then she gathered up her planner and waved at the barista. Might as well start on Rory's list. A day or two could pass before Ed answered.

The lovely reprieve she'd had from the pain when Gus massaged her jaws was wearing off.

He meant every word he'd spoken on stage? It sounded like he was proposing. He sounded sure, both then and now. How could he know? Her parents were no help. Dad wasn't an ideal marriage partner. Jess and Rory were better examples. If anyone ever loved their wives, it was those two. Did Gus love her like that? Or would he be an absentee father like her dad? Somehow, she doubted it. Gus was a mighty oak. Strong. Steady. Which brought a bigger question to mind.

Could she love him the way he deserved to be loved?

———

TAVO ATTEMPTED to hide his shock when he saw Sharla. Nothing could have prepared him for the contrast between the woman who had visited Valiant a couple of weeks ago and now. He hadn't encountered it often, but the air carried the distinct odor of illness no other scent could mask. Cheerful works of art covered the walls, and a vase of fresh flowers decorated the dresser. The quilt on Sharla's bed boasted bright colors and an intricate pattern. A knot of gratefulness formed in his throat. Sharla's housemate had taken care to make this place beautiful.

"Hi, T. Help me sit up." If Sharla noticed his gaping, she ignored it, instructing him how to slide his hands underneath her armpits to lift her. Tavo guessed she weighed around ninety-five pounds. The flesh below her prominent cheekbones looked cavernous. The rest of her was gaunt and emaciated, but her eyes gleamed with life.

"Hey, girl. Chased any criminals today?" He sat in a folding chair by her bedside. At one time, it had been their private joke. Their greeting after a long day of police work.

A lifetime ago.

Sharla's lips widened in appreciation. She remembered the joke too. "Roundin' them up in droves."

Roxanne appeared at the doorway. She distractedly pulled a hand through auburn hair that hadn't seen a brush in a while. When Tavo arrived, she'd met him and introduced herself with no accompanying frills, other than to explain Sharla lived with her now. The rest of the house was neat, clean, and homey.

She politely handed him a bottle of water. "Let me know if either of you needs anything." Silently, she and Tavo communicated their mutual grief. Then she vanished.

The room was quiet except for the soft purr of the ceiling fan. Sharla looked at it ruefully. "It's a toss-up. I get hot, and the breeze feels great, but if it stays on too long, I start hacking." As if to prove her point, she coughed, then sipped from the straw of her water bottle.

Tavo pulled the cord to turn the fan off. "Let me know when you want it on again." Rarely did Tavo feel helpless, but he did now. To believe this woman had once been so strong and vibrant ... it hushed extraneous words.

Sharla cleared her throat. "I've got documents." She picked up a manilla folder next to her. "Please read them before signing. If you have questions, we'll ask Roxanne. She's an attorney. And the friend who got me into church."

Despite the bleak situation, Tavo's mouth tipped up. "Sounds like a good friend."

"She takes good care of me. Drives me to doctor appointments. Reads the Bible aloud when I can't focus." She looked as if she would continue, then stopped. Instead, she handed him the folder.

The feeling she wasn't telling him everything swept over him again. He glanced through the papers. It all seemed pretty straightforward. He looked at Sharla. "Why me? I understand about your family, but surely, there's someone else ..."

A spasm passed across her face. "No. You're the one. I wasn't close to anyone else at SAPD. I'm leaving a little something for Roxanne, but it's only a token. Everything else rightfully belongs to you."

Her words stirred up more questions. However, her exhaustion was evident. Her eyes shut, then flickered open. He leaned forward to hear. "Your faith and your prayers saved me."

Tavo was relieved to see her chest rising and falling when her eyes closed again. She'd fallen asleep, though death seemed a whisper away.

Unscrewing the lid from the water bottle, he drank. He took the folder and thumbed through the papers. Strange. She'd named him as her beneficiary for a few investments, her savings, and some insurance policies. Why would she do that?

He recalled their brief visit. At the restaurant, she'd stirred her cup of soup but ate very little. Mostly, she'd shared how she came to Christ and asked him how things were going with Paige. At the football field, it seemed to matter that he take over her finances. Of course, he would. She deserved no less.

On the drive home, he prayed about the situation. A sense of conviction settled about how he needed to move forward. The questions he had about Sharla's request didn't matter. He simply needed to follow through and honor her wishes. As he prayed, the spirit inside directed him to another situation. And every time he tried to change the subject, the conviction only got stronger. Finally, he had to apologize for his attitude. Lay down his fears.

If he truly wanted to please God, he had to quit avoiding his mother.

"IS your shoulder healed enough to play hoops?" Mom bounced a basketball in Tavo's direction.

"I'm good for about forty-five minutes." Tavo caught the ball easily and aimed it toward the net, pleased when it sailed through.

A delicate blue sky lightened the oppressive heat. The park shimmered with water from underground sprinklers. A children's playscape sat mid-center, and walking trails wound through the green lawn. Except for the two of them, the basketball court was empty.

"Thanks for meeting with me." Mom had pulled her dark hair into a ponytail, and she wore a pair of Bermuda shorts and a T-shirt. Memories flooded Tavo's mind. She looked the same as when he was a kid.

Tavo shrugged, then wished he hadn't. He'd called her yesterday, though the desire not to whined loudly. The park was her suggestion. And she showed up with a basketball. Snagging the rebound, she slammed the ball onto the asphalt repeatedly. It occurred to him she was nervous too. She passed to him. He moved across the court, then passed it back. She shot, but it circled the net and bounced off. Grabbing it, she shot again and made it.

They played for a while, and let the ball carry the conversation. Within minutes, they had established a passing rhythm. Tavo didn't play as aggressively as when he did with

Jess or the other guys, but this tall, slim woman kept up. She also refused to cut him any slack. Her level of skill surprised him.

Finally, she stopped and bent over, hands on her knees. "I need a break," she called, between breaths. Seconds later, she rose and pointed to his hand. When she held her hand palm up, they slapped. "Great work. Sit with me?" Tavo found it hard to take his eyes off her as she led the way to a metal bench under a tree. She was a stranger. Also achingly familiar.

She pushed her sunglasses to her head and gazed at him. "You play well."

Tavo forced a politeness he didn't feel. "You do too."

Like a bumbling dinosaur, the awkward silence horned in between them. A mild breeze scattered brown oak leaves around their feet. Tavo's mother shifted on the hard surface. "I've always believed you can tell a person's character by the way they play ball." She faced him, her eyes suspiciously shiny. "I'm proud of you, Tavo. You're a man of integrity."

No thanks to you. A knot formed in his throat. "Why'd you leave?"

She traced the pattern on the bench with her finger. "I was unhappy. So when the coaching job came through, I took it."

Anger welled up inside him. "You had a family. We weren't important enough for you to stay?"

"I didn't ... say that." Her voice broke.

"But your actions ..."

"Were short-sighted. And the only way out."

What did that mean? "So that's it? You're back as if nothing happened?"

"No. I'll always regret what I missed. No way to get those years back." Anguish filled the words.

He frowned, moved by her lack of defense. "Now what?"

She blew out a long sigh, pushing at the damp tendrils of

hair that escaped from her ponytail. "I'm asking your forgiveness, Tavo. I hurt you and Rick."

A cynical snort rose in his throat. "And just like that, everything's okay."

"No." Her breathing hitched. "I made a choice, but I'm sorry for the pain I caused." Her noncombative answers unraveled him more than a shouting match.

His eyes squeezed shut. Truth was, his recommitment to God would insist he process this, however much he wanted to stay mad. *Help me, Lord.* He opened his mouth, not knowing what would come out.

"I need time."

His mother rose. "You got it. I'll be around." At his facial expression, a wry look flitted through her eyes. "No worries. Guess you've already learned I'm not a smother-mother." She clutched the basketball underneath one arm. He recognized the stance. A sad loneliness surrounded her. He could relate but was a long way from empathy.

Until this moment, he'd forgotten how often he and his brother had watched women's college basketball on television. Dad had often sat with them, uncharacteristically quiet. It was one of Tavo's favorite things to do.

Only now did he understand. They didn't watch basketball. They'd watched his mother.

CHAPTER TWENTY-THREE

What a bridezilla. Back at the coffee shop, Paige pasted on a bright smile as she showed a perspective client a mood board based on ideas from their last phone call. This wedding would add to her portfolio. *Focus, girl.* So far, none of Paige's concepts had interested the bride, though they were based on exactly what the bride said she wanted. Rather mercurial, this one. Paige adored the challenge. If only the bride's dominant color was a better choice.

Oh, well.

"You need to catch the nuances. I said charcoal. What you're showing me is plain old black." Lola had made whining into a fine art, but Paige could handle it.

"Of course. It's an unusual choice." This whole charade was a hoot. If the bride wanted charcoal flowers, then charcoal flowers it would be. Paige would sort out the color names later. And add some pink and white roses to soften that dreadful "charcoal."

The woman pored over a different mood board, this one featuring various styles of cake with black frosting. More

Halloweenish than wedding. Paige sipped warm coffee from a mug. Her mind wandered to her planner. She'd completed the tasks Rory needed, and Ed had flown off somewhere for the day. Or two. He'd been vague about when he'd return, but his next event was easy to plan. A beach weekend for select members of his last casting crew would be a cinch. Small. Private. Plenty of food and activities, and a large screen television. Ed's needs weren't all that different from everybody else's. Despite his superstar status, he was annoyingly normal, though she'd never tell him that.

"None of these cakes are what I had in mind." Lola's complaint broke through Paige's reverie.

"Okay. Tell me what you like and don't like about each cake." Paige used the same voice to put her siblings to sleep.

"Well, that frosting is too glossy." Lola pointed a black fingernail at the top left photo.

"Got it. A more subtle look. What about the flowers? Do you like those?"

As the bride squinted at the picture, Paige pulled out her phone. Dare she ask Gus to dinner? She hadn't seen him for a day or so. Oddly enough, she'd missed him. After hearing a few more of Lola's comments, Paige left her with a wedding planner's unique brand of catnip—a new bridal magazine. The door chimed merrily as she walked outside.

As she stepped out the door, however, a long white limousine drove through the parking lot and stopped in front of her. Her jaw sagged as Ed emerged from the backseat in a tux, holding a single red rose. Smiling demurely, he looked impossibly handsome.

He held out the rose. "Shall we dance?" He broke the spell and bounded up to her. "How's that for a Richard Gere impersonation?"

Dumbfounded, Paige searched for the proper response. "Uh, quite realistic?"

He stood close. No, he was crowding her space. The door stopped her backward movement. Ed followed. "Listen, I, uh, wanted to take you someplace nice, to—uh, make up for my rash behavior on karaoke night. I get in the moment and uh, maybe wasn't the gentleman I needed to be." Now he sounded like Hugh Grant—bashful with a bit of bumble thrown in.

A crowd was gathering on the sidewalk. Someone shouted, "It's him—Ed Clarkston."

Before Paige knew what was happening, a brawny hand grasped her waist and whisked her into the limo. Ed followed.

She recognized two men as part of Ed's security team. The one who shut her door climbed into the front seat, and the other got behind the wheel.

Paige whirled to face Ed. "Where are we going?"

With a mischievous grin, Ed placed his hand on hers. "Relax, hometown girl. I'm stealing you away for a proper date."

Paige sat back. A thousand thoughts whirled in her head. Ed excelled at playing different roles. Was this an act?

PAIGE HADN'T SHOWN up for their pool session. Again. Small waves rippled as Tavo moved the handheld exercise bells under the water. These workouts were so stinkin' boring without her. He switched to figure eights and accomplished two sets. Had their "talk" completely scared her off? If she had other plans, she would text. But if she didn't want to see him … No text was a sure sign it was the latter.

Funny. She hadn't acted scared at the coffee shop. When

he'd massaged her jaws, she seemed to appreciate it. Then Sharla called, and he'd been so consumed with the need to get to her, he couldn't recall Paige's reaction. He needed to tell Paige about Sharla.

Tavo traded the bells for small aqua fins and wound them around his wrists. A sigh escaped. When Paige wrapped his wrists with her small efficient hands, it was better. He liked her touch. Period. He kept his elbows at his sides as he moved his arms through the water. The resistance would strengthen his shoulder muscles. Paige's pretty face appeared in his mind, encouraging him to do another set.

By the time he finished with the arm fins, thoughts of Paige were erupting every other minute. Why was she so heavy on his mind? The only other person in the pool swam in the far lane. Tavo whispered, "Lord, I don't know what's going on, but you've put her on my mind for a reason. Please protect her. Help her and keep her safe from any kind of harm. Watch over her. I need you to take care of her when I can't."

Re-energized, Tavo made quick work of the rest of the exercises, though he was careful not to cut corners. Workout complete, he toweled off and slipped into his sandals. Paige needed to hear about his new commitment level. Or maybe not. He hadn't fudged, not one iota, but if she got the idea he didn't need her here … That wouldn't do at all.

The scent of chlorine surrounded him, and a soft haunting melody rose from within. A song he hadn't heard for years, but one he'd always wanted to sing. The Righteous Brothers performed a killer version of "Stand by Me." It made him want to find the lyrics and a soundtrack … after he talked to Paige.

He snatched his phone and glanced at the screen. Carlos's name appeared, then Miguel's. His mind whirled. What did Paige's brothers want?

Sitting in Peeps' deli, Tavo toyed with a foam cup. He'd filled it with coffee, but it wasn't hot enough. Carlos said they were close by. Said they'd meet him here.

That was fifteen minutes ago. They had about five minutes before Tavo decided they weren't worth the trouble. He drummed his fingers on the table, still praying for Paige. The need to talk to her was overwhelming.

Enough. The twins either got waylaid or weren't coming at all. Tavo rose and disposed of his tepid drink. Reaching for his gym bag, he spied the twins loping in. Good night. It looked like they'd run all the way. Their faces were red with exertion. Large wet circles appeared under their arms.

"Sorry, bro. Car trouble." Carlos stuck out a grimy hand. Tavo shook it, a little firmer than necessary. He let up when the younger man winced.

"Now that you're here, what's up?" Tavo sat back down and waited.

They pulled out the seats across from him and sat, looking nervous. They'd been little guys when Tavo hung out with Paige back in high school. He'd been around enough to tell them apart. Carlos was the bold one who usually did the talking, and Miguel had a mole on one ear lobe. Back then, Paige said Tavo was their hero. So much so, he'd had to be stern, so they'd give him and Paige some peace.

"First of all, we shoulda said it sooner, but we're sorry ... for acting stupid at the wedding reception." Carlos dropped his head, ashamed. Miguel nodded, his eyes not meeting Tavo's. His shoulder twinged as if to remind him of their immature behavior.

Must be his day for people to humble themselves. First, Mom. Now the twins. If only Ed would apologize for kissing his girl. Yeah, that would happen about the time pigs sprouted wings ...

"Did Paige make you do this?" He couldn't think of a better way to gauge their sincerity. When a surprised look appeared on both their faces, Tavo had his answer.

"Sis doesn't know we're here. She'd be mad at us if she knew we were talking to you."

"She wouldn't if she knew we're sorry." Miguel socked his brother in the arm.

"I think you need to tell *her* you're sorry," Tavo cut to the chase. "You embarrassed her because you acted like blockheads."

Miguel elbowed Carlos. "I told you he'd chew us out."

"We were being stupid." Carlos elbowed him back. "But you started it."

They argued, and Tavo resisted the urge to roll his eyes. Nothing had changed. Still communicating in their private twin language as if no one else was listening. "Are you done? Because I'm leaving." To make his point, because they weren't paying attention, he rose.

"No, you can't go yet. We got something else to tell ya." A note of panic clung to the words, only Tavo didn't know which twin said them.

"What is it?" Tavo was growing more impatient by the nanosecond.

"It's about Corona," Miguel said.

"Who's Corona?" Tavo asked warily. Nothing ever straightforward with the twins.

"The dude who works for Ed Clarkston," Carlos added.

Tavo's professional radar pinged. The guy who left the back door open at Ed's meet and greet. "What about him?"

"Word is, he's been buying drugs."

"How do you know?"

"We hear things," Miguel whimpered like a scolded puppy.

"I won't ask where you heard." Or how accurate they

considered the source. Chances were, they didn't have a clue. All Tavo had to do was stick around, and they'd eventually blab everything. So far, though, the details fit with what they'd told him previously.

Tavo filed it away for later. They didn't need to know he'd suspected Corona was dirty before now, but something else tugged for his attention. Paige often said the twins didn't have a good male role model. Well, they had a father, but his commitment was long distance at best. Small wonder they gravitated toward the wild side. Tavo desperately wanted to ignore the unction to step up. But if someone didn't reel them in ...

He was tired, and his shoulder ached. So hungry, he could eat the knobs off the fridge. The angst he felt about Paige tormented him.

He turned to Carlos and Miguel. "Here's the deal, guys. We'll go see about your car. Then I'll take you for a bite to eat. You hungry?"

Their incredulous expressions and quick agreement gave him a slight sense of guilt. Only slight. He still needed to find out what was going on with Paige. "Just give me a sec to connect with your sister. Do you know where she is?" At their blank looks, he took out his phone and shot Paige a text. No idea when or if she'd return it. In the meantime, however, he'd hang out with the twins. They needed help like dogs needed affection.

Tavo strolled out of Peeps, feeling lighter than he had since he'd talked to Pastor Mike. Purpose, belonging, and a reawakened passion banged around in his heart. The twins talked to each other nonstop, tripping over each other in their eagerness to follow him. Even as he shook his head, a chuckle rose in his throat. What was he getting himself into?

Tavo had never cared about saving the world. Truth be told, only a small portion mattered to him. Valiant had always been his passion. He'd always felt the call to protect and serve this city.

For now, it started with two young men.

CHAPTER TWENTY-FOUR

The view of Houston's skyline from Z on 23 Rooftop Bar surpassed Paige's expectations. She stood in the lounge corner area and looked at the night lighting on the surrounding buildings.

"Words don't do it justice, Ed. You told me I'd love it. It's ... magnificent." Paige's hands rested on the sturdy railing.

Ed leaned against her gently. "I thought you'd find it ... different."

She wasn't often at a loss for words, but Ed was right. She'd never seen anything that compared. He'd also been the perfect gentleman the entire evening. Still, deep on the inside, she felt ... wary. She'd seen his capricious mood swings. Part of her waited for the instance where she'd need to make a quick exit.

To her befuddlement and delight, they'd flown in his private jet to Houston and taken an Uber to this lovely place. He'd rented only one end of the lounge, saying he wanted to make sure other people were around so she'd be comfortable. His insistence that he only wanted her to have a special evening finally persuaded her.

This marvelous view was astounding, though her conscience insisted she'd grow tired of it. Even now, she felt closed in and wished, however briefly, for the uncluttered sky of Valiant.

Ed was dapper in a casual white suit, though he was careful to keep his hat on and didn't remove his sunglasses until darkness set in. Not being a celebrity tonight was his top priority. Or so he said. What he enjoyed was being incognito. Yet, he'd denied it when a server asked if he was Ed Clarkston. Paige hid a smile when Ed answered with a rakish Aussie accent, "I've heard the bloke looks like me, but tell me now, don't you think I'm better looking?"

No wonder he was famous. The man flexed in and out of roles like a chameleon. And now, he was giving her a charming side-eye.

"What?" As far as she could tell, he'd only had two glasses of wine. He seemed amused when she ordered lemonade with a twist of watermelon.

"You're breathtaking, Paige. And so ... sweet, I can hardly put two sentences together."

"Oh, nobody's sweet all the time, Ed. Least of all, me," Paige swirled the contents of her icy drink.

He tipped a hand to his brow. "I've seen you in action, dear. Homeless Sue—so quaint everyone seems to know her—didn't stand a chance when you twined your arms around her and claimed she simply had to let go of me."

A grimace stretched Paige's lips. "That was awful. Poor woman."

"Rather delusional, I'd say. But never mind about her." He leaned in so close she could smell the wine on his breath. She saw the heat in his eyes, but he slowly inched back. "If I kiss you, Paige. I won't want to stop."

"I've never met anyone like you. You're so unique, it makes

me want to be a better man." She shivered when he ran a thumb down one cheek. He seemed so sincere. The idea she could make him change increased her desire to initiate a kiss.

The effort it took to look away was tremendous. Oh, dear. This was feeling like she was in over her head. Frantically, she backtracked for something to say. Anything ... "I left my purse at the coffee shop. And my client. What am I going to tell Lola when she asks why I just disappeared?" she finished breathlessly.

Confusion knitted Ed's brows. "Always grounded in the real world, eh, Paige?" He seemed to think about it, then said, "Just tell her the truth. That I whisked you away without warning. And I'll autograph a photo for her. That always works."

"Sounds like a plan." It sounded too easy. Like he'd done this sort of thing before.

Sliding his arm through hers, he spoke earnestly, "You've torn me in two. I want to be the person you think I can be. And yet, you're so tempting, it's taking all my self-control not to ravish you."

He'd spoken the unvarnished truth. A shiver wound up her spine, and she edged away from him.

The words pricked her ever-alert conscience, but she brushed it off. Wisdom would dictate she not work for him anymore. Except it wasn't a perfect world. Mom needed those meds.

IN THE SMALL parking lot of the Thai restaurant Paige had chosen, Tavo waited outside his truck. Gray and purple clouds signaled dusk, but the warm muggy air made it a steam bath. He flicked away irritation. Again. She'd refused to allow him to pick her up, saying she'd meet him here. Good night. Didn't she know by now she could trust him? He should have insisted, but if she felt pressured, it wouldn't be a great start to the date he'd wrangled.

Locust song trilled through the twilight. Shrubs with pink snowball flowers lined the stone walkway. Pretty place. The overgrown trees made it feel secluded. Private. Not that he minded.

And here she came, streaking into the driveway like it was the Indy 500, pulling up next to his truck. He walked over and opened her car door.

She slid out gracefully in leopard print leggings and a white blouse. A tunic? He'd heard the term and thought it was correct. At any rate, she was stunning.

"Sorry. Were you waiting long?" Instead of answering, he kissed her on the cheek, breathing in the exotic scent of her perfume.

"What was that for?" She touched a hand to her cheek with surprise.

"So I wouldn't tell a lie." He grinned, dimples on full display.

As he'd hoped, she smiled and swatted his arm. "That was smooth."

He took her hand and tucked it into his elbow. When she didn't object, he led her into the restaurant. Once the server came and took their order, he happily gave her his full attention. "Tell me what's been going on with you, Paige."

She didn't quite look at him. "The usual."

When she didn't offer more, he took her hand and rubbed the palm. "Are you feeling all right? 'Cause we can get the food to go if that works better for you."

She swallowed some lemonade and winced. "Hot tea would be better. I'm fine staying here—with you."

He'd make sure she didn't regret it. Signaling the server, he ordered hot tea. After a few sips, she revived a bit. "Busy day, that's all." The dark circles under her eyes said otherwise, but he'd grant her time to change gears. Her stop button could use a little TLC.

Once their food arrived, they chatted with less awkwardness about their day, and Tavo was relieved to note she'd relaxed. "When was the last time you ate?"

Dabbing her lips with a napkin, her face scrunched. "Breakfast, maybe?"

"Half an apple on your way out the door," Tavo teased. Her smirk assured him he wasn't far off the mark. "Stick with me, doll. As long as I'm around, you will miss no meals."

When Paige finally pushed her plate away, it was mostly empty. Tavo's full stomach gurgled with what he was about to say next. "So tell me how things are shaping up with superstar Ed." Uh-oh. He didn't like the momentary guilt that flashed through her eyes.

"Ed's fine. We're on track for the beach party of the century." She twiddled with her napkin. "I think Valiant has been a beneficial influence on him. He's different now from when he first arrived."

Not what Tavo wanted to hear. She was also avoiding his gaze. Those bamboo curtains she stared at weren't that interesting. He phrased his next words with care. "I don't think he spends much time here. Isn't he usually in Houston or Dallas?"

Paige tilted her head to one side. "Maybe. But he's changed, Gus."

When she didn't elaborate, he pressed, "How?"

Again, the look of guilt and her cheeks turned a pale pink. "He seems sincere about becoming a better person."

A chill settled around Tavo's spine. "I suspect whatever he's telling you is a line, Paige. He acts for a living."

"I knew you'd say that. But aren't we supposed to hope for the best in people? Encourage them to change and all? Confusion and hurt fluttered around the questions.

"We can hope for the best, but only Jesus can change a person's heart. No way we can accomplish it by ourselves."

"I know these things." She frowned, deep in thought. A long sigh emerged. "But they're easy to forget."

"They are." He took her hand, unsure about his next move. "You'll figure it out, Paige. I trust you."

Her countenance softened. "Thank you for saying that. I appreciate your perspective." An impish gleam made her dark eyes glow. "Even if it includes your extremely biased opinions."

He squeezed her hand playfully. "It's not biased if it's the truth. As far as Ed goes, I still don't trust the guy ... and neither should you. Are you hearing me, Paige?"

"Yes!" she squealed as he tightened his grip on her hand, and they both laughed.

Tavo waved for the ticket. He smiled back at Paige, enjoying the color in her face and her spunky attitude. *Oh, my love.*

She gazed at him soberly. "I need to ask something."

"Fire away." He fisted his hands under his chin. So far things were progressing reasonably well.

"Who's Sharla?"

TAVO STIFFENED. Others might not notice, but she knew. Clouds swirled in her mind as she observed him. This was a question he didn't want to answer.

The silence became uncomfortable. He shredded a napkin bit by bit. "Someone from my past."

Not enough. "She called you in the present."

"It's not like that." His expression pleaded with her not to pursue it.

"Does your relationship with her affect us?"

She was only slightly relieved when he shook his head. "No, it's not like that."

"Like what?"

His fingers looked for something to do and found nothing. He wrapped his hands in his lap as if to get them out of the way. "There's nothing ... going on. I'm just helping her—" His jaw set as if that explained everything.

"Helping her how, Gus?" She wasn't sure what she expected, but it wasn't this sudden shutdown. His stern expression forbade any further discussion. As if she didn't need to know anything else about another woman in his life.

She made one more attempt. "Then help *me*, Gus. Help me understand why you can't talk about this person."

When he looked at her again, his eyes were red-rimmed. "I didn't know it would hit me this way. Sharla and I ... were friends." He paused, swallowing hard. "She's dying."

Oh. The server brought the tab, and Tavo busied himself with it. When he was done, he glanced at her, eyes still miserable.

"Why don't we go?" Paige hoped if they left, he would regain his composure. He looked as if he might weep, which would embarrass him.

Nodding, he rose. She tucked her arm firmly under his elbow as they walked out. Once they reached their vehicles, he leaned against his truck. She placed herself in the space in front of him and didn't object when his hands found her waist.

She looked up. They rarely stood like this because of his

height, but she sensed he needed the comfort. "I'm sorry, Big Guy." Her mind still teemed with unanswered questions.

He gave her a grateful smile. "Thanks. I didn't know that was going to happen."

"I'm here, Gus." She leaned her head against his chest and inhaled the faint scent of his freshly laundered shirt.

Though they parted with a promise to talk more later, he'd said little else. A deflated feeling followed Paige home. So much for their date.

CHAPTER TWENTY-FIVE

"Dad, I've been on the sidelines long enough." In the Chief of Police office, Tavo slammed the folders he'd been working on top of the file cabinet. He took a deep breath, savoring the mixed scents of leather and gun oil. He'd forever associate the smell with his father.

"It's not been a month. You bungled the first week by handing out tickets instead of going on light duty." His father calmly sat in a swivel chair, glasses on his nose, reading reports.

"I assumed that was light duty. I need to get back on patrol, sir." Tavo used a more respectful approach. He flexed his shoulder. It fussed, but only a little. Desk jockey duty—the fallback for those who couldn't hack the physical aspects of police work—was much worse than a tetchy shoulder.

"All in good time. What's the latest on Valiant's very own *celebrity?*" Dad spewed the word like a foul-tasting medicine.

Tavo crossed the small room in a few steps. "Appears to be minding his business here, at least. He jets to the metroplexes most weeks."

His dad favored him with raised brows. "And?"

Rats! If only the man wasn't so good at his job. "He's throwing a big beach party on Padre Island."

"And I suppose Paige is involved?"

Tavo shrugged, though the insinuation irked him. "She's planning it from beginning to end." He walked back to the file cabinet. Might as well keep his hands busy.

"She's good at that sort of thing?" It was the first time Dad had ever shown a speck of interest about anything related to Paige.

He held in a sigh. "Better than good. She's in the startup phase now, but with her personality and organization skills, she'll do extremely well." He couldn't resist a dig. "You might know that if you'd ever bothered to get to know her."

The only sound was the whir of the ceiling fan. Tavo clicked the button and pulled out the file drawer. He'd hung around Dad's office since he was a teen. Others saw organizing the Chief's files as a Dad-perk, but loose lips rarely bothered Tavo.

"Your mother mentioned you two finally talked."

File in hand, Tavo paused. "We did."

When he didn't offer anymore, Dad cleared his throat. Code for listen and pay attention. "Go easy on her. If true reconciliation is going to happen, it has to go both ways."

What would Dad know about that? Tavo found the *L*'s and stuffed the manilla folder into the slot.

"All I'm saying is you don't want to wait too long."

The remark reminded him of Sharla, though Dad couldn't have known that. Tavo gave him a sharp look. "What do you know that I don't?"

Dad regarded him steadily. "We need to talk. Regarding reconciliation, the longer it takes, the more everyone involved hurts." Their eyes locked.

"I'm trying." When he couldn't think of anything else to add, he spun back to the files and tucked them in the correct places. He hated filing.

On his way out, he paused at his father's desk. "Someone told me Clarkston's assistant—

Corona is his name—is buying drugs here in Valiant." As for how the twins knew, it'd be far better if that never came up. Tavo wasn't sure he wanted to know, much less inform the Chief of Police.

Dad sat up straighter. "Thanks for the info. I'll get someone on it."

"It needs a subtle hand." Dad would understand exactly how to handle it. Contrary to popular police shows, most drug arrests were quiet affairs.

"Got it." The older man scribbled on a memo pad. "Son?" Respect required Tavo to look back.

"Talk soon." The older man inclined his head. Tavo's stomach churned like a minor key jazz beat.

IF A TALK WAS IMMINENT, it might as well happen on a full stomach. Tavo had stopped by the grocery store on the way home. Now he puttered around the kitchen, preparing for dinner. The first step required loading the dishwasher. The steady rush of water running accompanied a quick rinse of dishes that had piled up. Once that was done, he sprinkled the green can of cleanser into the sink to rid it of stale food odors. A corner of his mouth lifted. Rick had nailed it. Tavo and Dad often chose the path of least resistance with grocery shopping and housekeeping.

Lax as their domestic skills were, Dad's insightful remarks in the office blazed a path of recall about Tavo's reasons for coming home. After years in San Antonio and Frisco, the need to make things right with his father had morphed into an emotional heartache that needed to be dealt with. Progress moved at sloth speed—slow and slower.

And he desperately needed to know if there was anything left between him and Paige except hard feelings, but that had proved more of a challenge. In the time since he'd been back, she'd hovered around his orbit but kept herself just out of reach. The date was a huge step forward, however weird it ended. He sighed. They still had too much stuff in the way—his past and her interest in Ed, for starters. They were by no means "together."

Dad's request for conversation uppermost in his mind, Tavo had bought large packages of chicken and sausage along with other fixings. The meat was grilling on the back patio, but the aroma permeated the entire house. He grabbed a carton of mac and cheese and readied it for the microwave. His father should be home soon. And Rick possessed a sixth sense whenever a real meal happened.

Tavo looked around the room as if seeing it for the first time. It fit the description of a bachelor pad, replete with dust and stacks of unopened mail. He corralled the stacks into a giant pile, then ran a dish towel over the table. That would do. A cleaning lady made infrequent appearances. Maybe it was time for her to come more often.

He opened a bag of salad and dumped the contents into a bowl. Oops. He'd forgotten dressing. Spying a packet buried in the greens, he pumped a fist.

His father entered after stomping his feet on the doormat in the garage. The broad smile on his face heartened Tavo. "I smelled something delicious the moment I opened the car door. What are you up to?" Out of habit, he clapped a hand on Tavo's shoulder. The injured one.

"Whoa!" Tavo sucked in a breath and kneeled. Not voluntarily.

"Oh!" The consternation on Dad's face as he leaned down was so comical that Tavo laughed, even though it felt like a hot poker had branded him. It helped when his dad joined in.

Still laughing, they rose. When his dad reached for him, Tavo hastily stepped around the counter.

"Let me get out of this uniform, and I'll help." Dad grabbed a longneck from the fridge and disappeared down the hall.

Tavo checked on the meat. When Dad came back, they finished the prep and had the meal ready in a short time. When Tavo volunteered to say the blessing, they bowed their heads. Rick strolled in just in time to hear the amen.

Dad and Tavo exchanged a knowing look, and Dad cracked, "What took you so long, Rick?" Tavo's younger brother grinned and held up a plate. The quiet joy of companionship reigned as they filled their plates and ate.

After the meal was complete, Dad patted his belly. "Great job, son. Before either of you takes off, let's adjourn to the living room. Need to tell you some things." He grabbed a second longneck on the way out of the kitchen.

Rick headed to the fridge. "Tavo, you want a beer?"

"No, I'm good with tea." Tavo had never developed a taste for beer. He quickly wrapped and stored the meat. Grabbing his glass, he made tracks for the living room. Procrastination fueled Dad's wrath faster than anything.

Rick sat on the other end of the large couch, bottle in hand. Dad had settled into his recliner with his legs elevated. The delicious meal threatened to curdle in Tavo's stomach as his father looked at him first, then his brother.

"Both of you know your mom's back in town." He rubbed a hand over his mouth. Tavo's heart sank. He didn't want to hear, much less talk, about his mother. Their meeting hadn't been terrible, but he hadn't addressed the forgiveness issue.

"I know it wasn't easy, but I appreciate the respect you've shown her." Dad's chest rose and sank heavily, as if the effort of talking about his ex-wife was enormous. "What you don't know is she and I have always communicated. For years, it was about you two, but lately, our conversations have shifted."

Tavo waited. Dad had a big hammer, and it hadn't fallen yet.

"We're different people now. She says I've mellowed, believe it or not." He chuckled ruefully. "We're considering dating again."

"Why'd she leave?" Tavo had already heard her answer. Now he wanted to hear Dad's version.

His father responded readily enough, though pain etched his features. "I don't need to tell you how harsh and controlling I was." Tavo bit his lip in agreement. The tongue-lashings had hurt them all.

"When you guys came along, I had no patience with her maternal way of doing things, though neither of us knew a thing about raising children. I thought being your father and the same gender that I knew best." He dropped his head, then looked up again with steely determination. "I was wrong, but couldn't see it, much less admit it. And"—He swallowed hard and his eyes moistened—"I mistreated her. There was never any physical abuse." He squeezed his eyes shut and paused. "But the way I talked to her still haunts me, though I've apologized and asked her forgiveness. So yeah, she was the one who left, but it was because of me, not you guys."

Unwanted tears slid down Tavo's cheeks and lodged in the creases. The pent-up emotion surrounding his dad's confession was choking him. Rick looked shell-shocked.

"I get this isn't pleasant, but please hear me out. Your mom is not an evil woman. She was young and found herself in an unsustainable relationship. I loved her, but my words and actions were unloving." His mouth twisted. "It took me a long time to figure out I was wrong and even longer to make amends."

He sat back as if exhausted. The silver in his sideburns had multiplied overnight. He looked ... vulnerable. They sat, mulling over the enormity of his admission.

"Does Mom know you're telling us this?" Rick was the first one to speak.

"She does." Dad's head inclined. "We talked about it. She would have come, but I asked her not to. You needed to hear from me about the role I played in our divorce. I also understand hard feelings." Tavo drew up straighter when Dad looked his way, but there was no accusation in his eyes.

His father kept looking at him. "Son, there's more, but you've already heard an earful. It can wait awhile." Tavo blinked. More? Dad was right about one thing. Tavo had heard all he could handle. He nodded, unable to say anything.

Rick asked a few more questions, but Tavo was through listening. He rose. "Are we done, sir?" Funny how tacking on that term of respect helped his brain to agree. Tavo needed to show his father deference. Despite everything, the man deserved it.

Tavo made his way to the kitchen and began the onerous task of cleaning up the kitchen. Minutes later, Rick joined him, then Dad. They worked together, communicating about cleanup details, otherwise lost in their own thoughts.

"If there's nothing else, I'll be in my room." Dad's confession hung in the air, and Tavo desperately needed space.

"How much can I take home?" Rick rubbed his stomach as if he was still hungry. When Tavo shrugged, Dad wrapped an arm around Rick's neck. "I'll supervise this knucklehead, so he doesn't take it all."

CHAPTER TWENTY-SIX

Tavo headed down the hall. He found the lyrics for "Stand by Me," but after a few poor attempts to sing the melody, he stopped. His timing was off. He strummed the guitar a while longer, then set it aside. Sighing, he dropped to his knees by his bedside. "Lord, I don't know how to process what Dad said about Mom." His insides twisted to the point he wanted to howl. Breathing hard, he said, "All I know is Mom left when I needed her. Now she's magically off the hook. How does that work?" His fists knotted. The ways she'd failed them came to mind, and he listed them one by one. As if to build his case.

Once his furious musings wound down, a small voice on the inside stated calmly, "You ran too."

His teeth ground with such ferocity, it made his head hurt. What? *You ran too.* Grabbing his short hair with both hands, he struggled to understand.

When did he run? Weary and drained of emotion, he waited. A memory appeared like a video clip in his mind. Surrounded by anxiety, he was packing to leave Valiant. Not long after high school graduation, he and Dad had argued again when Tavo told him he'd filled out an application for the police academy. It was only after Tavo left that he'd called Rick. The rational part of him wanted them to know he wasn't a missing person. That he'd left of his own volition.

"I had no choice, Lord." Anguish consumed him. Suddenly the picture Dad painted of his mom leaving appeared in stark reality. She'd thought the same thing.

Oh!

As Tavo absorbed this revelation, another ugly scene surfaced. The day Paige announced she was going away to college. Her face was lit up like a thousand candles. She didn't notice how her news crushed him. "Lord, she left me too." He panted for breath. "But—" he paused as the words tore out of him, "I forgive her. She didn't know how bad she hurt me." The heaviness subsided, but he waited.

Yet another scene of him packing a bag came to mind, and he recognized the apartment he'd shared with Sharla. She was in the other room crying, but he wouldn't talk to her. It felt as real as if it was happening all over again. He'd left her too.

Tavo stretched out on the floor, tears running down his face. "Lord, I've been so blind. I left too. More than once, I did what I hated." The scenes dissolved like ashes. Broken, he could barely utter the words. "I'm sorry. Forgive me."

He didn't know how long he was there, whispering his sins to God and asking forgiveness. The words slowly ebbed until the only thing left was one final hurdle. He groaned, casting it up. "Whatever You want. Anything at all." He pleaded for a way to move forward. The person he'd been tore at him, stealing the peace he craved.

Every joint creaked when he crawled to a sitting position. He hadn't held back anything. For now, there was nothing left to confess. The baring of his soul had led to an overwhelming thankfulness and a lighter heart.

How he'd face his mom was still a mystery, but the suffocating hatred had disappeared.

It was a start.

TAVO SCRUBBED a hand over the bottom of his face as he waited in Pastor Mike's office. The late afternoon sun streamed in a window, creating a dappled effect with the open blinds, but the room remained cool. The contents of shelves behind the desk looked to topple any moment. Books were piled haphazardly, newspapers overflowed their cubby holes, and photos perched precariously from every nook and cranny. A lived-in air permeated the small space. Pastor Mike entered, a steaming beverage mug in hand, and sat behind his desk.

"Sure I can't get you anything?"

The fragrance of Mike's drink wafted in Tavo's direction. Must be tea, since the smell brought Paige to mind. Shaking his head, he said, "If I get too comfortable, I might rethink my decision to come."

Mike acknowledged Tavo's confession with a small grin. Streaks of silver shot through his short hair. Tavo guessed he was forty-ish. Young for a pastor? Tavo had no clue. "Let's get to it then. Why are you here?"

Tavo inhaled a deep breath and blew it out. "I need to forgive my mom, but I can't. Seems the best I can do is not hate her, and God's responsible for that, not me." There. He'd cracked open his vault of secrets. The words hung in the air, taunting him.

Mike pursed his lips. "That admission tells me you're farther along than you think. Why can't you forgive her?" His no-tiptoeing-around manner encouraged Tavo to share the painful details. He'd prayed since the ugly meltdown in his bedroom and was positive this was the next right step.

As he related the circumstances of his earlier years, and Mom's sudden reappearance, his tight stomach unclenched by degrees. "So when Dad told us about them possibly getting back together, I got mad, but then the Lord showed me I run from things the same way she did." A pang radiated through the statement as his hands lifted in a "Now what?" gesture.

Pastor Mike asked a few questions, which Tavo answered readily. Already, he felt like it'd be impossible to keep anything from the man in front of him. Now he understood how Jesse had addressed his life-crippling anger issue, and how Rory had navigated his amputation with confidence. They'd had the same help Tavo was getting now. An enormous weight rolled from his shoulders. He didn't have to do this alone. He tuned back in to see a gleam in Pastor Mike's eyes.

"Now that you're with me, let me address the forgiveness issue. What I'm about to say isn't by any means original with me." He leaned forward, hands clasped on the desk. "The thing most folks don't understand is that to forgive is to let go. Of hurt. Anger. Jealousy. Whatever fills the blank. Our natural reaction is the opposite. We want to hang on to our hurts, but we only win by letting go."

His keen gaze focused on Tavo. "Sounds like you've done the hard part. Have you forgiven your mom? And your dad for the role he played?"

Tavo inclined his head. "I've said the words, but it sure doesn't feel like it."

"You don't go by how it feels. If you meant it, it's a done deal. You dropped your side of the rope in a game of tug-of-war. The war is over for you. But you've tugged the other way for so long, you need to reprogram your thinking. It won't happen overnight, but if you work at it, your feelings will change to reflect your new spiritual reality."

Tavo's jaw sagged. "Can that really happen?" Even as he said it, he knew it was possible. Jess and Rory were living proof.

"Yes, change can happen if you stay sincere and don't give up." Mike's slightly crooked smile reached deep inside Tavo, giving birth to a new hope. "And if you haven't forgiven yourself, you need to do that."

"I don't deserve it." The words popped out, a never-ending cycle of defeat.

"None of us do. But if we can extend grace, we need to accept it too. Otherwise, we're elevating ourselves above what God thinks, deciding we know best. Arrogance in disguise."

Oh. Could it be that simple?

"I have a suggestion for you." Pastor Mike leaned forward. "You seem like a guy not afraid of a challenge."

"Depends on what it is."

"There's that, but the cops I know have plenty of grit." He gazed at Tavo. A smile hovered around his lips. "I'm gonna ask a question, and I want you to give it some thought. Agreed?"

What did he have to lose? He'd been as transparent as a shard of glass, and the guy handled it like a pro. "Okay. Shoot."

"In the areas of your life that you struggle with—everybody's got those—ask yourself this: What would it look like if you stepped forward instead of running away?"

A grunt was all Tavo could manage. It was like Pastor Mike knew the reason Tavo had returned to Valiant. He'd wanted reconciliation, but it was proving difficult. If anything, the things he'd run from all those years ago had multiplied with warts.

He'd hoped to patch things up with Dad, but that was still thorny, and he hadn't expected to deal with his mother at all.

Progress with Paige was nowhere near what he'd imagined. And Pastor Mike said to keep stepping forward? Was that preacher talk for don't quit?

They discussed a few more things. Tavo rose when Pastor Mike glanced at his phone and stood. "Give yourself grace, Tavo. And time. I'm here if you need to talk again." Another grin appeared. "Now that you're coming to church, it'd be great for you to get more involved. Maybe join the worship team. I'm certain you'd get the opportunity to sing a solo every so often."

Tavo shifted his feet. "I know nothing about church music. My forte is the old classics."

Mike snorted. "It's not that big of a switch to sing about the One who saved your soul. Speaking of classic love songs, how's Paige doing? Still running full-tilt with her new business?"

"Now you're being nosy." Tavo rose. Placing a hand on one hip, he looked down at Pastor Mike. Tavo had never been above using his height to gain the advantage. He needed every advantage he could get on the topic of Paige.

Mike appeared more amused than intimidated. "Don't forget I was there the night you sang to her. You two were in your own private world. My wife's word for that is 'swoony.'".

There was no way "swoony" applied to his relationship with Paige. At any rate, it wasn't the preacher's business. Tavo waved. "I'll be around."

Pastor Mike's laugh followed him. Once Tavo had settled in his truck, his phone chimed. He glanced at the screen. The brief peace he'd experienced came to a screeching halt. Unknown number, but same area code as Sharla. Deep foreboding filled his chest as he answered.

CHAPTER TWENTY-SEVEN

A delicious cheesy smell penetrated Paige's tiny kitchen as she poked a fork into a large casserole of enchiladas. When in doubt ... cook a scrumptious supper and invite your besties. Donning kitchen mitts, she pushed the dish back into the oven. "About fifteen more minutes."

Standing nearby, Brenna Jacobs sipped from a plastic water bottle. "My mouth is already watering, girl." She opened a bag of chips and dipped one into a cup of salsa. "Oh, man. Jesse was so jealous when I told him you were making dinner tonight." She munched on the chip. "He claimed first dibs on leftovers."

"Rory beat him to it." Vi Spence joined her at the counter and snagged a handful of chips. "No salsa for these guys." She patted her tummy. "They tell me about it all night long if I eat hot stuff."

Concern rippled through Paige. Vi's baby bump had doubled since Jesse and Brenna's wedding. Rory said the doctor had already mentioned bed rest. Vi's tiny stature wasn't cooperating with a twins pregnancy.

"Why don't we eat in the living room like old times?" Brenna eyed Paige. She'd noticed Vi's fatigue too. "Starting now." She grabbed the bag of chips and strode from the kitchen.

"Yes, let's." Paige gently herded Vi into the living room, where Brenna sat in her usual place—a corner of the sofa.

Vi sank into a matching suede chair and reclined. She favored Paige and Brenna with a side-eye. "I know what y'all are up to."

"If it works—" Paige began, and propped her bare feet onto the coffee table.

"—then it's good." Brenna finished.

Paige exchanged a knowing look with Brenna, grateful for her presence. They were all thankful when the pretty, slender woman took the job as Peeps' accountant. Both Brenna and Vi had lived with Paige before they got married. She could admit it was lonesome without their daily presence. "So when's the marathon?"

"Still far enough away I can splurge now and then. Practices are grueling. Speaking of which, Vi, are you still doing massages? My legs could use your hands, but only if it works for you."

"We'll schedule one. Friends get priority bookings, as long as I don't get overbooked. Rory makes sure the front desk is aware of my limitations these days. Between the stress on my hands and carrying the babies ..." Vi's explanation helped ease Paige's concern. Both Vi and Rory were fiercely protective of the twins.

"If you're massaging friends, I'll sign up." Paige rubbed her cheekbones, making a mental note to ask Vi about facial pain later.

Vi grinned lazily. "Well, now. Friend thing aside, that'll

cost you. I want to hear about you and Tavo." The implication was clear. The ceiling fan whirred its agreement.

Paige considered avoiding any discussion about Gus but pushed the thought aside. She'd invited her besties over because she needed their advice. Following through would only be logical. "We've talked a little about us"—If brief and stilted conversations counted—"I told him I'm not ready."

"Ready for what?" Brenna eyes danced.

"Something deeper than friendship," Paige confessed. It was scary to bare her soul like this. "Ever since I said that though ... I'm consumed with thoughts of what dating him would be like this time around. But my work schedule makes it complicated. And to say Gus doesn't care for Ed Clarkston is a massive understatement."

"But you're done with Ed now, right? I see your point, though. Jesse couldn't stand PD." Brenna snatched another handful of chips.

"Remind me who PD is?" Paige held her hand out for the chip bag.

"Oh, he's the professor Brenna had a couple of dates with —made Jesse so jealous, I thought he was going to punch the guy right in the Peeps' lobby." Vi wore a satisfied smirk.

Paige remembered those days. Jesse was normally cool under pressure, but he'd been a hot mess about Brenna. "I've got one more event to do. I wonder what will go wrong this time. It's getting so I expect it. Now that I'm rethinking my relationship with Gus, it seems as if he's pulling away." If his warm arms encompassed her this minute, she wouldn't complain.

"Oh, I don't think that's the case. The way his eyes follow you around a room ... he's about to combust. It's obvious he's crazy about you. Back me up here, Brenna." Vi brushed at the chip crumbs on her skirt.

"True." Brenna nodded sagely. "He's with you every chance he gets."

"Like Jesse was with you, B.," Vi teased.

"Or how nuts Rory was about you, Vi. Poor guy. You didn't afford him the time of day until he gave you Cyrus." Brenna had been at the party when Rory gifted Vi with a guard dog for her protection.

"Granted, the man unearthed feelings I didn't know I had." Vi pressed her lips together, to no effect. A smile leaked through, revealing her happiness.

Paige envied their silly back and forth. If only she could be sure Gus felt the same way as he did two weeks ago. A lot happened since then. She didn't imagine the wall he'd put between them. The clock on the mantel chimed eight times.

"You should tell him, *mija*," Vi said gently.

A swell of yearning rose within Paige that she'd never experienced. She'd kissed Gus in high school, but they'd both been so young. This ... this was different. The guy she'd thought she'd fallen in love with in college hadn't come close to this. Ed won the prize for charming, but nothing about him was real or lasting.

"He deserves to know your feelings have changed." Brenna sniffed. Then her face scrunched. "Did you set the timer?"

A charred odor emanated from the kitchen.

"The enchiladas!" Paige scrambled to her feet and ran to the kitchen.

"Nooooooo," Vi wailed. "I'm hungry."

EVEN THOUGH TAVO EXPECTED IT, the news of Sharla's death devastated him. Her scent teased him, creating havoc with his senses, as Roxanne motioned him to a floral-patterned sofa. She sat across from him in a similarly fashioned chair. He gathered his scattered thoughts and tuned in to what Roxanne was saying.

"As I told you on the phone, the funeral is tomorrow. You can stay here tonight if you want. I've got plenty of room." Roxanne wiped a tear from her cheek. It comforted him to know the woman cared.

"How was she?" he ventured, not sure how to verbalize what he wanted to know.

"You mean at the end?" Roxanne supplied what he couldn't. Her eyes pooled again. "Tired. Sad about some things." Her look pierced him. As if she wanted to see deep into his soul. "More about that in a minute. Mostly, though, she was happy. I've never seen anyone with such vibrant faith. She knew she was going to heaven ... no fear of dying at all. No doubt in her mind she was going to a better place."

Wiping her eyes again, she sat in the chair with a small smile. "There's something else I need to tell you." She took a deep breath. "Hang on."

Hang on? That sounded like ... fear? Anticipation? He pushed through his mental fog to give her his full attention.

"... I hoped she would tell you herself." At her words, Tavo's consternation flowed unchecked. "She wanted to see how you were doing ... then she, um, ran out of time." Roxanne looked down as if ashamed.

Tavo's bewilderment mushroomed. Sharla had always been secretive. He couldn't imagine anything left now that she was gone. "What are you talking about?"

The lines on Roxanne's forehead tightened. "I wish she'd been the one to tell you, but ... you have a daughter."

Astonishment caused his mouth to fall open. "I ... what?"

She nodded regretfully. "When Sharla became a Christian, she felt a tremendous amount of guilt that you didn't know about. Her name is Heidi. Then she got the cancer diagnosis. When she visited you, I think she went to see if you were the same person she knew when y'all were ... together. She said little about the visit, but it settled her mind. When she returned, she seemed to just let go." Her gaze was earnest. "It would have been better if she'd told you herself, but it happened so fast. From one day to the next, she no longer had the energy for earthly things."

"I have a daughter?" Tavo's spine hugged the sofa back as he absorbed the news.

"Yes. You'll have to forgive me for being underhanded." Roxanne rose and walked to a small desk. Taking an envelope from the drawer, she held onto it and sat back down. "Sharla said Heidi was your child, but I needed proof. A side effect of being an attorney." She made a face. "So I took the bottle of water you drank from at your last visit and had the DNA tested for paternity."

Her eyes bored into him. "There's no mistake. Heidi is yours."

Tears filmed his vision. "I didn't know."

Roxanne's expression held a myriad of emotions. Grief. Regret. Sadness. "Sharla said you didn't. She said if you'd known, you would have married her. She, uh, couldn't face the prospect, knowing you didn't love her like that."

He stared at the large red numbers on a digital clock. The words held no accusation, but guilt consumed him. "How old is Heidi?" His ability to calculate had shorted out like a faulty light socket.

"She's seven. Sharla didn't know she was pregnant until after you left." Roxanne studied him. "Do you want to see her?"

"Yes." The stunned feeling was crumbling into curiosity. He wanted to meet his daughter.

Roxanne nodded. "Heidi's staying with a couple who have

other children. She needed a break from the grief, but there's something else." Her eyes were unreadable. This woman would be ferocious in a courtroom.

"Tell me everything." Tavo was done with secrets. His heart ached that Sharla hadn't trusted him enough to tell him, though he didn't blame her. Things hadn't ended well between them. Mostly his doing.

It was as if Roxanne read his mind. "I was there when she forgave you. After that, she only said kind things. She told me repeatedly that you're a good person."

The ache in his heart eased. That was the way he wanted to remember her too. "What else did she want me to know?"

A reluctant smile turned up the corners of Roxanne's lips. "She wanted you to have custody of Heidi."

The words shocked him to his core. The rational part of him insisted his life would never be the same. Nevertheless, his path was clear. No matter how inadequate he felt about being a dad, this little girl needed him. "I want that too. She's gonna miss her mama."

The lines on Roxanne's forehead relaxed, and her smile was now genuine. "Sharla said you'd want her. She said you'd be an excellent father."

Tavo's chest rose, despite his sore heart. "I will, er, I do ... whatever. May I see those papers?" He reached for the envelope.

She handed it to him. "If you're sure, there'll be other papers to sign. I made certain if you desired custody, there would be no obstacles." She made another face, this time as if something rotten had passed under her nose. "In the unlikely event her relatives come sniffing around, call me. No matter what they say, Heidi is legally yours."

The pain lessened its grip as gratefulness rushed in.

"Thank you, Roxanne. That means a great deal. Does she— Heidi know about me? That I'm her dad?"

Roxanne looked thoughtful. "Not that I know of, but Sharla ... well, sometimes she kept secrets."

How well he understood. Resentment raised its ugly head, but he swiftly brushed it away. "When do I get to meet my daughter?"

CHAPTER TWENTY-EIGHT

Tavo fiddled with his collar as he and Roxanne stood at the house where Heidi was staying. Roxanne gave him a once-over. "You look fine. Nervous?"

Yesterday, unreal as the news was, he'd been disappointed Heidi was at a swim park with the family she was staying with. As it was, Roxanne suggested he bring Heidi a gift, so they spent time at the local mall where she helped him pick out an item on Heidi's wish list. As the evening passed, Roxanne helped to ease his fears by sharing information about Heidi's life. In retrospect, the reprieve helped him over the shock. Though he'd slept little, alternately praying and punching his pillow all night, he felt more prepared than he would have been.

"Nervous, yes. But I'm looking forward to meeting her." The gift he held banged against his leg. He looked everywhere but at the door. Flowers bloomed in meticulously weeded beds.

They'd already decided on a plan. Roxanne would stay in the room with him for the initial meeting. Then, depending on how Heidi was acclimating, Roxanne would stay longer or let them have some time without her presence.

Once a man answered the door and Roxanne performed introductions, they entered. Tavo had already forgotten the guy's name but felt his scrutiny. He must have passed because the man led them to a cheerful room. Setting the gift on a coffee table, Tavo mopped his forehead with a handkerchief. Good night. Chasing criminals was baby stuff compared to this.

A door creaked open. A little girl with blonde hair ran to Roxanne and hugged her tight. "I've missed you, Roxie!" Her skin was golden from their swim outing the day before.

"I've missed you too, sweet girl." Roxanne returned her hug. Tavo watched them, mesmerized. Roxanne turned to him. "Come closer, Heidi. Someone wants to meet you." Heidi stepped toward him shyly. She had the bluest eyes he'd ever seen. Everything about her was familiar. This little one was a carbon copy of her beautiful mama.

"Mama said you'd come."

Tavo's insides were blowing like a sandstorm. "I'm glad she did." Oh, great. His voice matched his insides.

Heidi stared at him. "Mama told me about you."

"She did?" Tavo stalled, despite how much he wanted to know. Roxanne looked shell-shocked too. Talking to his daughter was scaring him spitless. He swallowed hard. Summoned his flagging courage. "What did she say?"

"She said you were tall as a giant, and you'd take good care of me."

That summed it up. He kneeled to meet her at eye level. "I will." He flexed his biceps. "I'm strong too."

Wide-eyed, she put a hand to her mouth and giggled. It helped him relax. He had no clue what he was doing, but he'd never met a kid who didn't love a show of strength.

She bit her lip, as if deciding to say more. Tavo leaned closer when she spoke. "I'm not supposed to tell, but—" She cupped a tiny hand to his ear and leaned into him. "Mama said you didn't know till now you're my daddy, but you'd love me the second you saw me."

Tavo silently thanked God Sharla had paved the way. The innocent, accepting way Heidi spoke the words broke the dam inside him. He wrapped his arms around her slight frame, careful not to squeeze too hard. Tears streamed down his face for the umpteenth time. He'd never been one to show emotion, but this situation came equipped with waterworks. "Your mama was right. I didn't know, but I love you."

She stepped back, watching him wipe his tears. "So I'm coming to live with you?"

"Heidi—" Roxanne began. Her eyes were wet.

Tavo caught her eye with a slight shake of his head. "You will as soon as we get things straightened out."

Heidi's lips drooped. "Because Mama's gone to heaven."

He regarded her steadily. "Yes. We're sad about that, but I'm happy I get to take care of you now."

She gazed at him critically. "For reals?"

"For reals," he answered solemnly, afraid to breathe, lest she not believe him. Oh, man. No wonder Rory was over the moon about being a father. Tavo couldn't describe the peace that had settled inside when he hugged her. His daughter. Joy chased away all his pending fatherhood doubts. He and this precious child would figure it out.

THE FUNERAL WAS every bit as hard as Tavo imagined. Heidi leaned against him and whimpered for her mom, so he plunked her into his lap and nestled her head into his chest. When her sniffles subsided, she reached for his hand. He squeezed and held on, hoping it comforted her as much as it did him.

The people in attendance warmed the generic room with their presence. It was reassuring to know Sharla truly had found a community of people who loved and cared about her. The preacher who did the eulogy knew Sharla well and shared poignant parts of their conversations.

When it was over, before Tavo could make his way to the aisle, two women appeared in front of him. His antenna alerted. They introduced themselves, though Tavo didn't remember what their names were. Only that one wore a ghastly shade of lipstick.

"Seems like you're good friends with Heidi. How did you know Sharla?" Lipstick crowded his space.

"We were friends." Tavo's lips firmed with resolve. His relationship with Sharla was none of the woman's business.

Fortunately, Roxanne chose that moment to ask when they were leaving for the reception. He gladly turned his attention to her and left the woman hanging. While they looked for Heidi, Roxanne laid a hand on his arm. "You don't have to go to the reception, you know. You just needed an out with those two, so I provided one."

"Which I appreciate. Will it help Heidi if I attend the reception?"

"I think it will help *you*. You might second guess your decision in the days to come, but if you hear how much Sharla loved God, then her procrastination about something so momentous as Heidi being your child will be easier to bear. Since I've known you, I can see why she wanted you to have custody." Roxanne touched a finger under a lash.

Tavo stared at her as the realization dawned. "You wanted

her too." Even as he said the words, he knew. "If I didn't want her, you would have been her guardian."

A flush stole up her neck. "Yes," she admitted. "But Sharla's clear direction was for you to have first choice."

"So I'm taking her away from you?"

"I've come to grips with it. You'll be a good father, Tavo. Granted, it'd be a lot harder to let go if you weren't already crazy about her."

Tavo nodded. Nothing about this was easy. "You love her too, though."

Roxanne sniffed. "Let's focus on the reception. I'll run interference from meddlers if you let me visit her."

Tavo squeezed her shoulder. "I can handle meddlers. But you never have to earn the right to see Heidi. I won't keep her from you. And I'll welcome any parenting tips along the way."

Gratitude shone in Roxanne's eyes. "Thank you. I'll miss the little imp."

PAIGE FURIOUSLY CUT through the water, splashing droplets into the air. Gus hadn't shown up for the last two water therapy sessions, not that she was counting. Nor was he answering his phone. She eased up on the strokes. This wasn't like him.

Unless ... she hated the option that sang to her like a bad recording. Panting, she held onto the plastic lane divider. What if he was friend-zoning her? She'd made it clear recently that friendship was all she wanted.

But that was before he sang to her on karaoke night. Or their chat at the coffee shop when she asked if he was serious about what he'd said on the stage.

She sliced the water again, breathing in the sharp chlorine

with every other stroke. Touching the side, she flipped under and began another lap. Recriminations tore at her. What an idiot she'd been. The fog that kept her from seeing had lifted. She loved Gus. She had since high school. But mistrust had lodged deep when she came home from college, and he hadn't been there. Now that she'd come to grips with it, she knew he hadn't left her. She'd left him. But not in her heart.

Never in her heart.

And now he'd disappeared again. She started another lap, but her rhythm was wrong. When she pulled to the side, the worried eyes of her brothers peered down at her.

"What are y'all doing here?"

"We're looking for Tavo," Carlos said. Miguel nodded.

"Why?" Her older sister persona still fit, though she hadn't used it in a while.

Carlos shrugged. "Cause we want to hang out with him."

"We've changed," Miguel added defensively.

"How?" She climbed the poolside ladder and stood beside them, daring them to explain.

Miguel mumbled an aside to Carlos. "She hates us." It was Carlos's turn to nod.

Paige did a double take. Exasperated, yes. Frustrated, definitely. But she didn't hate her brothers. Is this what they thought? Like Gus thought she'd never love him because she'd insisted on only being friends. What terrible mistakes she'd made.

"I don't know where he is. Have you been hanging out with him lately?"

"Yeah. He's cool, sis. Hey, you guys were tight once. What happened?" They both looked at her expectantly.

Now this behavior she understood. Inquisitive to the core. She shrugged. "We just … grew apart. People grow up." Their expressions indicated they weren't buying it.

Before she could enhance her story, Miguel said, "I'm thinking you need to hang on to him, Paige. He's a good one."

Carlos tacked on an addendum. "When was the last time you saw Mom? She misses you, *chica*." He looked at Miguel for confirmation. When he lifted his chin, they sauntered out, mission complete.

Guilt sliced through her. She'd been so busy with her normal PA job and planning events for Ed, she hadn't checked on Mom. Perhaps there was news from the insurance company. Or maybe she'd heard from Dad. A huff rolled up her throat.

She needed to visit, though it galled her to receive advice from the twins. Were they finally growing up?

CHAPTER TWENTY-NINE

Tavo walked into the pool area, taking care on the slick surface. His shoulder was crying for a workout, but he'd purposely chosen to arrive later than his normal session with Paige. She'd sent several texts. He'd answer soon, but for now, he needed time to think. That didn't always happen around Paige.

Someone slid into the pool beside him. When he turned, his mouth fell open. "Mom, what are you doing here?"

Holding onto the coiled lane divider, she shrugged. "I heard you were doing water therapy, so I hoped to find you here."

An awkward silence ensued as Tavo digested the news. Surprisingly enough, he no longer wanted to stay at odds. "You were looking for me?"

Instead of answering, she dipped her head into the water. When she came up for air, she rubbed her hands over her wet face. "Yes. I need to tell you something. First, let me do a few laps." She offered him a crooked grin. "It'll help with the nerves."

Talking to him made her nervous? Her transparency helped tamp down the skepticism that kept poking its head into his recovering faith. If she could make herself vulnerable, he could too. "That makes two of us. I'll be here when you're ready."

A grateful look passed over her features before she launched into a fast clip of the American crawl. He moved away from the pool ledge and began sets of the anchor punch and crazy arms. Ten minutes later, Mom pulled up next to him. Her rapid breathing slowed as she regulated it. Ever the athlete. But Tavo didn't remember her swimming. His childhood was a tattered blanket in need of mending. *All in good time.*

Her breathing might have slowed, but his was ramping up.

She began without preamble. "Your dad said he'd talked to you about why I left." Her eyes met his. "But he didn't explain everything. Nor did I." She shut her eyes briefly. "When you and Rick were little, I struggled with insomnia. It led first to sleeping pill abuse, then addiction."

Tavo felt his eyes widen, but he said nothing.

"I'd become a liability because I literally couldn't wake up at night. During the day, I was too tired to think straight." Her face crumpled, but she continued, "Your dad and I argued about it, but I wasn't ready to admit I had a problem. Then Reno got called out one night. When he drove home an hour later, he found Rick outside, toddling along the sidewalk. At three in the morning." She ended in a thin whisper.

Tavo didn't know Rick had ever gone outside, but yeah, his younger brother had a sleepwalking issue. He'd get up at all times of night and wander around for who knew how long. When his body became fatigued, he'd climb into bed with someone else or fall asleep in strange places. Never in his own bed. Shortly after Mom left, Tavo had moved into Rick's room to help corral him. Somehow, he'd stumbled on the solution of a nightlight. Something about the soft glow soothed Rick enough that the sleepwalking mostly ended.

The memory of raised voices and a sense of angst rose from deep within his psyche. A small child wandering around outside with no protection was a parent's worst nightmare. No wonder they'd argued. And how difficult for his mother to relive those awful moments.

"Mom," he began, "You don't have to—"

"Yes, I do. Your father doesn't deserve all the blame. He told me I had to get help or leave. I left."

The hard line of her mouth softened. "But God ... God helped me get a job I loved. Getting away from Reno helped too, especially at first. For years, we only communicated about you and Rick, but it's ... become more. We've talked through almost all of it—"

So much made sense now. "Dad told us about the role he played. How hard he was on you. But he seems genuinely sorry."

A sad smile peeped through. "Yes. I'm sorry too, for all of it. When I justified my actions, the depression only got worse. It was only when he insisted I give up my rights to you and Rick that I hit rock bottom."

"Why would he do that?"

"He didn't trust me alone with either of you because of the addiction." Her eyes pleaded for understanding. "He was right. I went to a Christian counselor because I didn't want to lose my job. With her expertise, we uncovered the root causes of my insomnia. Once that happened, real healing took place.

"Reno could have washed his hands of me, but he never did. He stayed in contact. Because of that, we still care for each other. Now we're attempting to find out if what we have is sustainable."

That word again. Yes, for any relationship to continue, it

needed maintenance and support. And honesty. If Mom could share the worst part of her life, so could he, though he wasn't sure how he'd get through it.

"Mom, I need to talk to you and Dad."

She searched his face with a decidedly maternal look. "Okay. I'm meeting him at the deli in about forty-five minutes. If you want to meet us there, I'll let him know." No asking Dad ahead of time. No keeping him to herself.

She'd picked up on what he didn't say like a pro. Like a survivor. It strengthened his resolve. "I'll be there."

He had to tell them about Heidi. The part about Sharla was bound to disappoint them. His past actions disappointed him. A phone chat with Pastor Mike had helped. He wasn't too keen on telling Rory and Jesse either, though Mike had encouraged him too, saying it was never too late for accountability partners. But first, Mom and Dad. His hope was they'd fall in love with his daughter the way he had. Instantly and completely.

He groaned. His shoulder was tetchier than usual.

HIS PARENTS HAD FOUND A RELATIVELY quiet corner in the crowded restaurant. Dad sat with his back against the wall. An old law enforcement habit—keep the entire room in view. After minor chit-chat throughout the meal, Tavo pushed away his half-eaten salad. He'd rummage in the fridge later tonight, but for now, the impending talk had stolen his appetite. He nervously swished the tea in his glass, and Mom's eyes bored into him. *Tell us now.* How she could read him after her lengthy absence was a mystery he'd yet to solve.

He set down his glass, taking the cue. "Got something to tell y'all."

When his father's brows raised, Tavo swallowed hard. "I apologize for not telling you sooner, but I didn't know."

Briefly, he shared the facts of when he lived in San Antonio, how he and Sharla had been friends, and then lived together. His stomach heaved. "I heard from her recently. She told me she had cancer."

Mom's eyes softened. Dad waited for the other shoe to fall. As Chief, he'd certainly had enough practice. Unfortunately, what Tavo had to share next would confirm his wariness. He took a breath. "She died last week. Um ... after she died, I learned we had a child. Sharla made it clear she wanted me to have custody." He frowned. "There's more, but I have a daughter. Her name is Heidi. She's seven."

The shock and bleakness of his parents' expression almost unraveled his resolve. He held eye contact for a moment, then looked away.

Restaurant noise happened all around them. A server strode by with a loaded tray. A toddler in a booster chair cried for more soda. Flatware clattered to the floor as a small child unwrapped a cloth napkin.

Silence reigned at Tavo's table.

"How do you know this is your child?" Dad's voice was hard and unyielding.

Tavo answered readily. "The woman Sharla stayed with is a lawyer. When I visited, she took a DNA sample. I didn't know she'd done it, but her motives were right. I have the papers to prove paternity. There's no question." He picked up a spoon to keep his hands busy.

Dad plopped back against the booth cushion, assimilating the news. Long moments passed. Mom leaned toward him. "Do you want her?"

This, Tavo knew, though he had no clue how to be a father. "Yes, ma'am. I've never wanted anything more." Except Paige.

Tavo plunged into the awkwardness. "Heidi is staying with people I trust while I get things worked out. I … um, I need to move out of your house, Dad."

Dad's stare pierced him like a sword. *I'm sorry.* Tavo's chest loosened enough to breathe when the ache finally relented. Even more surprising was Dad's response. "I wouldn't mind having my granddaughter around while you figure things out."

He shrugged at Tavo's incredulous expression. "You got things out of order, but that's water under the bridge now." His hand drifted toward Tavo's mother. "Your mom's been working on me. I focus on other people's inappropriate behavior and mistakes and have a hard time letting it go." His lips pressed together. "So I'm telling you now, when you bring this child—Heidi—home, I'll welcome her as a grandfather." He blew out an exhale. "It'll be good to have a woman around again, even if she is a little thing."

Flabbergasted hardly described how Tavo felt at his dad's pronouncement. Then Mom chimed in. "I just signed a lease on an apartment here in town, but I'm at loose ends job-wise. I'd consider it a privilege to help any way I can."

"You would do that?" Dad looked as astounded as Tavo felt.

She nodded slowly. "I coached big girls for years. Having a part in my granddaughter's life would be pure joy … if that's okay with you." She sought Tavo's face. A painful longing etched her features.

"I'll take your help, Mom." When her eyes watered, his moistened too. The changes in both his parents were miraculous. He set down the spoon he'd been fiddling with.

Suddenly, Mom didn't look like a middle-aged stranger anymore. She was the mom who'd taken him to school and doctored his skinned knees. "Tell us what she looks like." She playfully hit Dad's arm, then clasped her hands together with excitement. "Hair color, eyes, height. Maybe she'll have basketball genes."

A laugh spilled out as he scanned the table. All three of them had dark hair, brown eyes, and olive-toned skin. What would they think of his blonde fairy-child?

CHAPTER THIRTY

P aige pressed the tea bag into the spoon, pulling together her unwieldy thoughts. Mom spoke across the large marble counter of the island in the kitchen. "You're spoiling me with these visits, *mija*. Come sit with me." She made her way to a small sitting nook.

"I'll be there." Paige opened a small box of packaged sweeteners. A window seat behind the dining table boasted several plant varieties. A smile tugged at her lips. Mom had the greenest thumb ever.

"What's going on, Paige?" Mom set her phone on the narrow table next to her chair. A stack of devotional books and a Bible took up most of the surface area.

"I want to know how you are doing." It was mid-morning, but the dark smudges under Mom's eyes suggested a lack of sleep.

"I'm fine." A wary tone had entered her voice as if she suspected Paige's motives.

"Is there an update from the insurance company on the medicine?"

"No. I didn't expect one."

"What about Dad? Did you get in touch with him?" Paige pressed.

Mom's eyes narrowed. "What's this about, Paige?"

Oh, for the love. "I can help with the meds, Mom."

Surprise etched lines into Mom's forehead. "Wha … No. Your dad and I will figure it out. I don't want you to pay for my medicine, Paige. *You* need it for your business."

"Not if Dad doesn't help, or the insurance doesn't come through."

"I'm not worried about the ifs, and neither should you. Now tell me about your karaoke event. Your version is bound to be more credible than the gossip floating around."

Oh, maybe not. She shared the highlights, at least the musical ones. She left out Ed's kiss and Gus's onstage remarks.

Her mother sighed wistfully. "I miss Gus's singing."

"He's better than ever. More confident." Paige took a deep breath. There wouldn't be a more perfect opportunity to give her jumbled reflections breathing room. Mom had always been a safe place for confidences. She'd certainly had enough experience with five children and a mostly absent husband. "We went to dinner the other night. He says he still has feelings for me." Paige twiddled with her cup and took a sip, avoiding eye contact.

"He'd be a fool not to," Mom's response was loyal but …

"You've always been in my court, Mom. Your opinion is biased." Nonetheless, it soothed Paige to hear it. Her confidence about Gus lay at the bottom of a deep barrel. He hadn't been in touch, nor had he been at the pool. Had he finally moved on?

"Look at me, *jita*." Her gentle tone contained a hint of steel. "That boy has a good heart, and he's turned into a fine man. I'd tell you if he was wrong for you. Gus got the best from both his parents. Such a shame his mom left."

The woman standing with Gus's dad. The puzzle pieces fell into place. "I think she was at the karaoke event." Curiosity overcame her normal reticence about digging into other people's lives. "Did you know her? Why did she leave? We were just kids. Everything seemed hushed up."

Mom's lips pursed. "We were all so young. Mostly, I knew *of* her. She played basketball in college and wanted to go pro but fell in love with Reno. We didn't travel in the same social circles, what with your dad being gone so much."

All the time was more like it. "And? ..."

A sigh escaped. "Gus's dad and I were friends in high school. Once your dad and I started dating, I didn't see Reno much." A mix of sadness and amusement filled her expression. "Reno wasn't fond of Victor, so it was the end of our friendship. I was glad when Reno met Marie. Sorry when they split up. She was good for him."

"Why didn't he like Dad?"

A girlish giggle bubbled up Mom's throat. "Reno excelled in sports but was competitive to a fault. That Victor consistently beat him in track didn't set well." Her gaze seemed far off. "Your dad could run like the wind. He won the state meet our senior year."

"Why didn't you tell me any of this before?"

"You didn't ask," Mom laughed. "And what does it matter? I fell in love and never looked back."

Yeah, Paige saw how that turned out. Dad was gone on missions far more than he was ever home. As if Mother read her thoughts, she said, "Love is a funny thing, Paige. I wish he'd been around more when you and your siblings were growing up, but it never happened. Somewhere in the journey, I decided to stay and let the bitterness go." She leaned closer, her voice nearly a whisper. "If I had to do it all over again, I'd still choose him. These days, I pray each of you will get to know him. He's talked of retirement. Time to let God give back the years 'eaten by the locust.'"

Dad retiring? The news stirred a longing inside of Paige to become acquainted with her father. But she wouldn't hold her breath. A spotlight beamed into her heart. Could her non-existent relationship with her dad have played a role in her ability to trust Gus? What if she admitted her desire, and he left? He'd done it once. They'd worked through her misunderstanding and assumptions, but her heart was slow to catch on. Dad had left repeatedly, taking part of her with him every time.

Could she break loose of this well-traveled rut of wrong thinking? Dare she trust Gus with her feelings?

PAIGE STOOD at Gus's door. Her stomach mimicked a soupy sea and sabotaged any peace about talking to Gus. Yet here she was. Though it was late morning, her long white blouse already felt damp. The rest of her ensemble included zebra-print leggings and red sandals. Clothes helped her confidence level. If she could get a word out. Ever since she'd aired her heart with Brenna and Vi, then Mom, her desire had mushroomed. After the worst first meeting ever with a potential client, she knew her attraction to Gus had to be dealt with. Her knees were swimmy as if they might not hold her up. *Where are you, Lord?*

Taking a deep breath, she rang the doorbell. A strange car was in the driveway. Maybe this was a bad time. She should have noticed it earlier. The weakness in her knees intensified. Standing was becoming an issue.

She heard footsteps, then the door creaked open. Gus's father appeared. Less than thrilled to see her, of course, but that wasn't news. Something akin to pity passed over his face. Well, that was a first. The urge to know why flitted through her mind. "I'm, uh, looking for Gus."

Before his father could answer, Gus appeared and stood in the open doorway. Guilt burned through his features. He opened his mouth, then hesitated. For too long.

If she left now, maybe she could process his strange reactions. "Ahh, this is a bad time." She took a step back. "I'll, uh, ... just give me a call later." Her stab at a cheery tone failed. As she turned to go, a small feminine voice asked, "Who is it, Daddy?"

Daddy? Paige sought the person who said it. A little girl with platinum blonde hair wormed her way past Gus's dad and slipped her hand into Gus's. Shock set in, and everything happened too fast.

Gus's father had disappeared, but a woman—a very pretty woman with auburn hair—stepped into the area he vacated. "Heidi, not everything that happens here is your business. Especially visitors. Let your daddy talk to his guest."

Shooting Paige a look of chagrin, the woman attempted to take the little girl's hand, but Heidi planted her feet, and asked again, "Who's this?" She stared at her with unaffected curiosity.

"This is Paige, a, um, a friend of mine." Gus inclined his head toward the woman. "This is Roxanne."

As if that explained everything. A dagger slipped into Paige's heart. She didn't know the breadth of what was going on, but it was enough. Her legs threatened to buckle under her, but she needed to leave now. The smile she pasted on trembled, then cratered. Roxanne's concerned look only hastened her steps. Paige stepped to the sidewalk. If only she could get to her car without falling.

"Paige, wait!" Gus caught up with her. When she didn't stop, he said, "Let me explain, Pep."

Almost there. She reached for the handle, but Gus slid between her and the car. He clasped her shaking hands. She tried to yank them back. "Move." The emotion clogging her throat made it a one-word command.

"Will you let me explain?" he pleaded.

She couldn't look at him. Distress and anger clouded her vision. When he showed no sign of letting go, she bit out the first of a thousand questions. "Why did that little girl call you Daddy?"

———

TAVO SHUT HIS EYES. Why hadn't he seen this coming? Pastor Mike said it would help if Rory and Jesse knew. Tavo hadn't forgotten about Paige, but he'd been so consumed with Heidi and his new role that it had been easy to relegate her to the back burner. Now she'd learned he had a child in the most awful way possible. *Lord, I need your help now.* How to handle this? He only knew of one way.

When Paige moved impatiently, he said softly, "Because I'm her father." Sighing, he let go of her hands. Grabbing them wasn't a smart move in the first place, though he'd never hurt her. His quick glimpse of her face showed he already had.

"Can we talk?" Heat from the car radiated against his skin.

"I need to go."

"Not without the facts." He couldn't let her leave without knowing how it happened.

She continued looking down. "Sure." She didn't sound sure at all. He couldn't blame her.

"Walk with me." He took her hand tentatively and led her to one side of the house. Once she knew where they were going, she tugged her hand loose. She made her way to a concrete bench. Stiffness had replaced her natural physical grace.

At one time, the tiny corner had been a place of beauty with various flowers. It had been in disarray since Mom left. Paige sat on the bench, a mask settling over her lovely features.

Not wanting to crowd her space, he sat close to the edge. An awkward silence ensued. She crushed a beetle bug under her sandal but said nothing.

He cleared his throat. "When you left, I was miserable." At her "don't-blame-this-on-me" look, he held up a hand. "None of this is your fault." He waited, hoping for a shred of ... something. When she didn't respond, he continued.

"We've talked about why I moved to San Antonio ... What I left out was Sharla, the friend who had cancer."

"Had?" Paige shot him a questioning look.

"She died last week. When I went to the funeral, Roxanne told me about Heidi."

"Sounds like you and Sharla were more than friends," Paige fingered her red necklace. She sounded more sad than accusing.

Gus expelled a long breath. "We lived together for a while, but I never loved her ... not like ..." He ran a hand through his hair. "Eventually, I took a job in Frisco and left."

"You didn't know?" Deep grooves lined Paige's forehead.

"No. We didn't talk again until recently." Tavo hung his head. "I've talked to Pastor Mike about it. Paige, please believe me. I was so caught up in the logistics of having her here, I wasn't thinking ... about anything else. I'm sorry. Roxanne brought her this morning. Heidi was meeting Mom and Dad when you came."

Paige's rueful smile tore at him. "And I spoiled everything."

"No!" He struggled for words. "I've been preoccupied ... when I realized you didn't know ... well, here we are."

He faced her. "I love you, Paige. You're it for me. I couldn't make it work with Sharla because ... I never stopped loving you. I still do. I just got consumed ..."

Two fat tears pooled in her eyes and cut twin rivers down her cheeks. "Thank you for telling me. Even if my timing messed things up."

He longed to wipe her tears away, but he wouldn't touch her. Not when they were at such a horrible crossroad. His anxiety kicked up a notch. He hated that she took the blame. And the polite way she said it, disguising her emotions like this sudden great chasm between them was nothing.

Her tear-ravaged face urged him to speak again. He couldn't let her go like this. She'd retreat and friend-zone him forever. "Give me time, Paige. Give us time. I know me having a daughter is a huge wrinkle—" He stopped. Heidi changed everything.

He couldn't push her into loving him or his child. Nor would he want to. It wouldn't be fair to any of them. If they were to be together, Paige would have to make the move.

Another thought left him reeling. This was the woman who didn't want kids.

There was nothing else to say. If only she'd stay in his orbit a little longer. But that would make it about him. His hemorrhaging heart. What about her heart? He had hurt her, possibly beyond repair. *Oh, God, what have I done? I can't fix this. Please mend what I've broken.*

With wooden steps, he walked her to her car and watched her white Jetta roll down the street. Her careful driving both relieved and bothered him. Was this slow exit a preview of what was to come?

CHAPTER THIRTY-ONE

Tavo felt as if his head would burst. Roxanne had stayed overnight in a hotel and spent the morning acclimating him to Heidi's needs, the school she would attend being foremost. He'd never considered school would be a major decision. One he had no expertise with. His mom had stopped in, something he found himself grateful for. She'd sensed his bewilderment and asked Roxanne questions Tavo wouldn't have known to ask.

After checking out campuses all day, he was ready for a break. But first, dinner. He herded Heidi and Roxanne into his favorite diner. They all needed comfort food tonight. Heidi, who possessed more energy than the K-9 Belgian Malinois at the station, bounced around the seating area, taking in the homey décor and atmosphere. Mom had begged off, saying they could fill her in later.

Due to the popularity of the evening special, the only seats left were at the larger tables in the back. Gus was relieved to let Roxanne discuss the menu options with Heidi and order for her, though he paid attention. Once drinks were served, the tight band encircling Tavo's head lessened. How would he manage without Roxanne? The responsibilities and endless details of parenting were swamping him.

He bent his head toward Heidi, answering another of her endless questions. In his peripheral vision, two people slid into the seats in front of him.

Carlos and Miguel.

"Sup, bro?" Probably Carlos. Tavo craned his neck, searching for the tell-tale mole, but the angle was wrong.

"Where ya been, homey?" the other twin asked. "Haven't seen you at the pool. Or the basketball court."

Tavo found it easier to address the twins as one unit, since he was never sure which one he was talking to. He needed Paige to refresh his memory, but that wouldn't happen any time soon, if ever. Before he could answer, though, Heidi intervened. "Who are they, Daddy? Why are there two?" Her lower jaw sagged as she stared at them.

"Heidi," Roxanne started in, but Tavo missed the rest. The sheer surprise on the twins' faces reminded him most people didn't know he had a daughter. Questions would have to wait. Paige approached with leaden steps.

Tavo's head hammered again. Her glow was missing, and he was the one who'd taken it away. *Help me, Lord.* Speaking in an even tone that didn't betray his quaking insides, he said, "Hi, Paige. You've met Roxanne. She's giving me the lowdown on how to care for Heidi." He turned slightly in his seat to face Heidi and Roxanne. "You know Paige. These are her twin brothers, Carlos and Miguel."

"Twins!" Heidi squealed. "That's why they look alike, Roxie."

"I'm guessing it's the first time she's seen identical twins."

Roxanne gently placed her hand on Heidi's arm. Tavo watched the interaction closely and stored it away for future use. Her simple touch had the magical effect of calming down the excited child.

"Can we sit here? Y'all got plenty of room. That way, we don't have to wait for a table." One twin said it, but both nodded as if it was the perfect solution.

"Guys! You don't just invite yourselves to someone's table." The arcs of Paige's delicate brows communicated much more.

"It's okay, Pep." Tavo grasped the opportunity. The twins would entertain Heidi. Both he and Roxanne could use the break, plus he'd get the added benefit of chatting with Paige. If she didn't freeze him out.

One twin asked if he could show Heidi the arcade room. The other reached for her hand. Tavo and Roxanne exchanged quizzical expressions, but Paige spoke up, "Not so fast. If Gus says it's okay, there are rules."

Tavo held Roxanne's eye a second longer, then inclined his head a fraction.

The twins perked up. Paige eyed each of them sternly. "You stay with her all the time. Never leave her side. Got it?"

"Easy peasy," one twin chirped.

"Lemon squeezy," the other finished. Grinning, they slapped high fives.

Paige rolled her eyes, but Heidi stood between them in a flash, eyes shining. As if she'd found her two new best friends. Each twin took a hand and wove her through the tables.

"How long will they be back there?" A line deepened Roxanne's forehead.

"Until they run out of money," Paige said dryly.

"I'll check on them in a few minutes," Tavo reassured her.

The worry line fading, Roxanne turned to Paige. "We need a server over here to get your order."

"No worries. I ordered take out since it's so crowded, but once the twins spied Gus, they wanted to stay. I'll let the server know."

Once the two women got the orders squared away, Tavo rose. "Be back in a minute." He attempted a casual, "I-got-this" vibe. Truth was, the unrelenting pressure of fatherhood and the qualms about Paige had slung a wrecking ball into his emotions. Thrusting a hand in the back pocket of his jeans, he strolled to the arcade room. His life had become a loud noisy pinball machine with no place to think.

———

THANKS, *Gus.* Paige fumed silently. What on earth was she going to say to this woman who knew things about Gus that Paige didn't? They seemed comfortable with each other. Had they spent the day together?

Roxanne placed a napkin under her glass. "I take it this is a shock, Tavo suddenly being a dad."

Paige inclined her head a fraction, trying to find words ... any words that might smooth this over. Before she could respond, Roxanne spoke again. "Sharla is, uh, was my friend. There's no question Heidi is Tavo's child, but I know for certain he had no idea." Her voice was gentle. "I'm an attorney. Reading people comes with the territory. He reacted exactly as Sharla said he would—a good man who wants to do the right thing."

Every nerve Paige possessed flamed to life. The woman sitting across from her couldn't know her well-meaning words jabbed into a fresh wound. She went with what she knew, though it hadn't occurred to her until this second. "Gus will be a great dad."

Sadness knotted Roxanne's brows. "I know, and I'm

grateful. I couldn't leave her otherwise. He said I can visit regularly, which I plan to take full advantage of."

Roxanne's visiting might be great for Heidi, but Paige hated the idea. Jealousy stuck to her insides, and she couldn't shake it.

"You know he's going to need a support group. People who love him and accept Heidi. He's trying, but he doesn't know anything about being a dad." She arched a brow at Paige.

Like Paige knew anything about little girls. As quick as the fib came, she pushed it away. She'd practically raised her two younger sisters. Among a thousand other things Mom had depended on her to do, she'd fixed their hair and got them to bed on time.

"You're the one who got away," Roxanne murmured. "Sharla said someone had already claimed his heart. I'm guessing it's you."

Paige wanted to cover her ears. "We've just recently reconnected, and neither of us knows what will happen." She truly didn't. Even if what she'd stuffed down for years refused to stay buried. Even if she'd belatedly come to grips with how much he meant to her. He had a child to care for now. Paige couldn't get in the way.

Roxanne's narrowed eyes suggested she didn't buy Paige's explanation. She leaned forward as if to share a confidence. "That gorgeous man needs a wife, and Heidi needs a mom. Are you up for it, or are you going to let them settle for second best?"

Somewhere during this excruciating conversation, their food had arrived. Gus headed back with the twins and Heidi in tow. Heidi skipped to the heavy beat flowing from the arcade as if this was all part of an exciting adventure. Paige's heart hitched. It would be great fun to curl those thick blond tresses into long spirals.

TWO WEEKS LATER, Dad had already kicked back in his recliner after supper. Heidi was in his lap, still wearing the cute plaid jumper required at the private Christian academy he and Roxanne chose.

The last Tavo heard, Heidi was explaining why she'd rather go to work with G, her shortened version of Grandpa, than go to school. *Give it your best shot, doll.* He'd quickly learned if anyone could convince Dad of anything, it would be his granddaughter. Even now, his father rumbled in response, using a soft tone Tavo rarely heard growing up. Dad had also been coming home earlier, opting to take calls from home instead of spending long hours at the office.

Mom usually dropped by most school nights. The three of them would watch the kid's channel on television until Heidi's bedtime. Their help afforded Tavo the time to play his guitar. It helped him wind down and recharge. The instrument had become a solace amid the sea of changes in his life. Something he could count on.

They were slowly settling into a routine of sorts, though Tavo desperately missed Paige. He needed the easy back and forth with her. Her encouragement. The comfort of her presence. But she'd reverted to staying just out of reach. The pool sessions came to a halt because of Heidi's after-school schedule.

Things had changed in a way he couldn't fix. He adored Heidi, but having her in his life didn't fill the Paige void. Would she still love him now that his past mistakes had manifested in a sweet little girl he loved more every day? Would Paige believe he'd known nothing about her? If she'd talk to him, he'd find out. What if she'd already decided and didn't want him to know? Vulnerability had never come easy for her.

He finished putting dishes in the dishwasher and cleared the table. One more thing that had changed. Now that Heidi was living here, he and Dad made sure dinner happened, though Tavo suspected they had a way to go with healthy food choices. Dad had lived like a bachelor for years. When Tavo moved back home, nothing changed. It was just two single men instead of one. Tonight's takeout wasn't the greatest, but Heidi had eaten it with no complaints. That was progress. Her definite preference for chicken over beef had them scrambling the first few nights.

His coming and going had never been an issue, but now he had to consider Heidi's schedule. His brow pinched. Would Mom be open to putting Heidi to bed? It was all so new. He wasn't sure. But he had to see Paige or go nuts.

A knock sounded on the front door. That would be Mom. No one else he knew would drop by unannounced unless … Heidi's high-pitched squeal gave it away.

Rick.

Tavo walked into the living room in time to see his brother grab Heidi out of Dad's lap and swing her around like a ragdoll. Despite his angst about Paige, a smile stretched his lips. His chest expanded when Mom entered shortly after Rick. She held her arms out, her mouth in a big O. Rick set Heidi down, and she dashed over to Mom for a hug.

Yep. It was official. Every member of his family was over the moon about Heidi. He gave silent but heartfelt thanks to God their family dynamic was knitting back together, though it was still too soon to know if it would last. "Got a favor to ask." His grin widened at Mom's arched brow.

If God would move on his behalf with Paige, his world might make sense again. An eternity had passed since they'd seen each other at the diner. Still too soon for a deep conversation, but if she'd accept his presence, it'd be a baby step forward. He'd ask Mom if she would make sure Heidi got to bed on time. If so, he'd take his guitar. Paige had always loved it when he sang. Music had a way of slipping under the strongest defenses and frayed emotions. It used to soothe both of them. If he could just get his foot in the door.

CHAPTER THIRTY-TWO

Filled with trepidation, Paige closed the door as Gus carried in his guitar case. Blast it all! He knew she wouldn't turn him away, even if he showed up unexpectedly, but no way he'd be happy about her late meeting with Ed. Hopefully, it wouldn't come up.

He stood away from the ceiling fan. His facial expression communicated wariness and ... heat? Longing? A pleasant sensation tickled her insides. "Would you like a cup of tea?" Good grief, where was her brain? She should know better than to ask that.

Gazing at her for a long moment, he said, "If it's in a glass with ice."

When his dimples twinkled, her nervous giggle helped to break the awkwardness. "Coming right up." She made her way to the kitchen, vowing to get her foot out of her mouth.

Once the dust settled after she'd showed up at his house and met his daughter, Paige had thought long and hard about everything that had happened. Yeah, it sucked she'd been at the bottom of his need-to-know list about Heidi. It also hurt that there had been another woman. It had driven her to fall on her knees before God, something she wasn't good at and didn't do enough. He'd given her the strength to forgive Gus, despite the daily wrestling matches with doubt. The hurt had lessened but still poked its head up at the worst moments.

To her complete amazement, however, when God uncovered the layers that lay over her heart, what remained was a desire to be with Gus. She'd missed him. How her heart soared when he appeared on her doorstep. Only she didn't know how to navigate through the pain and misunderstanding. Several hurdles stood in the way.

Pulling a large glass from the cabinet, she retrieved the pitcher of iced tea from the fridge and poured it, halfway expecting him to appear behind her. What would she do if he did? Much as she wanted him to wrap his arms around her waist, that shouldn't happen. Their physical chemistry would present more obstacles than solutions.

When he didn't appear—had he sensed her vulnerability? —she carried the glass back to the living area. A vague disappointment curled at the bottom of her spine. Placing it on the coaster across from the sofa, she moved to the other end, wrapping her fingers around the handle of her teacup.

Gus reached for his glass and drank half of it in a giant gulp. Her lukewarm tea had no appeal. His spicy aftershave drifted to her. It drew her to him, even as she glued herself to the cushy seat. He was fresh-shaven and wore a clean short-sleeved button-down and jeans. She soaked him in, willing him to slide nearer.

She kept forgetting why they couldn't do that.

His burning gaze melted her thoughts. Muddled the reason why she sat on the far end of the sofa. Without a word, he stretched his arms, beckoning her to him. Dazed with longing, she stood. Her legs wobbled as indecision and desire warred for dominance. When she stepped back, he shook his head as his lips formed the word *no*. Light on his feet, he closed the distance. His arms wrapped around her. The exhale she'd been holding onto released as she nestled against his chest. The clean smell of his shirt tickled her nostrils. This was exactly what she wanted.

He took her chin and tipped her head back, his eyes deep pools of emotion. Giving her time, his mouth moved toward hers. She leaned toward him and brushed her lips across his. Taking the permission she'd offered, his lips covered hers. Oh, how she'd missed this.

She sank into him, letting him possess her mouth. He kissed her with the hunger of a starving man. Her desire matched his. Time stopped, and the world shrank to just the two of them as they bridged the long years apart. Finally, she pulled away to catch her breath. His forehead found hers, his breathing erratic.

Her cheeks warmed as he found her ear and whispered, "Mm. We have to talk." His eyes probed her face again, as he flicked a thumb across her lips. "And kiss."

As that delightful thought registered, she leaned toward him, yearning for a repeat of his lips on hers. The reality of their situation gave her no warning. Its sudden trample through her mind doused her happy dream like a pail of icy cold water.

Things were different now. Gus had a daughter. The one person in the world Paige could never come between. She took a reluctant step back. Confusion replaced the glow in his eyes. "What?" His arms tightened on hers as if to keep her.

He wanted her, but she couldn't stay. Not when he'd loved someone who'd forever be out of reach.

"What just happened?" Hoarseness lowered his voice.

"We can't do this, Gus. Not when you love someone else."

The dimples winking in his cheeks belied his bewildered expression, but he slowly released her. "What are you talking about? I've never loved"—he paused, as if not sure he wanted to say the rest—"anyone but you," he finished shakily.

"Sharla …" Paige couldn't finish as tears blurred her vision.

"I didn't love Sharla."

She impatiently wiped away the tears. "Heidi …"

Weary resignation passed over his face. "Yes, Heidi. I lived with Sharla for … I don't know … months, maybe. I was miserable without you, but we've talked about that. The lines got fuzzy once I stopped going to church. We were both broken, and … I knew it was wrong, but I gave in to the temptation of having someone, even if I didn't love her. Once the newness wore off, it tormented me. That's why I … left."

He faced her. "I'm not proud of what I did, Paige. But God's forgiven me. I'm covered by His grace. He made something beautiful out of the worst decision of my life. So, yes. I have Heidi."

The muscles beneath his jaw rolled like marbles under a blanket. "I love you, Paige. I have since we were kids. But you have a decision to make. If you want me, I'm yours. But Heidi is part of my world now. If you can't accept that …" His eyes moistened.

He backed up and moved around the coffee table. "I need to go."

Tears gushed down her face. She didn't want him to leave. Not like this. But she had no answer. Her inclination to smooth things over had deserted her. The words froze on her lips.

Her silence hung heavy in the room, an encumbrance neither of them could get around. He turned his back on her, boots thumped relentlessly across the wooden floor. The door banged shut behind him.

TAVO WAS ALMOST BACK to Dad's before he remembered his guitar. It was still at Paige's ... along with what remained of his heart. He drove into the driveway and cut off the engine, attempting to think past the brick in his throat. Every breath stabbed. Going back to the source of hurt filled him with greater pain, but he needed his guitar. If he couldn't have Paige, his aching soul needed the consolation it would provide. Steady. Consistent. No confusion.

With resolve, he backed out of the driveway. He drove slowly, mindful of the speed limits. The focus on driving was pure self-defense, protecting him from feeling the pain of her rejection. He only had to get the guitar. That's all. No more talking. The knife thrust deeper. No more kissing. Mentally, he heaped great shovels of dirt to bury that lovely kiss away ... far, far away.

Driving the familiar route, his eyes registered landmarks along the way. The convenience store on the corner he'd told Paige to stay away from because of the shady business the owners conducted. The elementary school he and Roxanne had decided on for Heidi. The small banking branch Paige used ... he pulled up into her gravel driveway alongside a car he didn't recognize. A fancy BMW, by the looks of it. He laid a palm on the front hood. The engine was still warm, but he already knew it would be. After his hasty departure, someone else had come.

He jogged up the veranda steps. Turning the crystal knob, he cracked the door open. "It's me, Paige. I'm only getting my guitar." He stepped inside and halted.

Ed Clarkston held Paige in a tight hug, but she broke away. She stared at Tavo, dismay etched into her forehead, and she swiped at her cheeks. "You're back." Relief and confusion filled the words. Clarkston resembled a cat with a bowl of cream.

Tavo wanted to knock the guy into next week, but controlled his reaction. Barely. "I forgot this." He strode over to the mantle. Between the door and the mantle, anger jangled his thoughts to the point he forgot why he had returned. Fortunately, he spied his guitar. Muscle memory kicked past his rage. He clutched the black case to his chest as if it was a lifeline. Gripping the handle, he made to leave.

"Don't go like this, Gus," Paige pleaded.

"Crappy timing," Ed muttered at the same time.

Disentangling herself from Ed, Paige followed Tavo out the door. "This isn't what it looks like, Gus."

He spoke through clenched teeth. "So tell me what it is, Paige. Because I thought you were kissing me with all your heart thirty minutes ago."

Paige's face crumpled. A rosy glow came to her cheeks, and she stared at him. "I've wanted to kiss you for a long time."

Astonishment broke through his anger. "You have?"

Before he could process the words, the image of Ed hugging her stormed back into focus, effectively blocking her entreaty. "And now you're in Ed's arms. That doesn't work for me, doll."

She'd moved closer to him and gripped his arm. Had the nerve to look exasperated. "I was upset about the way you left. He noticed and was just being kind."

"Looked like something else to me." He brusquely shook off her arm.

"We had a meeting planned, but you showed up. We … I didn't get to tell you." Paige didn't know her words were crumbling him into pieces. He'd been in this place before with her.

Gus tightened his grasp on the case handle and stomped down the stairs to his truck.

The automatic check in his side mirror showed Paige still

on the porch. She looked bereft, her face stricken and teary. How could she look like that when she'd been playing him all along?

She'd wanted to kiss him? He mashed the accelerator harder.

CHAPTER THIRTY-THREE

P aige's hands shook as she ripped the package open and plunked a teabag into a cup. At least she didn't have to contend with Ed. He'd left abruptly once she made it clear she didn't need any more hugs. He'd caught her off guard. Now, on top of everything else, Gus was furious with her.

A thin tendril of steam shot from the gurgling tea kettle. She poured boiling water into the cup. Her chest rose in a deep breath as she inhaled the minty aroma. Despite the awful circumstances, Gus coming back for his guitar made perfect sense. He needed the comfort after her dismal failure to bridge the gap between them. What was wrong with her? Why couldn't she come to grips with him being with someone else?

Then the business with Ed. The perfect storm. She rubbed her blazing jaws. The hug wasn't what it appeared. *Never again.*

She wrapped the tab around the teabag and squeezed the excess liquid into the cup. Adding sweetener, she carried the hot brew into the living room. The presence of two very different men lingered. Her eyes squeezed shut, even as a leftover tear rolled down her cheek. Gus's wonderful kiss felt like a dream. She'd felt so ... complete. Like the years that had separated them were finally over.

Then he'd acted as if their being together depended on her. As if she couldn't accept Heidi. Didn't he understand Paige's hesitation wasn't about Heidi? It was more about pecking order. He said he loved her, but he'd told her that before. Then he left town. Now his daughter would always be first in his affections. Paige didn't know where she fit anymore.

She blew on her tea and took a tentative sip. Taking the cup, she pressed it against one jaw, then the other, hoping to ease the pain. "Lord, give me strength," she whispered. If she could just get through this beach event for Ed, she could figure things out.

When she'd come back in the house after the futile conversation with Gus, Ed had wanted to pick up where he'd left off. With her in his arms. Trouble was, she'd appreciated his hug. Too much. Gus's untimely return woke her up. She'd opened the door to Ed's caress. What a stupid thing to do when she knew his "kindness" was superficial.

A shiver prickled her skin. She rubbed her arms with her hands. Ed and Gus's reactions replayed like a bad dream. One so honestly indignant. The other was plain mad. She set her cup on the coffee table with shaky hands.

She would tell Ed she couldn't plan his beach party. Even as the thought formed, a cringe rose within. Part of her work ethic was to deliver. She'd never backed out of a job, no matter how difficult the client.

A small voice inside insisted she didn't have to work for Ed.

Her phone chimed. She patted her pockets, then around the sofa and found it wedged between the cushions. Once Gus kissed her, she forgot about it. That man knew how to kiss.

Cherish the memory, girl. You've run him off for good.

Her heart aching, she glanced at the phone screen. Several texts from the twins. What had they done now? She scanned the contents. *Oh, no!* Her hand covered her mouth.

Punching in numbers, she bit her lip and waited. When the other line clicked on, she said, "I'm coming." The phone still glued to her ear, she leaped off the sofa and ran to retrieve her purse.

PAIGE PUSHED her car door shut. She winced at what Gus would say about her driving, but this qualified as an emergency. She hurried along the sidewalk to Mom's front door. Turning the knob easily, she slipped inside. The serenity she usually felt here had fled, replaced with a jittery fear. Miguel said she'd fainted and hit her head.

Blood smeared the kitchen counter and floor. More blood appeared on the towels in the sink. The tell-tale metallic smell tainted the air. Paige avoided the urge to hold her nose. She tiptoed around the mess. "I'm here." The preternatural quiet only added to her concern.

"Back here," a feminine voice called. One of her sisters. She hurried down the hall to the master bedroom and rushed to her mom's side.

"I'm fine, *jita*," Mom's pale skin and wan expression contradicted the words. A gash on her forehead was swelling and turning blue. Taking a breath, she rubbed her chest.

"The twins found her in the kitchen." Carmen patted Mom's small hand. "We think she passed out and hit her head on the way down." Her sister gave Paige a worried look. "I've been asking what happened, but she's a little loopy. I sent the twins for more bandages."

Paige placed a hand on her younger sister's shoulder. "You did good, Car. Why don't I spell you for a bit while you get Mom some water? Maybe clean up the kitchen?" Paige breathed a brief prayer of thanks. Carmen handled difficult situations better than their other sister.

When Carmen rose with a grateful look, Paige moved into the space next to Mom. Paige gently pushed a stray lock of her hair to one side and took her hand. "Can you tell me what happened?"

"I would if I could. I was watering the flowerpot on the island—the roses still have a bit of life." Her lips pursed. "My arms felt tired. Then nothing ... until Carlos. He looked so scared."

"Carlos is fine, Mom. He was only concerned about you. You don't remember anything else?"

"The kitchen needs cleaning up." Mom shifted as if about to rise, but stopped when Paige shook her head.

"Carmen's seeing to it. Your job is to rest." Paige peered at the bump on her mother's head. Surprisingly, the gash was more of a nick, though the amount of blood made it seem much worse. "What's the update on that new medicine the doctor prescribed?"

Mom moved her head from side to side, not appearing to be in pain. "No news. But I've told you that's not your problem, *jita*."

"Falling is a problem, Mama."

"I've got another appointment next week. We'll see what the doctor says then."

Paige wanted to bang her head in frustration. This family of hers. Nobody listened or paid a lick of attention to anything she said. She prepared herself to stay the night. If she wasn't there to supervise, everyone would sit around bemoaning the circumstances, and nothing would get done.

Despite her discomfort with Ed, she'd make his beach party happen. He paid well, and the medicine was no longer an option.

CHAPTER THIRTY-FOUR

Yes. Paige stood at the end of a driveway on private ocean-front property, miles from the Padre Island National Seashore, and observed the magnificent condo the owner rented out to the rich and famous. Her mouth turned down. Because only the rich and famous could afford it. Personally, she thought the fee horrendous. It was a classy bed-and-breakfast on the water, not the Taj Mahal.

A tiny shiver slid down her spine. Palms surrounded the stately two-story building. Short squatty sagos, palms with thick trunks and fronds that swept the sand, and tall ones resembling windmills. Pristine white trimmed the windows and railing, and complemented the sandy-colored stucco. Paige clasped her hands together like a small girl. Her favorite feature of the mansion was the splendid stairway rushing like a waterfall down from the second-floor balcony to the ground level. A lovely throwback to another era, it captured the elegance of Hollywood's early days.

She took a deep, relaxing inhale of the salty air and strolled along a sidewalk that led to the back. Gulls cried overhead. The balmy wind teased her hair into a knotty mess.

As much as she appreciated the sheer majesty of the condo, she loved the water view more. Cupping her hands over her brows, she gazed at the body of water off the Texas coast.

Waves swelled in rich indigo waters and crashed noisily along the flat shoreline. They beckoned her to come swim. Her skin prickled with anticipation.

Soon.

Her phone rang. Ah, the delivery truck. She gave instructions to the kitchen entrance and hurried to unlock the door.

Later that afternoon, the first of Ed's entourage arrived. Claude, the security guy recommended by Gus, helped retrieve baggage. He unloaded as Paige greeted the guests. Though she'd studied their photos, she'd privately given them quirky nicknames.

Paige had expected questions, tours of the mansion, and the desire to see the ocean. She quickly learned, however, that their first interest was finding the bar. And to her dismay, she only remembered the aliases she'd given them, not their real names. *Never again.* Fric, a pretty blonde, said she needed a drink before she could even think about anything else. Frac, the other blonde, agreed. When Paige could spare a minute, she'd look over the guest list again. What was wrong with her brain?

Tic, Tac, and Toe followed shortly. The sultry brunettes. Their smoky-eyed perusals torched lesser beings. Squealing noises ensued from the bar once they found Fric and Frac.

Mo and Jo, then Henny and Penny, arrived together, their British accents quite charming. After a flurry of introductions, they happily followed the well-trod path to the bar. The ever-increasing din left no question about the amount of alcohol being consumed.

As the morning stretched into afternoon, more guests arrived. Ed's tardiness frustrated Paige. She had sent texts throughout the afternoon to keep him apprised about guest arrivals, but he hadn't answered. They'd mostly communicated by text since she'd refused his advances. Gus's perspective cleared up her rose-colored view of Ed, though she hadn't wanted to see or admit it at the time. He acted like a sullen child who hadn't gotten his way.

Any response from him would have helped settle her nerves. She'd had appetizer trays sent in mid-afternoon, but the increasing clamor suggested his guests were getting restless.

As she and Claude coaxed tipsy people out of the bar toward the buffet, Ed finally made his appearance. His guests cheered. Paige sagged with relief. The evening was saved.

He made the rounds with hugs and kisses for all. Some of the affection transpired on a playful note, but other kisses took a decidedly fervent slant. Then he made a beeline for her. "As usual, everything is perfect. Would you be a dear and get me a drink?"

Paige stared at him. He gave a short laugh at her shocked expression. "Ah. That wasn't very polite, was it? Now you know why I need a drink." He slipped his arm through hers. "Or better yet, show me the way. I have something to speak with you about."

Her jaws twinged as she glanced around the room. She wasn't sure how to handle this latest version of Ed. The others were at the buffet, dishing up the catch of the day and sides. Healthy. Vegan choices available. At his gentle nudge, she started. "Sorry, I'm still in planner mode. The bar is right around the corner." She led the way with misgivings. Was relegating her to the role of a servant a subtle form of retaliation?

Once Ed ordered his drink and took a few swallows, he gazed at her appreciatively. "Better. Please forgive my lack of manners. Do you ever drink?" He offered her one, but she declined. For pity's sake, she was working.

"No, thank you." She didn't elaborate. The single crease between his brows suggested a preoccupation with something other than her beverage preferences.

He swallowed more of his drink, though gulps might be more precise. "I have a proposition for you." Uh-oh. A warning bell clanged inside of Paige.

"The police arrested Corona, my PA, today in Valiant." Ed studied her face.

Paige's eyes widened. "What happened?"

"Possession of cocaine." He watched her until she twitched with confusion.

"I'm sorry." Paige didn't know what else to say. Corona had always struck her as sneaky and underhanded ... and he looked like a drug user. Not that Paige had tons of experience picking them out.

"Did you know anything about it?"

It was the second time that evening Ed surprised her in an ugly way. "Me? How would I know anything? I've only seen him once or twice."

Ed polished off his drink and waved for another, then seemed to reach a decision. "Sorry. I can tell you're as innocent as a dove, sweet one." He leaned so close, she inhaled the scent of his fragrant aftershave. "I'd like to offer you his PA job."

Paige gasped. *Not* what she was expecting. Ed chuckled and brushed his lips across her forehead.

"I need someone I can count on, Paige. You're dependable and have proven yourself. You handle my moods like a champion." He flashed her his million-dollar smile. "Think about it, and we'll talk particulars later."

Was he crazy? Or just that self-assured? Paige tore her eyes from his. The magnetism of his personality threatened to draw her in again, but she took a deliberate step back, both mentally and physically. "I, uh, need to see to the guests."

With a satisfied expression, he reached for his fresh drink. "Oh, my little hometown girl. I'm certain they'll see to themselves."

"No, I ... they'll ... oh, never mind." She fled the room. It smelled of alcohol and risky decisions. She regretted taking this job with every minute that passed.

CHAPTER THIRTY-FIVE

A glorious dawn broke early Thursday morning with the promise of a sunny day. Flat clouds in hues of rose and canary yellow shot across the sky. Between her busy day and the lull of ocean waves, Paige assumed sleep would come quickly last night. But no ... her pillow seemed made of rocks. She left the small abode in the second outbuilding and headed to the main kitchen. So far, the best perk of this gig was not having to stay in the main house with the guests.

"Hi, Mondo." She greeted the chef as she made her way to the coffeepot. The chef nodded and kept stirring the sauce on the stovetop. French toast sizzled on one griddle, thick slabs of bacon on another. Her appetite flickered to life at the mouth-watering scents.

Once she'd fixed her mug, she slid into a tall bistro chair at the counter. She pointed at the coffeepot when Claude wandered through. In her mind, he'd already proved his mettle, pitching in to help wherever needed.

"Did our guests get to bed at a decent hour?" Her lips tilted upward. The midnight hour had come and gone by the time she left, though most of the party guests showed no signs of slowing down.

"Oh, I dunno about sleeping, but most were in their rooms by two." His answer was straightforward enough, but he looked away.

Was he not telling her something? "You checked the pool?"

He nodded. "Throughout the evening and after everyone retired." When they'd gone over his responsibilities, he'd added pool checks to the list. She was thankful for his knowledge. Her imagination was all over the place these days. No doubt she'd misread his body language.

Paige didn't anticipate many early birds. She'd learned not to expect any responses from Ed, text or otherwise, before noon. She helped herself to a slice of crispy bacon, then motioned to Claude. "Fill your plate. Mondo always cooks a ton."

Strolling outdoors with her coffee, she angled her head so the sun shone directly on her face. The heat eased the pain in her jaws. It improved when her schedule slowed down. The idea of limitations was tough to accept. She loved her life. Cutting back made her feel like a slacker.

Ed's offer poked its odd little head into her musings. What did she know about running a celebrity's schedule? Even as she toyed with the idea, she knew deep down it would never work. Ed wouldn't stay in Valiant long, no matter what he said. And contemporary Hollywood wouldn't suit her at all. The glitzy lifestyle wasn't for her. She wouldn't have a minute's peace if she accepted. A close-up personal job with Ed wouldn't lead anywhere good.

He had no savvy about the things that mattered. Money was ... convenient. She appreciated his generosity, but she loved Valiant. The people for whom weddings and family events were special. Christians attended church and sought

God's guidance for their lives. Her lifestyle was completely foreign to Ed. He didn't understand Rory or Jesse. Pretty much despised Gus. In retrospect, the only logical conclusion for his inebriated kiss at the karaoke party was jealousy. Gus was a hard act to follow when he sang.

Her hand went to her mouth. Gus would bellow long and loud if he knew of Ed's offer. Gus cared about her as a person, even if he no longer wanted a relationship. It was who he was. Strong. Steady. Her hero. Only she'd seen it too late.

The sea boasted a deep emerald green this morning. The swells broke into frothy waves along the shoreline. As the sun rose higher in the sky, the water would warm up. Perfect for boogie boarding or a swim. Paige loved pitting her skills against the water. She'd planned a moonlight swim into the itinerary for those who were interested. A memory the guests could take home.

Sighing, she made her way back to her mansion on the sea. Her enthusiasm for this job faded by the hour.

Per her prediction, the morning had been quiet. By lunch, most of the guests had made an appearance. Mondo had provided what amounted to a giant charcuterie buffet of exotic meats and finger foods. The guests swooped on it like seagulls. They mingled in clusters around the room, eating and laughing. And many trips to the bar.

Shortly after lunch, Penny, sporting an enormous pair of cat glasses, waltzed over to Paige. Henny followed behind her dressed in flashy Elton John style.

"Darling, we're striking out on a day trip. Methinks we must see Elon Musk's brainchild. Call us an Uber?" Paige set aside her mostly untouched plate. The two young men engaging her in conversation moved on. She'd dubbed them Rock and Roll because of their long hair and love for music. She'd run dry of chit-chat, but they still looked at her as if she was part of the charcuterie board. *Not going to happen, fellas.*

"An Uber? No problem. I'll warn you though, it's a drive to South Padre. Are you sure you want to go such a distance?"

Penny exchanged a knowing look with her partner, then said, "Quite certain, dear. We came to support Ed—the man is such a love—but as for the others ..." She flicked a hand in dismissal. "Let's just say Space X is bound to be more entertaining."

The woman spoke loud enough for the others to hear. The Five—Paige's collective name for the single women—tossed scornful looks their way. Their skimpy bikinis and sheer coverups clearly communicated a desire for attention. But that wasn't her problem.

"If you're ready, I'll call for an Uber." Paige pulled out her phone and made the arrangements, hoping for an end to the petty jealousies floating around like so many balloons at a party.

Once Henny and Penny had gone to wait for their ride, she walked through to make sure the other guests were comfortable. The Five stood to one side, eyeing Ed and the other men. The brunette who appeared to be the leader announced she was going to hang out at the pool. When the rest of the gaggle followed, Paige found herself caught between a mental eye roll and relief. She strolled over to the two other couples still in the room. They'd segregated themselves into their own group from the start. Paige mentally referred to them as The Others.

"We're thinking of renting a four-wheeler. Driving up and down the beach is a good way to kill time," one man said. When the rest of the group nodded, he continued, "I saw sand dunes when we drove in. It'd be great fun to rocket up the soft hills." He nudged the woman next to him. "Haven't heard you scream in a while."

The woman gave him a playful swat on the arm. "At least I've got company today. Your driving is enough to make anybody scream."

Oh, dear. What sort of wild ride was he planning? Paige cleared her throat. "We're on private property here. Just be mindful of the boundaries. National Seashore law prohibits dune buggies within its boundaries."

The wild-ride guy scoffed. "Legal, schmegal. I'll drive wherever I want. What are they going to do? Confiscate my license?" The woman beside him tittered nervously. The other couple shared an irritated look.

Paige kept a bland expression. Texas law enforcement came as a surprise to most out-of-state visitors. Ed sauntered over with a wink and ribbed the man about his behind-the-wheel adventures. He'd either had firsthand experience as a passenger, or the guy had quite the reputation for reckless driving. As they conversed, Paige slipped away to the kitchen for a cup of tea.

Rock and Roll moved toward the pool. No surprise there. Ed finished his chat with the couples renting the four-wheeler and followed the two young men. It stung to realize he planned to ogle the girls too. The Five had already shown their willingness to supply the eye candy.

She took a sip of her beverage. Usually, she found a cup of tea soothing, but not today. Grabbing her phone, she headed outside. There was something so solid about the ocean. Steady. Not fickle.

Who Ed hung out with wasn't her business.

CHAPTER THIRTY-SIX

By Friday afternoon, the smoky fragrance of a slow-cooking brisket emanated from the mansion's kitchen. The rich, meaty aroma reminded Paige of Gus's cookouts, but the comparison ended there. Her morale warred against the petty hostilities and ongoing complaints of Ed's guests, and the copious amount of alcohol consumed grieved her spirit. Sweet as some of them were, these were not her people.

Paige ran lightly up the stairs in response to the shop lady's you-need-to-come-now message. Sandals snapping, she crossed the landing to the All Things Texas boutique. A popular perk of the out-of-the-way estate was a fully stocked gift shop. Expensive souvenirs, from children's gifts to furniture overflowed in the small niche. The posh items were way over Paige's budget, though the other women had spent hours shopping.

"Hey, Greta, what's up?" The shop owner was already making tracks for her, shaking her head. Her haughty air had been off-putting at first, but when Paige had refused to take offense and stayed friendly, the woman had loosened up.

"Let's step outside. There's only a couple of women shopping, but they're not the ones I suspect."

Well, that didn't sound promising. Paige followed her, and they stood in the bright landing area, an inviting echo of the individual rooms. The color scheme of beige and blue complemented the wall on one side. Photos of seascapes created an ethereal effect.

Greta leaned toward her. "We have a kleptomaniac on the premises." Her silver eye shadow sparkled, as if in conspiracy with her tale.

The furiously whispered accusation rattled Paige. "What?"

"It's true. I've had several expensive pieces go missing. My inventory is small, so it's easy to keep tabs on sales."

"Surely there's another explanation—" Paige began.

She stopped when the other woman shook her head. "It's as plain as pineapple pie. There's a thief on the loose."

Paige's sigh ended on a shaky note. "Well, make a list of what you *think* is missing." Another thought occurred to her. "Do you have any idea who may be responsible—if someone is, um, taking items?"

"It's one of those blondes, I'm sure of it." Greta crossed her arms as if she'd already nabbed the guilty party.

Paige thought back over the last two days. One of The Five? Their MO was to flirt with any male in the vicinity. Paige wasn't on the second floor often, and the women's rooms were down the hall. It'd be a snap to slip things out in a large purse. She'd tell Claude about Greta's suspicions. He probably had training for this kind of situation.

A door slammed downstairs. Squabbling and curses filled the air. Now what? Maybe if she wasn't available, whoever was mad this time would simmer down of their own accord. Her job description didn't include babysitting.

Decision made, she swung the other way, intent on exiting

through the side stairway. And bumped into Ed. Wearing a goofy smile, his arms folded around her. "Now this is fortuitous." His slurred speech tipped her off. He was drunk. A sweet odor emanated from him. Maybe drunk and high.

She returned a lesser version of his hug and stepped back. He was buff in a Brad Pitt way, but not as tall. Still quite handsome, but the veneer was wearing thin. Smiling, he leaned in again and held her upper arms. "So, when are you coming to work for me?"

The last thing Paige wanted was to answer *that* question. She stepped back again, shrugging out of his hold. "About that ..." She frantically thought how best to say it. "As ... enticing as your offer is, I have prior obligations I can't let go of. Regretfully, I need to decline." She gazed at him earnestly, hoping he would simply accept her explanation.

No such luck. In a wink, his eyes hardened into a glare. He grabbed her upper arms again and tightened his hold until she gasped in pain. "You never thought I was good enough for you, Miss Morality." He spat it like a curse.

Paige vigorously shook her head. "I don't think that. Ed ... it ... it has to work for both of us, that's all."

Abruptly, he let go of her, his features twisted in a sneer. "You know, I thought you were different, but you're just like all the rest. You're only interested in the money." His hands plowed through his perfect hair.

As she opened her mouth, a deep voice said tersely, "You can't reason with him, Paige. Just leave. I'll take care of it."

Pulse racing, she stared at Claude. When had the security guard entered the room? Jerking his head toward the stairs, he mouthed *Go*.

She fled down the stairs.

TAVO'S PHONE rang as he opened his truck door. Paige. They hadn't talked since the evening they'd kissed. The same one that had ended so dreadfully. He shut the door and leaned against it. Heart thumping madly, he schooled his voice. "Hi, doll."

"Hi, Gus." Silence ensued. Tavo waited. Was she already regretting the call? "What are you doing tomorrow night?" She sounded breathless.

Nothing now that you're not in my life. "Let's see. Saturday? ... Don't know that there's anything planned." The understatement of the year.

"I, um, was hoping ... can you come to Padre Island?"

Her thready voice gave it away. Something was making her nervous. "What's going on, Paige?" It came out sharper than he intended. Occupational hazard.

"Nothing to worry about. Mondo's planning a fabulous dinner, and, uh, there'll be a moonlight swim ..."

A moonlight swim didn't interest Tavo, but Paige would be all over it. "Is Ed behaving himself? What about his guests?"

Soft laughter filled his ear. "Oh, he's fine. Did you know Corona was arrested? Ed asked me if I knew anything about it. Then he offered me the PA job."

Ice invaded his heart. "What did you say?"

"I said no. He, uh, didn't react well, so I was hoping ..." She babbled on, totally out of character. She'd downplay what really happened, but the fact she'd called ...

Something had frightened her enough to ask him for help.

"When do you want me to come?" Even if his weekend was chock-full, he'd clear it.

"Oh, tomorrow afternoon. Not early. Dinner won't start until seven."

"I'll be there."

"Thanks." Relief and something else filled her voice. "It's probably no big deal ..."

"Steer clear of the guy, Pep."

"That won't be easy. I'm making a mountain out of a molehill. Everything will be fine."

Everything was not fine, or she wouldn't be calling. "Do it for me, doll. Ed's not the genial guy people think he is."

Her quiet acquiescence told him all he needed to know. She was in over her head.

WHEN TAVO'S PHONE CHIMED, he blew out a giant exhale. Now what? A conspiracy was afoot to keep him in Valiant. He glanced at the screen and knew he had to take it. One did not ignore calls from the Chief of Police. He listened, then clicked off. Another delay. He picked up a pair of sandals and stuffed them into the bag he'd been packing.

At the police station, he strode in and waited outside Dad's office. Through the window, his dad talked to John Ochoa. When John joined the force, there were already two guys with that name, so he went by his last name. Over time, it got shortened to Ochee. Small in stature, he made up for it with skill. Tavo had learned to trust Ochee's instincts. When his father saw Tavo, he waved him in. "I've got calls to make, but I need you in the loop." He peered at Tavo's dress shirt and slacks. "Where are you going?"

"Paige called yesterday. I'm meeting her at the event she's doing for Ed at Padre Island." He cringed inwardly. Sharing personal info with Dad wasn't always the best policy.

The older man gave a noncommittal nod, then said, "Well, that's timely. Give him the update, Ochee, while I start on these calls." He looked at Tavo. "Don't leave until I've briefed you."

Dad wasn't normally so mysterious. "A briefing for what?"

Ochee's white teeth flashed. "As you know, we arrested superstar Ed's assistant Corona for cocaine possession." Tavo's curiosity deepened at the mention of Ed. "Seems Corona's been tattling on his boss for a better deal." Ochee shook his head and made tsking noises. "Ed Clarkston is a very naughty boy, hoss. Chief's seeing if someone higher on the chain wants to follow through with criminal charges."

Tavo's brows shot up his forehead. Best news ever, as far as he was concerned.

His co-worker looked downright gleeful. Ochee had a strong sense of justice and the smarts to get it done. "Clarkston is a first-class slime ball who dabbles in criminal activity. Illegal drugs. A nasty temper with women. Abuse. Possible rape." He rubbed his hands together.

A cold chill wrapped around Tavo's spine. Paige was in terrible danger. "Is there enough to hold him?"

Ochee lifted a shoulder, then let it drop. "If Corona's info pans out, we've got enough to extradite him. We'll serve up A-lister Ed a Texas-sized headache."

That suited Tavo. He'd love to see the guy get his comeuppance. His urgent need to see Paige intensified. "I'm headed to Padre as soon as I get the green light." He angled his head toward Dad's office. "What can I do in the meantime?" He had to stay busy, or else he'd pace a groove in the floor.

Ochee brightened. "You can help me."

Tavo impatiently followed him to their desks. Precious time was slipping away. Swallowing hard, he made an effort to trust the Lord with the entire situation.

Two hours later—about one hour and fifty-five minutes longer than Tavo preferred, Dad reappeared. Tavo and Ochee had worked through a mound of paperwork that would have made several grown trees weep.

His face was grim as he motioned to Tavo. "Come with me."

Tavo followed him outside. Dad wheeled around to face him. "What do you know about the Padre Island event?"

"Not much, but I can make a call."

His father studied him. Most people wouldn't catch the tell, but when Dad was deciding something, one brow twitched ever so slightly. Like now. "Make the call, then tell me everything you know." Tavo pulled out his phone.

Minutes later, he clicked off, frowning.

"What'd you find out?" Dad had given him space for privacy with the call, but now he was back.

Tavo's heart was in his throat. "Don't know what you're hoping for, but if Claude's right about what he's seen, you've got a corroborating witness for charges."

As Tavo filled him in, Dad listened intently, his jaw grinding with each new revelation. "Okay. Let me get a couple of things firmed up, then you can go."

"I need to leave now."

"No. Not until I release you." Everything within Tavo clamored to argue. With effort, he stayed silent. He sensed Dad was teetering on the edge of not letting him go. Better to win a battle than lose the war. Dad's posture was unyielding as he stepped back into his office.

Agonizing minutes passed before his return. "Okay. It's set. The locals aren't thrilled, but the FBI has jurisdiction. I convinced the Padre Island Chief it's better that way. Let's hope it's true." His gaze was fierce. "It will be quick and quiet. Around dinner time. They know you're an officer. Your only job is to protect the innocent. No going after Clarkston."

Tavo shot his father a tight smile. "Protect the innocent"

was code for giving Tavo the leeway he'd need to take care of Paige. "Thank you. How will they know it's me?"

"I gave them your physical description. Not too many guys your size, so I'm hoping they'll figure it out." His mouth slanted. Beneath his ferocious brow line, dark eyes pierced Tavo. "Need I reiterate? You have one job, *mijito*. Just one."

"Got it, *Padre*." Tavo's jaws clenched. Maybe he and Dad were gaining ground. If he hit the road now, he'd make it in time for dinner.

CHAPTER THIRTY-SEVEN

On his way out of town, traffic had slowed to a crawl on Highway 77. Good night, this was Valiant, not Houston. Tavo gripped the steering wheel in frustration, then craned his neck out the window. The line of cars didn't look too long. He needed to text Paige. If only this traffic would move. As he inched forward, the situation unfolded. A car exiting the freeway had sideswiped another vehicle on the access road, but no EMT van had arrived.

Gazing at the wrecked vehicle with a practiced eye, Tavo gasped. He recognized the car. The driver's door had caved in. Checking his rearview mirror, he bumped his truck off the road into the weeds. Sirens sounded in the distance. He ran toward the car, heedless of the gawking onlookers. The driver had lost control and careened into the strip of grass between the lane and the freeway. A woman slumped over the steering wheel at a weird angle. Strange that the window was smashed, but the airbag hadn't deployed.

Tavo sprinted to the vehicle. This couldn't be happening. He spoke loudly through the broken glass, "Can you hear me?"

The woman stirred, then sank back onto the steering wheel. He stepped back and scanned for the emergency vehicle. Nowhere in sight. To his surprise, the driver's door opened. One foot emerged, then the other. When the woman tried to rise, Tavo gently pushed her back. "You need to sit. The EMT will be here in seconds." He pushed a tangle of hair back from her bloody cheek. She gazed at him, confusion clouding her dark eyes.

He crouched inside the car door. Emotions choked his throat at her dazed condition. He placed a hand on her knee. "You're gonna be all right, Mama. I'm right here. Help is on the way."

A tear rolled down her cheek as she placed her hand on top of his.

Minutes later, the EMT techs had helped her out of the car onto a gurney. Tavo stayed by her side, but hit speed dial on his phone. When a voice answered, he spoke into the device. "Dad, Mom's okay. She's been in a wreck. They're taking her to the hospital. She's conscious and recognized me."

"What route? And what's the ETA?" His father's vibrant voice had reduced to a hoarse whisper.

Tavo gave him the info. "Mama's okay."

"I'll meet them at the hospital."

"Do you want me to follow the van in?" The question tore at him. Tavo didn't want his parents at the hospital alone, but the urgency to get to Paige overwhelmed him. With Mom hurt, Dad could easily insist Tavo stay in town.

Silence. Tavo waited, hardly daring to breathe. "No. Rick will come. You stick with the plan."

Relieved Dad made the decision for him, Tavo released the breath he'd been holding. A wave of tenderness swept over him as they shut the doors of the vehicle. They would take care of her. Concern tasted much better than the resentment he'd carried for years. Something on the inside flared again, demanding his attention. Paige's well-being gnawed at him. He started praying again.

———

IT WAS CLOSE TO DINNERTIME, and Gus still hadn't shown. If Paige attempted to list all that went wrong this weekend, midnight would roll around before she was done. At least Mr. Wild Ride had calmed down—or was too drunk to fuss anymore.

The group who'd taken the four-wheeler out had returned by Uber. Sure enough, they'd become stuck while joyriding in the dunes. They'd also overlooked the teeny-weeny fact that they'd driven out of the private property zone. Paige swallowed the "I-told-you-so" that longed to jump out of her mouth.

The beach police impounded the four-wheeler and issued Mr. Wild Ride a stiff fine. Hence the door slamming and cursing. While the party guests slept, Paige and Claude spent the morning getting the four-wheeler back. She'd taken his suggestion and hidden the keys.

The Five and the rest of the pool groupies broke the diving board. Clowning around, they wanted to see how many bodies it could hold. The idea had been to make an epic splash when they jumped off, but the board snapped before that happened. Their adolescent behavior horrified Paige. They thought it was hilarious. Someone said it mimicked a scene on *Saturday Night Live*, so they'd watched reruns of the show all afternoon and performed crude riffs on the various show segments.

Ed acted as the ringleader. Since Paige had turned down the PA job, he'd ignored her and made a show of cozying up to the lead brunette. Paige vacillated between indignation and sadness.

Henny and Penny's return had been the only bright spot. They'd regaled the others with colorful descriptions of the inspiration they'd received from touring Space X. Penny insisted her creativity had tripled. Henny claimed he was brainstorming a new play based on the experience. Their outlandish opinions and antics diverted her from the heartache of seeing Ed act so immature.

Mondo signaled dinner time. Still no Gus. Paige had the sinking feeling he concluded the drive and another evening with Ed wasn't worth it. She'd pushed him into agreeing to come. A strong feeling of disquiet washed over her. She sorely missed his solid presence.

Standing in the dining room entrance, she announced the post-dinner activities—a disco dance for those interested, followed by a moonlight swim. Enthusiastic clapping came from most of the guests, though Ed shot her a dark look. The brunette's livid expression threatened to set Paige's hair on fire. With a stiff smile, Paige lifted her arms in invitation. "Time to fill your plates, Texas-style. Enjoy!"

While the guests awaited their turn at the buffet, she moved through them, chatting about the disco dance and swim. Once everyone had their food, she planned to take her meal in the kitchen with Mondo. She'd previously asked him to make plates for Claude and the deejay in charge of the dance. How she wished it had been Rick instead of another stranger. Gus's brother had apologized for the video episode, but it was more than that. He was part of her tribe. The people she did life with. People who loved, forgave, and accepted each other, warts and all. The ones who didn't hang on to divisiveness like a perverted trophy. And she knew down to her bones if she and Gus couldn't overcome their differences, he would still care for her as a person. He'd already proved that with Sharla and

Heidi. If only Paige could get on board with the way his life was now …

After dinner, she found Mondo. "Marvelous job, chef. You made everyone's taste buds happy." She omitted the fact she preferred Tavo's brisket. Something about the way he seasoned the meat … Guilt sliced through her. The guests had gobbled up Mondo's food as if they shared the lead in *Cast Away*.

Music pumped from the ballroom. Most guests had vacated the dining area. Paige had instructed the deejay to start the program at eight o'clock sharp. If she knew Ed's group at all, they would follow the music.

"You gonna join us?" Paige didn't miss Mondo's wistful look. He'd worked hard all weekend. No one would care if he took a break.

"Let me finish cleaning up. It'd be nice to see something other than the kitchen." He hustled back to work with a spring in his step.

As Paige entered the room reserved for dancing, her heels clicked on the hardwood floor. A server handing out glow-in-the-dark accessories gave her an orange necklace, a bracelet for each wrist, then held up a pair of glasses for her perusal. Ever changing swirls of color lit the dark room. Paige declined the glasses but snapped on the necklace and bracelets. The server held up another pair of bracelets and pointed to her ankles. Paige shook her head no, but the woman snapped them on anyway.

People gyrated to the songs, drinks in hand. The accessories made them glow. The rainbow of color from the disco ball wreaked havoc with the darkness. She peered closer. The Five had changed from their dinner clothes into the requisite bikinis and coverups.

Everyone embraced the dancing with wild, overblown abandon. Thrilled this event was almost complete, Paige loosened up a bit, though her jaws pounded. Once Mondo showed up, they danced. Paige's tension drained a tad. Before long, though, she'd need to escape the ear-splitting music.

"Feels good, doesn't it?" Mondo's face and neck were shiny from exertion. Paige nodded, moving her feet in time to the beat. Shimmying away the pain of Gus not keeping his word.

She turned and bumped into Brunette Number One. What was her name? Something cutesy—Barbie? No ... Cookie. That sounded right. Cookie had a scowl for every occasion. The current one aimed at Paige shouted "Roadkill." How special.

Cookie waved a finger—made longer by spiky painted nails —in her face. "Only guests on the dance floor."

Astonished at her audacity, Paige shouted above the noise. "Says who?"

A nasty grin sliced Cookie's face. "Me. I'm Ed's new PA." She leaned forward to make certain Paige heard. "It's time for you to make tracks." She walked her fingers in the air, then laughed hysterically.

Heat and ice ran through Paige simultaneously. The betrayal stung. She wouldn't trust Cookie to lace a pair of shoes without an ulterior motive. If it was so, Ed's crass actions had climbed to new heights.

Or maybe Paige was seeing him for the first time.

CHAPTER THIRTY-EIGHT

Shaking with anger and hurt, Paige left the party. Her sandals crunched on the gritty caliche as she followed the winding path to her room. As she packed her bag, the new red swimsuit she'd bought glimmered in the moonlight shining through the small bedroom window. She fingered it, longing to feel the surf against her skin. At this time of evening, the water would be cool and delightful.

She wondered how many others had overheard the hurtful conversation. Surely, no one else would object to her going for a swim. Just a quick dip to clear her head. Then she'd figure out what to do next. She shrugged off her sweaty clothing and slipped into her bathing suit.

Paige struggled with the authenticity of Cookie's words. Had Ed really made her his new PA? He wasn't one to think deeply about decisions. He was more whimsical and impulsive. Paige debated taking off the glow accessories, then decided it was too much trouble. She marched out the door.

Cookie might have a say about whether Paige stayed on the premises, but she wasn't in charge of the ocean.

A full moon wreathed the beach in pale yellow light. A night breeze fluttered the fronds of the palm trees surrounding the mansion. The grotesque shadows vied with the moon's glow. The roar of the disco music competed with the rhythmic sound of ocean waves.

Paige ran toward the shore, loving the bracing feel of the water as she waded out deeper. Invigorated, she swam parallel to the shore, completing stroke after stroke until her arms were jelly. She kicked until her calves cramped.

Treading water, she peered at the beach to re-orient herself. Oh, wow! The mansion seemed a mile away. Bouncing to touch the bottom, the water was just over her head. She rolled to her back and floated to conserve energy before swimming to shore. The starry sky twinkled and winked at her.

TAVO EXITED HIS TRUCK. Deafening music flowed from a cavernous house. He ran to the ornate door. The knob turned easily under his hand. The empty living area stretched out before him. What if the guests had caught wind of law enforcement headed their way and fled? He squeezed his phone as if it would spill Paige's whereabouts. She hadn't answered his calls. Claude hadn't either.

He dashed up the stairs to a large dark room. Ah, the disco dance. Paige's excitement had been palpable when she'd brainstormed the idea with him. He rushed in, then stopped. A few people were dancing. Others were lounging on chairs and sofas, making out. The pungent aroma of weed floated about the room. He strode up to a couple entwined on the dance floor. "I'm looking for Paige."

The brunette glared at him but said nothing. Okay. Forget subtle. His voice rose above the din with every ounce of authority he could muster. "I'm looking for Paige Munoz. Who can tell me where she is?"

A man wearing an apron walked toward him. "Paige was here until that chick,"—he pointed to the brunette—"told her to go home."

"She left?" That didn't sound like Paige at all. His mind flipped through possibilities. "Who are you?"

"Mondo, the chef." Concern furrowed his brow. "Has something happened to Paige?"

Anxiety made Tavo's voice rise. "Show me where the garage is and tell me everything you know."

As they shuffled down the steps, Mondo said, "Paige was killing it—had everything running as it should. I've cooked for these types of gigs plenty. Can't tell you the number of times, things run late. Hours late. But not with Paige. Then that chick told her to leave … something about working for Ed. It made no sense. Why would he replace Paige in the middle of a gig?"

It made sense to Tavo. Dad had taught him never to rule out jealousy as a motive. Mondo opened the door to a garage where Tavo spotted a white Jetta. "She's here somewhere." His mind worked frantically. "What did she have planned tonight?"

Mondo pursed his lips. "She announced dinner, then talked up the disco dance … oh, yeah. A moonlight swim. The way she talked about it made me want to go, and I don't even like salt water."

Tavo's heart plummeted. Of course. "Which way's the beach?"

Mondo's eyes reflected the fear consuming Tavo. "This way."

Winding through a short hallway, Mondo pointed toward a room with floor-to-ceiling windows. The way Tavo had come in. He spied a door on the other end and hustled outside.

People stood in clusters, some talking, but everyone gazed out to sea. One couple argued loudly. Tavo dashed to them. "I'm looking for Paige. Have you seen her?"

"I told you it was Paige!" The woman looked at Tavo, tears mussing her heavy makeup. "She's still wearing the glow rings —I saw them flashing. Ed's in the water too, and now they're both going to die."

The couple's distress knotted Tavo's stomach. This was no ordinary swim. Before he could formulate a question, the woman bawled, "She's so far out, we thought she was in trouble. When Ed heard, he jumped in to rescue her. He's such a love, that way, but it's been too long." She gave another shrill cry. "Too long. They've both drowned."

Tavo's cop skills kicked in. "Call nine-one-one. Tell them we need the Coast Guard ... lifeguards, whatever they've got." The woman stopped crying long enough to grab her phone. Tavo peered out to sea again. Hard to distinguish anything because the moonlight cast a silvery glow on the moving surface.

At a distance, tiny lights like fireflies winked off and on. Much closer, a shadowy figure sloshed through the surf.

Ed.

Tavo kicked through the sand to the water. "Where's Paige?"

The mega-star shook his head. "She swam away from me and got too far out." The words sounded matter of fact, like it was all in a day's work, but Tavo caught the "how-dare-she" undercurrent. Someone handed him a towel.

"You left her?" Tavo wanted to rattle Ed's brains loose.

"I came back for help. Someone needs to call nine-one-one." He drew a ragged breath and mopped his face.

"Already done." Tavo shucked off his boots and threw his phone into one. His shirt followed. A new swell of fear mushroomed. Could he do this? He'd made progress in the pool, but this was an ocean. Nothing to steady him.

"What are you doing?" Skepticism filled Ed's words.

Tavo gritted his teeth. "I'm going to get Paige." *Help me, Lord. I need the courage of a lion.*

Visions of Rick's frightened face all those years ago rose to the surface and crippled his thinking. Tavo breathed hard. He grabbed a stray surfboard and waded into the stiff, menacing surf. His knees threatened to lock. He pushed back the darkness that wanted to overwhelm him and took step after excruciating step. The water itself seemed evil, determined to keep him from his goal.

Lessons learned long ago punched through his fear. When the water deepened, he hoisted himself onto the board and paddled with his arms. A wave crashed. He swallowed salt water, then spit it back out. Regulated his breathing. All the things Paige had taught his reluctant heart about swimming.

What atrocious thing had Ed done to make Paige risk her life?

Choking back panic, he kept going. Sometimes, you had to do things afraid.

PAIGE FOUGHT for every stroke to tear herself free of the rip current. She'd gained some distance, but her strength was gone. She floated along like debris tossed by the waves, but it wouldn't last. The next wave submerged her. She attempted to surface, but another wave buffeted her, drawing her back toward the rip current. If it snagged her again, she'd never make it out. An eerie sense of calm enveloped her. The breath she'd gulped was gone. *Lord ...*

CHAPTER THIRTY-NINE

Where was she? Tavo peered through the watery crush. There! Her head popped up, then bobbed down again. He maneuvered the board in that direction. Just a few more feet. Another wave nearly tore it from his hands. He coughed, spat out water, and yelled at the waves, "Not going down. Have to find her!"

He moved forward. Something bumped his body. He thrashed in that direction, searching under the water. Green and orange lights twinkled. His fingers tangled into a mass, and he pulled.

Paige's hair. Oh, thank God! He struggled to grasp the rest of her. His other hand scrabbled the surfboard into a prone position.

Tavo shouted, "Get on the board." No response. Her limp weight sagged against him. He clumsily gripped her waist and heaved. She splatted onto the board's surface. Her head lolled to one side. Non-responsive. His heart quaked.

His feet touched the sandy ocean bottom, stabilizing him somewhat. He checked her wrist for a pulse and wanted to weep with relief. He leaned over and wedged her body against his to hold her in place. Lowering his mouth to hers, he began CPR. One breath. Quick compressions. Another breath. More compressions.

The waves tore around them. "Come back." He blew another breath into her mouth, timing the span between compressions. And again. "Come back to me, Pep."

PAIGE WANTED to stay in this sweet, quiet place, but the walls were giving way. Water roared in her ears. A body pushed against hers ... talking ... a watery bed cradled her.

Vile-tasting sea spray came up her throat. She tried to sit up. An arm surrounded her as she coughed up salt water. Where was she?

Everywhere, water frothed. She breathed in salty air and coughed again. The rest of her was numb. A face appeared in front of her. Gus. Talking, but she couldn't hear, then he pointed. Her eyes followed his hand. Two shadows moved toward them. Why was it so dark?

She stared back at Gus. "Why aren't you wearing a shirt?" He threw back his head and laughed. Joy, solid and deep, rippled through her confusion.

The shadows turned into men with faces. Then things got hazy again. Gus wouldn't let go of something. A board? Jostling back and forth. More loud talking. Gus sounded mad, but the men insisted on taking it.

Paige remembered packing to leave. Swimming in the moonlight. Ed's rough kiss in the water. Slipping out of his grip. The rip current dragging her away.

Why were men carrying her on a surfboard? They splashed onto the beach. Gus followed through the surf, looking both elated and confused. He told the men, "I got her." His knees buckled, and he fell. Another man rushed over to him.

"Think you can stand?" A lifeguard asked Paige. She nodded and stood up. When she swayed, he grabbed her elbow and assisted her into a chair.

She peered around him. "I need to see Gus."

"It would take more than me to keep him away," the lifeguard chuckled. He glanced over his shoulder. "Here he comes now."

Henny and Penny rushed over to her, clucking like chickens. Gus shooed them away. Another man, this one in a uniform, walked toward them. He shook hands with Gus and asked a question. They both looked at her, then Gus answered in a tone she recognized. Whatever the officer asked, the answer was no. The man spoke again, this time louder. Gus's appearance was a mess, but he stood his ground. Yep. Covered with sand from head to toe, but on the inside where it counted most, he was rock solid. She tuned back in to what he was saying.

"We'll stay here or in town, but she nearly drowned tonight and needs to rest."

Nearly drowned? The mild breeze on her wet skin made her shiver. Other official-looking men and a dog searched the perimeter, but Paige didn't know why. Where was Ed?

Then she heard him. Standing between two men in uniform, he protested loudly. When he turned, she gasped. The silver handcuffs encompassing his wrists winked in the moonlight. Were they arresting him? As quickly as her jaw unhinged, she clamped it shut.

She looked at Gus, who'd been watching too. He held his hands up and shook his head. Hm. He knew something. She was sure of it.

With mild surprise, Paige realized she didn't care what

happened to Ed. She only felt sorrow for the awful choices he'd made.

None too steady, she rose and gripped Gus's hand. She attempted to dust off the sand, but it had turned to mud. Looking forward to getting rid of the grit, she gripped Gus's hand. He looked at their clasped hands, and a slow smile lit up his face. Something shifted in the chocolate depths of his eyes, and he gave her hand a gentle squeeze.

She didn't let go. Never again would she let go.

CHAPTER FORTY

Gloved hands on hips, Paige gazed at the droopy flowerbeds in her front yard. Their neglected state smote her conscience. A robin flit around the veranda and perched on the back of the swing. The morning was warming up, but she still had about an hour before the heat would drive her back inside. Reaching for a determination she didn't feel, she marched to the weediest bed and plopped down on her knee pad. It was where she did her best thinking, aside from the pool. Her swim routine and helping Gus with his shoulder therapy had gone the way of her flowerbeds. Too busy pursuing her new business and making the funds to help Mom.

It was time to find herself again. Listen to God. Get back to doing the right things instead of inventing her own path. She attacked the weeds with savagery.

The purplish half-moons she'd observed under her eyes this morning gave evidence of long sessions at the police station and a restless night. Her personal items remained at the mansion because of its crime scene status. She'd left her contact info with the police at Padre Island and drove back to Valiant yesterday. Finally at home, she delved into the activities that gave her comfort. She'd cooked a batch of enchiladas, drank tea, and watched a silly movie. Peace, however, had proved elusive.

She needed to pull out her planner and move on, but her mind refused to settle. Everything still felt undone with the last event. She'd only heard tidbits of the conversations that bandied around the station, but Gus told her Ed faced serious charges. It sounded like some sort of raid or sting took place during the moonlight swim. Gus had been reluctant to share more, and she didn't push. Ed Clarkston was history in her book.

A dirty feeling lingered. It stung that Ed had pointed out her motives were the same as everyone else's. It galled her even more that he was right. She'd taken advantage of his celebrity status to help her mom and launch her event business.

Moisture clouded her vision. She sniffed and stopped weeding. Sitting back on her heels, she whispered, "I'm sorry, Lord." Then the tears came in earnest.

Bottom line? She hadn't been content to wait for God's timing. Her true friends had thrown plenty of red flags, but she hadn't listened. She'd wanted to help Mom and convinced herself that doing gigs for Ed was the way to make it happen. As it was, Ed still owed her a final payment, but she wouldn't pursue it. She'd use the money he'd already paid her for the expenses incurred. If she couldn't figure something out, Rory would know. If she could bring herself to ask.

Tears rolled down her face as shame gnawed its way to her core. Other impure motives, once hidden, sprang up for attention. Ambition. Vanity. Pride. Her goal was to be the go-to event planner in Valiant. At the root was a deep insecurity. She didn't want to depend on anyone else.

Gut-wrenching sobs broke from her throat. God hadn't been in her equation for success. She'd paid him lip service but hadn't allowed him to work through her fear of being like her mother. So she depended on her strength and determination.

With her focus on self, she'd been easy prey for Ed's seductive ways. Worse yet, she'd sensed his predatory nature, but decided she could handle it. The evening in Houston rose in her mind. Her skin prickled. She'd put herself in a dangerous position, but God had still protected her. And again in the ocean. She hadn't been in peril until Ed's supposed "rescue."

Amid her recriminations, a car door shut.

Gus.

Too late to run into the house and hide. She wiped at her face, hoping to disguise her utter brokenness.

He must have sensed her mood, because he said nothing. Oh, horrors. Did he see her dreadful meltdown? He just wrapped his long arms around her in one of his forever hugs. The strength and comfort he provided calmed her trembling body. She sagged against him, completely spent. He snagged her hand. "Let's sit on the swing."

Once they sat, he handed her a handkerchief. She mopped her eyes and face, wishing for makeup. "Sorry. I'm a real mess this morning."

He pulled her close and tucked her into his shoulder. "You're beautiful, Pep." He took her hand again. Moisture gathered in his dark eyes. "I'm glad you're here beside me. I was so afraid ..." He sniffed and looked away.

"I don't know how you missed the rip current." Her insides lurched.

"God guided my steps. All I could focus on was getting to you."

She turned his chin back to her. "You hate the water."

A grimace stole across his features. "Yeah, not my favorite, but I had to rescue my gal." He nuzzled her ear. "My future."

His future? A tiny seed of hope sprouted into life. Gus still wanted a future with her, despite her awful mistakes? "About that ..." The rest of it died a quick death. The thorny issues that had driven them apart needed to be discussed. Only she had no heart for it. Not after he'd saved her life. Vanity kicked in. And certainly not when she looked like a train wreck. Good grief. She smelled like dirt ... and weeds ... and ...

Gus gently claimed her mouth before she could object. The insistent pressure of his lips chased away any thought of makeup. One impression stood like a beacon, beckoning her forward, making it easy to return his kiss.

This man loved her just the way she was.

PAIGE OBSERVED the thriving houseplants while her mother puttered around the kitchen, making tea. When the teapot whistled, she poured boiling water into two mugs. Paige pulled her attention from the miniature garden to plunk a tea bag in her mug. She sniffed appreciatively as the fragrant peach aroma rose with the steam.

Mom headed into the sitting nook. Paige followed, mindful of the hot liquid in her mug. Once she sat, her eyes roved around the room and found her mother's forehead. The bump had faded into a bruise. A fresh-looking scab covered the small gash, but her eyes were clear. She took a cautious sip of tea. "I'm enjoying these visits."

Paige wanted to hang her head. "Well, you can expect them on a more regular basis now that I'm done with Ed."

"I saw on the news that he'd been arrested. Drugs, was it? It sounded like you were right in the middle of it."

Gus had been hesitant but shared the specifics when Paige asked. Now she wished she hadn't. "A large stash of cocaine, but I knew nothing about it." She omitted the part about the Rohypnol, the date rape drug. Ed was planning quite the party. Gooseflesh prickled her arms. The danger she'd been in had a sobering effect.

"I'm hoping to stay off the journalist's radar. The negative fallout won't help business." Her eyes met Mom's. "I made some bad assumptions, but I never dreamed it would turn out this way. Working for him was a colossal mistake. But I wanted to help—" she broke off, unable to finish. The way she'd tried to fix things was still too fresh.

"You wanted to help me with the meds."

Paige grimaced. "Yes, but I was doing the wrong thing for the right reason, if that makes sense." She was relieved to hear her mom chuckle.

"You've always had a big heart, *jita*. Too big. You can't take on everyone else's problems. When your dad called, I told him about it. I don't know how he manages, but I got a call from the doctor's office this morning. They approved the insurance for the prescription."

Paige's brows lifted. "He got it taken care of?"

"He did. I understand your doubts, him being gone so much, but Paige," Mom's dark eyes bore into her. "He's realized how his long absences have affected all of you."

"Mom, you have the patience of a saint. It's taken him eons to discover he has a family." She couldn't keep the sarcasm out of her voice.

"You need to give him a chance. Nowhere does it say in the Bible that reconciliation is easy or convenient. It's a commandment, though, that we love one another. Just do your part so you can have peace. Leave the rest up to God."

The hint of fire in Mom's expression helped the words sink

in. "You're right. Doesn't mean I have to like it, though." She broke into a grin at her mom's narrow look. Might as well have a lighthearted moment before she delved into her reason for coming.

Mom sipped at her chamomile tea. The lemony scent wafted toward Paige and soothed her. A cycle in the dishwasher thrummed. The comfort of home.

"How's Gus? The twins told me quite the tale about him rescuing you." Mom's forehead knitted with concern. "You're part fish, so how did that happen? He's never shared your love of the water."

Of course, the twins would tell whatever they'd gleaned from less-than-reliable sources. Paige sighed, then gave her a brief rundown, leaving out the scary parts. Like being knocked around by the waves with no strength left. Or the sensation of her lungs bursting for air. Not to mention the brief out-of-body experience when she felt cocooned by something far more powerful than Gus's arms. "I'm fine, Mom. Gus is my hero these days ... but, um, I met his daughter."

Surprise flashed across Mom's countenance. "He has a daughter?"

Paige nodded. "She's seven. The cutest little blonde you ever saw." She could see Mom doing mental calculations, and she hurried to finish. As if saying it fast somehow lessened the relentless truth that the man she'd never stopped loving had fathered a child with someone else. "Heidi's mom died recently. Gus didn't know about their child, but now he has custody. So Gus has a little girl." The last sentence babbled out like a noisy brook. Paige winced. She was repeating herself.

Mom's eyes crinkled in the corners, and she gave a long exhale. "How are you doing with this news?"

"I'm having a hard time wrapping my brain around it."

Paige's voice was barely above a whisper. The news had slammed into her world with meteor force.

"Do you love him?"

The question was soft and nonthreatening, but it brought the situation into focus. "Yes."

Her mom nodded, unsurprised. "Then you have a decision to make."

Paige searched her face. "Gus said as much ..." To her dismay, her eyes had moistened. At least Mom was a safe place.

Mom set her mug on the pile of books next to her chair and stood. "This calls for a hug, *jita*, like when you were a girl. Growing up is tough, but if you let grace cover the hurts, you'll find one glorious rainbow after another."

Paige went into her mother's arms, sorely needing the comfort only her mom could give. She and her siblings used to fight about who got to hug Mom first. Until she assured them there was no end to her love or her hugs.

A little blonde girl with sad eyes rose into Paige's consciousness. Heidi no longer had a mother to hug. Sympathy pushed aside the jealousy Paige had experienced ever since she'd learned Gus had a daughter.

Paige would never be Heidi's biological mother. Yet, even as her Mom's arms surrounded her, Paige knew she could be a safe place for Heidi to grow up.

She bowed her head to the Almighty and made a choice.

CHAPTER FORTY-ONE

Heidi bounced along beside Tavo as they navigated a walkway at Peeps. "Where are we going, Daddy?" She said the word "Daddy" often as if trying it on for size. Tavo hoped it fit.

"I want you to meet some friends of mine," he said, for the third or fourth time. He'd lost count. This little gal was fond of questions. "Here, grab my hand. We're going inside, and you need to stay with me." Her tiny hand slid into his sweaty one. He'd chosen powerlifting practice to make Heidi's presence known to Rory and Jess. Maybe it would cut down on the inevitable questions. From Rory and Jess, and the little girl whose hand Tavo held.

As they stepped into the large practice room, Heidi's eyes widened. He chuckled. It must look like a circus to her. Loud music blared from speakers. A ginormous American flag took up an entire wall. Young men and women hoisted heavy weights and yelled at each other. He squinted. Yep. Rory was on the floor, giving instructions to a small group. Jess sat on the aluminum bleachers, hands clasped behind his head.

Heidi's question broke into his reverie. "Do you do that?" She pointed to a team member lifting a barbell with a hefty amount of weight on each end. The effort had screwed his face into a ferocious scowl.

"I did before my shoulder got hurt." He'd already answered a slew of questions about why he wore the shoulder brace.

"Were you as strong as him?"

"Mostly." His mind had moved ahead to the impending conversation.

"Are you still strong, Daddy?"

Her vulnerable tone sliced through his musings. He seized the moment. Kneeling, he looked into her solemn face. "God made me very strong, so I can take care of you *and* fight the bad guys."

For reassurance sake, he tucked her arm possessively through his as they made their way around the gym. He'd also learned she could flit away like a butterfly without a tether. Jess, looking relaxed in khaki shorts and a Peeps polo shirt, rose and shook his hand. His dark eyes bristled with curiosity as Heidi scooted behind Tavo. Rory joined them with a whistle still in his mouth.

Tavo turned so Heidi could observe them. "I want you guys to meet my daughter." He grit his teeth at Jesse's double-take. The whistle fell out of Rory's mouth. Forcing the brick down his throat, Tavo turned to Heidi. "Wanna shake hands with my friends?" He crouched eye level with her and pointed. "This is Jesse. He's the boss around here. And this person"—he pointed again—"is Rory." Rory had recovered enough to give her a wink. Tavo stood, not letting go of her hand. "Heidi is seven. Her mama has gone to heaven, and she lives with me now."

He'd found the easiest explanation was usually the best. Heidi's acceptance of him as her father helped him roll with it. Even now, she was more interested in Rory's whistle than any careful explanation. Rory sensed it too, because he unhooked it from his lanyard and wiped the mouthpiece on his shirt. "Do you want to blow it?"

He rose when she nodded. "Tavo, why don't you make the rounds on the floor while we go outside and make good use of this whistle?"

Tavo dipped his chin. Rory's take-it-in-stride manner encouraged him more than his friend would ever know. Rory held out his hand. Heidi took it easily, and they made their way outdoors. Jesse looked on with amusement. "Watch out, dude. He'll give her anything she wants." He scrutinized Tavo closely. "Sounds like a big change. You doing okay?"

Tavo scuffed a boot heel, then kicked at an imaginary speck of dirt. "All right, I guess." Honesty insisted he say more. "I didn't know I had a daughter until a week ago."

"Ouch." Jesse's eyes shone with sympathy. "Does Paige know?"

He stretched his neck and rolled it around his shoulders. "Oh, yeah. She found out the worst way possible. We've not talked much since." Technically, it was true. They'd kissed. Argued. He'd fished her out of the ocean, and they'd kissed again. So no, not much talking.

"Give her time, but don't leave her hanging. Make double-... no, triple-sure she knows how much you love her."

"That's not the issue." He sighed heavily. "Paige has never wanted kids ... now she has a ready-made family. If she wants it."

Jesse's brow cocked in disbelief. "Paige is a natural. When we were growing up, she was always mothering us. She just needs time."

Tavo didn't remember it that way. Friends, yes, but there had always been a spark of something more between them. "I don't know." Tavo looked at a group of young men on the floor yelling comments at the women. They were accomplishing squat. "I need to do rounds so the guys will lift instead of flirt." He took a step toward the practice floor, but Jesse caught his arm.

"Paige needs to know she's got your heart. I'll check on Rory. Make sure he's not buying Heidi three kinds of ice cream." A wistful smile split his grim countenance. "She's a keeper. Brenna and I are looking forward to having a family of our own."

PAIGE SAT in her favorite chair at her favorite coffee shop, desperately trying to stay calm. She couldn't bring herself to visit Tavo's house again. Standing at the door, on the verge of declaring her love, then finding out he had a daughter? Nope. Still painful, but she was adjusting. Moving toward the only thing that made sense. This meeting might help with that.

She'd asked Gus's parents to meet her here—well, she'd asked Marie, and she agreed to bring Gus's dad. Paige wasn't sure if she had invited a lion into her den or if she'd jumped headfirst into a fiery furnace. Only she had a goal to accomplish. This way, she'd know right quick how to proceed. Gus's dad was not one to beat around the bush. He was as old-school as they came, and her idea ... wasn't. A sip of tea trickled past the lump in her throat. What if he outright refused?

The chimes on the entrance door rang, just as the espresso machine shrieked. Paige nearly dropped her cup of brew. Marie entered first, then Gus's dad. Mom had called him Reno, though Paige wouldn't dare. However, knowing the man possessed a first name made him a little less scary.

Paige inhaled a breath, redolent with notes of vanilla, and strived for composure. She rose and hugged Marie, then shook

Reno's hand. If he noticed how her hand trembled, he gave no indication. His usual sternness had given way to curiosity. Paige hoped that's what she spied on his face.

Reno consulted with Marie about her choice of beverage and glanced at Paige. She merely raised her cup. Her voice wasn't cooperating yet. He afforded her a tiny nod and made his way to the counter.

"Thank you for inviting us, Paige." The bruises on Marie's face from the car wreck were slowly fading. Terrible as the accident was, it heartened Paige to know Gus's late arrival on that fateful night was beyond his control. "Tell me, how is your mom? I haven't seen her in years."

"Mom is great. It will thrill her to know I saw you."

"You were little when, uh ..." The older woman's face flamed.

Oh, dear. Not where Paige wanted this conversation to go. She defaulted to newsy chitchat. "I'm their oldest. Would you believe I have four siblings?"

"Five in all? Oh, my. And I thought I was busy with two." Marie recovered quickly.

"Yes. And the last two are twin boys. They're eighteen." She made a comical face. "Going on thirty."

"Reno mentioned you and Tavo are dating again." Marie checked Reno's whereabouts. "I'm guessing this meeting has something to do with that."

"It does." Paige longed to share with a sympathetic party but decided against it. Saying it once would be challenge enough. "I'm really glad you're here ..." she trailed off, unsure how to address Gus's mother.

"Call me Marie. And please relax if that's possible. I've already told Reno he's not allowed to bark or bite." A hint of mischief shaded the words, helping Paige feel less tense. Someday, she'd tell Gus what a lovely woman his mother was.

They chatted until Reno returned with two cups of brew. Her nerves had subsided somewhat. Reno's piercing stare rattled them back to life. Sitting straighter in the chair, her chin rose.

"Paige, I haven't seen you since high school ..." A spasm of something cracked his granite features briefly. Finally, he said, "You've grown up."

She wanted to slip into the crevices in the vinyl flooring. Of all the things she'd expected, the Chief of Police floundering for words wasn't one of them.

Marie came to his rescue. "High school was a long time ago. That was then, and this is now, so to speak. It's a pleasure to see the beautiful woman you've become."

"Yes. That's it exactly." Reno's features softened as he glanced at Gus's mother.

Unbidden tears filled Paige's eyes. "Thank you." She took a breath to say more, but her throat had closed up. The pause grew awkward. She struggled to get the words out.

She set her cup on a small side table, so she wouldn't spill it and clasped clammy hands together. "First, I'd like to ask for your blessing." She paused, summoning the courage to finish. "Then, if I have your blessing, I'm going to need your help."

Reno opened his mouth. At that moment, the espresso machine screeched again. Paige silently commiserated with the machine. Once the noise stopped, Reno ignored the warning look Marie shot his way.

"Why do you want our blessing, Paige?"

CHAPTER FORTY-TWO

Tavo was reliving a bad nightmare. He stood in Dad's office, hands on hips, struggling to keep his temper. Desperately trying not to roar at his father. Also his boss.

"Dad, it's been eight weeks. The doctor and the physical therapist have cleared me. What more do you need?"

Tavo's ire didn't faze the man sitting in front of him. Glasses halfway down his nose, Dad had the gall to act as if adding a week of vacation after eight endless weeks of light duty was no big deal. For cryin' out loud, it was a doggone mountain. "I need to get back out there, Dad. I've been cleared to work."

"Not by me, you haven't. Before you come back, I need the assurance your brain and body are in tiptop shape. Lots of changes in your life these past few weeks. Take some time off. Think about things. Your mom and I can handle Heidi."

The absolute last thing Tavo needed was more time to think. He'd go crazy with nothing to do. Of all people, Dad knew that. He'd always touted the "hard-work-helps-whatever-ails-you" philosophy. So why was he keeping Tavo from patrol?

Now, Dad wore his legendary not-budging look. *Help me, Lord.* It made no sense. The trouble was, he was also hearing it internally—deep on the inside. The right course involved giving up what he had assumed was standard procedure. Respecting Dad's authority as his father and his boss. Leave off the wrangling.

"Sign these papers and get out of here." Dad pushed a stack of papers at him and laid a pen on top.

Tavo exhaled long and loud. This submission gig was eating him alive. He plopped heavily in the chair and started signing where the arrows pointed. When he finished, he slammed the pen down on the desk. "Satisfied?"

Other than giving him a stern look, Dad ignored the sarcasm.

Tavo huffed out the door, grousing under his breath. He climbed into his truck and stabbed a number on his phone. If he didn't talk to someone, he'd blow sky-high.

———

"GLAD I WAS BETWEEN APPOINTMENTS." Pastor Mike sat behind his desk, his hands wrapped around a fresh cup of tea. Faint lines on his forehead suggested a strenuous day. "What brings you here?"

Tavo shifted uncomfortably in the chair. Second thoughts about coming threatened to derail his decision to ask for help. "Got too much time on my hands." Briefly, Tavo related Dad's insistence on another week off. The warmth and sincerity that flowed from the man sitting across the desk shored up his sagging spirits.

Again, the tea fragrance drifting in his direction reminded

him of Paige. He'd tackle the thorny subject of the woman he loved next.

"Sounds like your temper could have taken a backseat. Overall, though, I think you handled the situation with as much grace as you could muster. Life doesn't happen with perfection. You're taking the week off, right?"

"As if I had a choice," Tavo muttered.

"You always have a choice, and you made the right one." He studied Tavo. "Your heavenly Father won't come down on you for a flawed reaction. He knows we're a work in progress. What else?"

In for a penny … Tavo inhaled a deep breath and blew it out. "I don't know what to do about Paige. She baffles me."

His mood soured at Mike's unsuccessful attempt to hide his smirk. "What's the problem?"

Mike's expression sobered when Tavo explained about Heidi, how Paige found out, and how they'd reconciled. "On one hand, our relationship has reached a new level, but she won't talk about the future. Not at all." He scratched his head.

"I suspect she needs time. A man with a child changes things." Mike leaned back in his chair.

"I get that. But …" It confused him how *right* things were— they talked for hours on the phone, and she sent memes and texts daily. To say nothing of her response to his kisses. His blood warmed thinking about it.

"I've assured her of my love several times. When I bring up anything long-term, though, she changes the subject." Last night when he'd broached it, she pulled his face to hers and kissed him until he forgot his name. Definitely swoony.

"Patience, Tavo. Hang on to your hope. There was nothing fake about her feelings for you the night of the karaoke event." He came around the desk and sat in the chair next to Tavo. "Let's pray about this. Work helps to take our minds off things.

God's help is even better. He'll get the tension tamped down to a sustainable level."

"SLOW DOWN, sugar plum. You're too far ahead," Paige called.

Heidi slowed, then turned and ran back. "Why do you call me sugar plum?" Her blue-eyed stare suggested she wasn't complaining, merely curious.

"Cause you're not too big, like a sugar plum, and you're just so sweet, it makes me want to eat you!" Paige grabbed her for a hug and twirled her around.

It was amazing what time together could do. Years of her ingrained older-sister habits had fallen away, replaced with a new wonder for children. It had started with this enchanting little blonde. Once Paige made her mind up to embrace Heidi and cast off the jealousy, the Lord had started a whole new thing inside her heart. Even if it was a secret. Along with other secrets.

The only part she hated was Gus, out of necessity, wasn't in the loop. She was banking on him being surprised, but thoroughly pleased with her plan. Pulling it off, however, was like hoisting a piano up a flight of stairs. He was getting antsy at her seeming lack of interest in their future, but it wouldn't be long now.

Heidi pointed to a swing. When Paige nodded, the little girl ran to it. Paige envied her energy. When she wasn't busy with this event, she lay awake at night worrying something might go wrong.

This was her third visit alone with Gus's daughter. His mom had agreed to let Paige spirit Heidi away for bonding time once they knew what she was planning. Everyone was on pins and needles with the task of keeping Gus none the wiser. Paige's chief concern at the moment was Heidi saying something she shouldn't, bless her chatterbox-y heart.

Paige pushed Heidi until her arms hurt. When she stopped, Heidi jumped out of the swing. She ran and hugged Paige. "I'm hungry."

A chuckle bubbled up Paige's throat as she hugged Heidi back. "How about we go to my house for a corn dog and apple slices?" Since she learned the child's favorites, she'd kept her pantry stocked with them. Children weren't so different from grown men ... their stomachs led the way.

"Yes!" Heidi bounced up and down, then took Paige's hand. "I love you, Pep." She grinned as if she knew a secret. "But Daddy ... he loves you different."

Paige's heart tilted crazily as she swung Heidi's hand. "You think so?"

Her blonde head nodded seriously. "I can tell by the way he looks at you."

"How does he look at me?" Paige held her breath.

Heidi chewed her lip, thinking about it. Adorably so. "Well, you call me sugar plum, and your eyes turn soft and pretty when you say it." She paused, as if thinking again, and then she shrugged. "Daddy loves me because I'm his little girl. But you're different"—She stressed the words to make Paige understand—"you're *his* sugar plum."

Out of the mouth of babes. Paige's heart swelled almost out of her chest.

CHAPTER FORTY-THREE

M uch as he adored her, Tavo was ready to strangle Paige. She needed to attend a friend's wedding, she said. To check out the competition, she said. Would he go as her plus-one? And wear his tux? When he'd made a face, her eyes flashed as if him saying yes was the most important thing on the planet. Then those dazzling lips moved with a one-word question. *Please?*

He'd caved. Now, it irked him to no end that he'd agreed. A wedding, of all things. Was she trying to pile on the misery? The only upside was a possible conversation about their own wedding. Just thinking about it made his insides feel like a worm on the end of a hook. She was going to bail on him again. Despite what the pastor said, Tavo knew her. The last few weeks had been too good to be true.

He stood at her front door. The gentle breeze didn't help in the least. The tux was too warm. His collar itched abominably. Then Paige appeared, and he forgot to breathe.

Her knee-length white flowy skirt and short red jacket fit the dressy casual requirement. By comparison, his tux seemed overdone, but she'd asked specifically for him to wear it. Getting past the grumps, he feasted on Paige again. She'd swept her hair up in a super cute style, and her sparkly necklace and bracelet looked new. "You look lovely."

"Thank you." Eyes shimmering, she took his arm. "You're quite handsome tonight."

"Thanks," he said, wincing at the flatness of his tone. "Remind me why we're doing this?"

She swatted his arm. "You know why."

"Paige—" he began.

"There's a stop I'd like to make ahead of time." She had the audacity to wink at him.

Still exasperated with her, he tucked away the need lapping at him like those infernal waves in the ocean. *Patience.* The next time he broached the subject, she wouldn't wiggle out of it. But for now, he'd drink in her beauty for as long ... He couldn't bear to finish the thought. Instead, he swallowed hard and waved his arm in a long, low flourish. "Your wish is my command."

She gave him a tremulous smile and hurried down the veranda steps to his truck. He followed with leaden feet. He'd never seen her look more stunning, but she was also acting ... brittle ... nervous. He hung on to the hope he'd felt earlier in prayer. It lasted a nanosecond, then dissolved into dread.

Was she going to end things?

PAIGE HOPPED up the stadium steps to the very top. Gus followed. One moment, he was exhibiting patience, and the next, he was too quiet. Hard to blame him. She took the prize for ditzy this past week. She gave the concrete bleacher a cursory sweep with her hand, mindful of her freshly manicured nails, then sat down, hardly daring to make eye contact. Willing her face and insides to cooperate, she patted the space next to her. As the time grew closer, her ability to stay cool waned. It would require every ounce of grit and finesse she possessed not to prematurely spill the beans.

The worst of the summer heat had passed, leaving cooler days and pleasant evenings. A soft breeze caressed her, as if assuring her everything would go according to plan. A couple of guys were putting out speakers and a mic on the green football field below. Nothing Gus would question or pay attention to, she hoped. The sky was a perfect cerulean blue, with whitish-gray clouds undulating like water.

He sat beside her with a bemused expression. He surveyed the field briefly before turning to face her. Either he didn't notice, or his eyes simply weren't taking in the details. Just as she'd hoped.

"What are we doing, Pep?" His soft question wasn't referring to their physical location. It almost undid her resolve.

Instead of blurting out the truth, she licked her lips. "I wanted to come here for old time's sake. What this place represents. Revisit our history a little."

The vertical lines beside his lips creased, but the dimples stayed hidden. "We have history here. But that was a long time ago." He looked at her warily. "I'm more interested in our relationship now."

She glanced at the field, then back. "Can we reminisce? It's been a while since we've talked about high school."

He stared at her, as if trying to read her mind. Resignation passed over his face. As Paige swallowed the rock rising in her throat, he said, "*We* actually started in junior high. You were always late to class. That day in the locker room ..."

Relieved, she joined in with a laugh. "The day you saved

me from those two thugs. How you were there at just the right moment ..." She shook her head.

"Oh, that's easy. I knew your schedule and followed you ..."

"You followed me? That's creepy."

For the first time that evening, a mischievous grin streaked across his countenance. "Probably. I had a crush on you."

"We were both late to class that day." Paige made a face like it was the worst thing ever.

"Because the school paparazzi showed up."

She peeped at the field again, trying to keep track of their conversation. "They emblazoned our picture on the front page of the school paper. Made it look like something was going on, but it wasn't." The men setting up equipment were gone. She shot a quick prayer to heaven.

They chatted through a few more memories, but the lines on his wide forehead were deepening into a somber expression. Suddenly, he started talking. "What are we doing, Paige? I'm glad for the progress we've made, but you're still holding me at arms-length. I'm sick of being your boyfriend ... if that's what I am.

"I want more, Paige. But you won't talk about more." His face turned red. "I can't keep doing this—" He cut off mid-sentence because Heidi was climbing the steps. Paige relished the consternation etching across his face.

She pressed her lips closed. They both watched his daughter bound up the last few steps. She wore a white dress with a short red jacket and red sandals. Her hair style was a carbon copy of Paige's.

Gus stared at her, then back at Paige. Confusion pulled his brows together as if he didn't know where to start. Finally, he settled on Heidi. "What are you doing here, sweetmeat?" He reached for her, and she went readily into his arms.

Heidi glanced at Paige for confirmation, and then said to Gus, "Paige says you want to marry her."

A giggle burst out of Paige before she could stop it. Gus's helplessness was just too funny. When Heidi looked at Paige again, she gave a tiny nod.

Heidi faced her dad. "Do you want to marry Paige?"

He gazed at Paige nervously. "We haven't actually talked about it, but ..."

"Paige says she's waitin' on you." Heidi's clear steady voice was everything Paige had hoped. Just like they'd practiced.

When Gus's mouth fell open, Heidi gave him a hug. "I want Paige to be my new mama."

Tears pearled on Paige's lashes. Heidi created that last line all by herself. She glanced down at the field again, fighting for composure. Her phone buzzed. She took a surreptitious peek. Everything was ready.

"Am I done now?" Heidi looked at Paige even as she relaxed in her father's arms. At Paige's nod, Heidi skipped back down the way she came.

Gus stared after her, a question forming on his lips. Paige cut in, "She's fine, Gus."

He cocked his head. "What's going on?"

She scooted closer to him. Time for the big question. "Would you like to get married tonight?"

Astonishment, wonder, and delight passed over Gus's face in quick succession, followed by a quizzical look.

Paige pointed to the center of the field. "We gave each other our first kiss right down there during a homecoming game halftime. I'd loved you for a long time, but that was the first time I realized it. Then we got separated ... and lost our way." She took his hand, willing the sudden shyness away. "But no more. You're the only man I've ever loved. The one I want forever. Would you like to share our first kiss again, this time after we say I do?"

For a few interminable seconds, he said nothing. Then he stood and held out his hands to her. When she rose, he placed his hands on her waist and lifted her onto the bleacher. Standing eye-to-eye, he searched her face. Paige bit her lip under his scrutiny. Finally, he spoke. "You know that's what I want." His eyes had lost the dullness and now sparkled with a new light. "But here? Now? You want to get married on a football field?"

She wilted with relief and leaned into him. "Yes. I wanted the bright lights again, like all of heaven is smiling down at us. Like we're the only two people in the world." At his look of incredulity, she added, "No crowd though. Just family and our closest friends."

"I've had plenty of time to think about it. As much as I love to plan weddings, the emphasis on lavish appearances can overshadow the simple joy of joining two hearts together. I wanted our wedding to be about us, not how everything looks."

Butterflies danced in her stomach. "That said, the reception will be traditional—also for us, but for our families too."

Somewhere in her little speech, he'd wrapped his arms around her waist and clasped his hands against her back. "I have no doubts about your ability to plan an event, Pep. But you don't want an engagement? I don't have a ring ... or—" His hands fell away to grip her shoulders. "We need a license ..." His head moved sideways, though his eyes still looked wildly hopeful.

He was so close, his breath warmed her face, melting her heart into a puddle. "I don't need an engagement. And I know you. You won't rest until there's a ring on my finger. But for the sake of the ceremony, your mom and dad have loaned us theirs —only a loan—until that happens."

He held her even closer. "So you've been planning this—for how long? Cause I've been thinking the worst." She enjoyed his embrace for a short, sweet moment, then he pulled back. "But that doesn't solve the need for a license. I'm not settling for anything less than legally marrying you." Paige wanted to burst with laughter at his adamant words.

"Already taken care of."

"But how?"

Laughing in earnest, she put a finger to his lips. "Shhh. Trust me, Gus. Everyone will be eager to tell you how we kept it a secret."

He studied her, then opened his mouth as if to ask another question. But Paige was done with questions. She feathered her lips against him. He kissed her gently, then moved to her cheek and her ear. "Okay."

"Okay, what?" Paige pressed through the haze. It was hard to think with him so close.

"I'd love to marry you. Tonight." A brow lifted. "Why is Heidi dressed like you? You're not going to wear a long, white dress?"

"No. A long dress with a train doesn't work with this venue." She waved a hand toward the field. "And when I asked Heidi what role she wanted at our wedding, her only request was to look like me." She choked the last words out. His child had captured her heart. "I'll tell you about that too, but the connection we've developed is far more important to me than a traditional wedding gown."

His eyes moistened. "You're all right with helping me raise my daughter?"

"She'll be my daughter too, in all the ways that matter."

Before she could say more, he claimed her mouth with his.

The sound of people cheering broke their kiss. They looked down at the field where friends and family were shouting and beckoning them to come down. Their phones chimed simultaneously.

Gus waved to them. His dimples winked in the twilight. He turned back to her. "Let's not keep them waiting."

Paige's jaws ached, but this time it was because she couldn't stop smiling. She twined her fingers through his. "Or us, love. We've waited long enough."

CHAPTER FORTY-FOUR

S till shell-shocked, Tavo gripped Paige's hand as they navigated the bleacher steps. Perhaps to make sure it wasn't a dream. He and Paige were getting married. Tonight! He squeezed her hand, reassured when she squeezed back.

As they reached the bottom and stepped onto the grassy sideline, Rory was the first to extend a hand. "Way to go, Chief. I take it you said yes?"

Jesse nudged Rory aside and enveloped Tavo in a firm hug. "He'd be a fool not to."

"You guys are in on it?"

Paige had stepped away to hug Brenna and Vi but was now by his side again. Snugging her arm through his. "They were. No way I could have pulled it off solo."

"So I owe them thanks for making our wedding happen?"

"Well, it hasn't happened yet, dude. Let's get you to the church, uh, the ceremony on time." Rory clapped him on the back. "Relax, Tavo. Everyone's been doing her bidding the last two weeks. She's taken care of everything."

Paige took his hand, and they made their way to the center

of the field. Slowly. Between hugs and well-wishes. A joyful calm had spread over the group. His parents had joined them. Paige's twin brothers each held one of Heidi's arms, swinging her in the middle. Her peals of laughter carried across the balmy air.

He glanced down at his soon-wife-to-be, falling more deeply in love with her every second.

"You're sure about this?" she asked.

"A surprise wedding? I've never loved an idea more."

"It's informal. Out-of-the-box."

He caught the note of worry and allayed any second-guessing. "You chose well, Pep. I spent so many hours on this football field, it's like home. And now that you've convinced me you want to get married here for sentimental reasons"—he smirked—"and not the clash of the titans, I'm all in." The tic of concern in her brow needed to be kissed, so he obliged. Then the spots of color in her cheeks needed kissing as well.

And so it went until Pastor Mike cleared his throat. "C'mon, you two. Let's get you married before you set the night on fire." The sky had darkened through a display of tangerine and pink streaks as the sun gradually descended.

The instant they took their positions in front of the preacher, the stadium lights whooshed on. The group clapped with delight. Someone hollered, "Let's get this show on the road!"

Tavo looked down at Paige's sudden movement and followed her startled gaze. White party chairs had magically appeared from somewhere. Her mother sat on the front row next to a slim man Tavo didn't recognize.

Paige held on to his arm for support. "Dad's here."

Tavo turned her chin, willing her to hear him. "Your mom knew about this, right? He's come home to be at your wedding, Pep."

She gazed into his eyes for what seemed like forever, and her breathing lost its erratic pace. "It's a surprise, that's all."

"Yeah, well, we've got that in common tonight, don't we? Let's get married, and we'll chat with him at the reception. I'll be right by your side." *Lord, help us.* He and Paige were finally at the altar. For pity's sake, nothing else needed to get in the way.

He continued to hold her with his eyes until the shock wore off. Finally, she nodded, and they both looked at Pastor Mike.

"Are you all right now, Tavo?" he asked in a low, teasing voice.

"So I was sitting in your office, pouring out my angst, and you knew all the time." Tavo pretended disgust. "If anyone asks, I've never been better. I'm thrilled to marry Paige. Right now!" Mike's excitement was contagious. Or was it the other way around? He looked at Paige, and she murmured assent, even as she squeezed Tavo's hand.

Tavo's chest swelled as Pastor Mike proceeded to marry them.

To be perfectly honest, he remembered little of the actual ceremony. Except when they promised to love each other for as long as they lived, and Paige's clear strong "I do." Cameras and phones flashed. Jesse and Rory stood next to him with huge grins. Nothing, however, compared to Paige's glow. She lit up the entire field brighter than the stadium lights. Somewhere along the way, she'd taken off the red jacket, and the result was a short snazzy wedding dress. He adored the opening in the back that allowed her bare skin to peek through. Stylish. Very Paige-ish.

When the preacher pronounced them man and wife, Tavo whooped louder than anyone else and kissed his wife with a fervency that made the sunset blush.

TAVO'S JAW slacked as they paused at the entrance of the venue. The place looked like something out of a storybook. An old world garden of sorts. Austin stone adorned the walls with bright pink flowers cascading out of every crevice. A mini waterfall gurgled on one side. Someone had strategically arranged large vases of red roses around the room. White twinkly lights cast a warm, cheery glow.

"It's beautiful. Like a fairy tale." He inhaled the fragrant aroma. Roses had always been her favorite.

Paige's hands covered her mouth. She bounced with excitement. "I knew they'd come through."

Her enthusiasm captured the girl he'd fallen in love with— only now she was his wife. "Who do you mean by 'they?'"

Paige gave him a knowing smile. "I might have planned our wedding and reception, but I wanted the night off. So my rivals became my friends."

"How did you do that?" Tavo acknowledged his parents as they walked through the door. They gaped at the exquisite setting. Paige might have contracted the physical labor, but her trademark elegance shone through every aspect of their marvelous surroundings.

"There will be plenty of events in my future. If the planners in Valiant combine our forces when we need help, we'll all win. So I invited 'the big three' for coffee, and we hashed it out together. They listened to what I wanted and agreed to make it happen."

Tavo caressed her face with his hands. "I'm glad you made a way for this night to be special for us."

"Oh, babe, we're just getting started." The impish twinkle in her eye warmed his neck.

"How's the pain these days?" He tenderly stroked her jaws.

"Mm. Better when you do that. But ... enormous improvement since I stopped working for Ed."

"That's all in the past, Pep. Nothing will spoil this evening or our future." He leaned in for another kiss, but stopped when someone cleared his throat. Loudly.

When Tavo turned, Dad grasped his hand and simultaneously transferred an envelope. Then he enclosed Tavo in a bear hug. "For your honeymoon."

Astonished, Tavo didn't respond, and Dad guffawed. "You thought your old man had finally lost it when I gave you a week of vacation instead of more hours."

Several things clicked into place. "You were in on it?"

"I couldn't have done it without his help," Paige interjected with a demure smile. "If not for Marie's encouragement, I wouldn't have been brave enough to ask. She also lets me have time with Heidi."

What was in the envelope? He opened it and thumbed through a thick wad of hundred-dollar bills. Eyes wide, he looked up to see the merriment on his parent's faces. "So you gave me this and vacation time?"

"And your signature to make our marriage legal," Paige murmured.

The memory of Tavo slamming the papers on Dad's desk came back with a vengeance. Mortified, Tavo ran a hand over his face. "I was so angry at you."

"Oh, you were livid."

Roxanne stood nearby in a shiny emerald-colored dress, holding a bulky package. Tavo turned slightly to include her in their circle. The delightful blend of food flavors filling the air made his stomach growl.

"Oh, I don't want to interrupt." Roxanne's eyes reflected the opposite. As if part of her longed for a close-knit family.

"You're not interrupting. I'm glad you're here." He made introductions, nodded to Dad, and steered Roxanne into a small alcove. Two large bougainvillea covered with pink blooms flanked the space on both sides.

Paige joined them, placing a small hand on his back. He couldn't get enough of her touch. His eyes strayed to the gift.

"I, uh, this is probably not the best time to give you this, but I don't know when I'll get over here again ..."

"You want us to open it now?" Paige. of course, knew what needed to happen. Tavo held her close.

"Yes, if that's all right. It's really for Heidi, but I wanted both of you to know ... hear about it first."

Tavo took the package. At Roxanne's nod, he tore the white paper down the middle. A beautiful frame held a single piece of stationary with what looked like a scripture written on it. Puzzled, he looked at her.

Tears pearled her lower lashes. "It's the last thing Sharla wrote. I wanted Heidi to have it, but it will be special to you too."

Tavo gazed at the colorful piece of paper encased within the glass. He recognized the loopy cursive as Sharla's. He read the words aloud, "'I know that my Redeemer lives, ... and after my skin is destroyed, this I know, that in my flesh I shall see God, whom I shall see for myself, and my eyes shall behold, and not another. How my heart yearns within me.'"

Roxanne cleared her throat. "It's from the Book of Job. She loved those verses so much, she wanted to share them with Heidi—and you."

Paige's eyes had filled. "We'll cherish it. And we'll make sure Heidi understands what the verses mean and why her mom wanted her to have them."

As his wife enclosed their new friend in a hug, tenderness filled Tavo's heart and healed the broken spot that had ached for so long. God had forgiven him and answered his countless prayers for Sharla's salvation. She was now living her happily ever after.

Mom had been hovering just out of earshot, but now she stepped up, her gaze on the picture. As Paige related the story behind it, Mom murmured to Roxanne, "This is special." She extended her arms as Tavo hefted the frame. "Let me take care of it for you." Once he handed her the picture, she faced Roxanne. "There are some people who would love to meet you. And I could use a little advice about Heidi. She's my first grandchild, you know ..."

Tavo caught Roxanne's wistful look as the older woman slipped an arm through hers and gently steered her toward a small group of women. Another gap in his memory closed. Mom had always been quick to help others. Even from this distance, it was obvious she was introducing Roxanne to Paige's mother. Between his mom and Paige's, Roxanne wouldn't have a secret left by the end of the evening. Paige had observed it too. When one delicate brow lifted knowingly, he acknowledged it with a grin.

To his delight, Paige took his hand. "I think they're waiting for us to dance."

He lifted her hand to his lips. "Nothing I'd like better, Mrs. Morales."

CHAPTER FORTY-FIVE

Paige sighed with contentment as she rested her cheek against Gus's shoulder. The stiff feel of the tux fabric rubbed her cheek, and she reveled in the comfort of the spicy cologne he wore. They swayed to the strains of Elvis Presley's rendition of "Can't Help Falling in Love." He held her snugly, his large hand covering the keyhole on the back of her dress, the other holding her shoulder. Never had she thought she'd be in the category of brides who recognized their wedding dress the instant they saw it, but this dress had made her a believer. It didn't hurt that Gus loved it too.

"I'm loving every second of this, Paige." He tipped her face up and planted another kiss on her lips. Her arms tightened around his waist. She couldn't get enough of him tonight. All too soon, the dance ended. She stood, her arm on his, wishing for another kiss when someone tapped her shoulder.

When she turned, her mouth fell open. "May I have the next dance?" her father asked. His eyes strayed to Tavo, as if asking for permission. A flustered feeling rose, trampling any rational thought. Marie's words echoed deep in her spirit. *That was then. This is now.*

Paige took in her father's sharp appearance. He'd always been lean and wiry, but it startled her to see he barely reached Gus's shoulder. His ebony hair, streaked with silver, was as straight as hers, slicked back off his forehead, and tethered into a short, don't-mess-with-me ponytail. His eyes were fierce, as if he meant to reclaim something he'd missed, though a small corner of his mouth drooped. As if he wasn't as sure of himself as he appeared. The slight movement reminded her of the twins.

"Paige?" Gus's soft query gave her the strength she needed. She squeezed his hand, and then nodded to her dad, afraid her voice wouldn't cooperate.

A familiar love song sounded in the background. The consummate gentleman, her father escorted her to the dance floor, though her movements were stiff. His long absences played with her emotions. *That was then, this is now.* "I'm glad you came, Daddy."

A small smile creased his lips. "I've missed too much. But not this. Not your wedding."

Still at a loss for words, Paige kissed his cheek. He moved his hand from her shoulder and clasped hers tightly. "I love you," he whispered. Then a wry expression flitted across his face as his head angled toward Gus. "But that one's been hanging around, mooning over you for years. Now he's too big to mess with, so I'll concede," he teased, drawing her closer. "You picked a stellar guy, Paige. I'm happy for you."

"Thanks, Daddy. It took me a while to figure out Gus is what I want—all I want." Even now, as he chatted with Claude and Ochee, his eyes found hers. Her knees turned to jelly at their molten depths. She returned his look with a saucy wink and focused on her dad. "Mom says you're thinking of retiring." Their feet moved in rhythm to the music as if they'd been dancing together for years instead of minutes.

"Retiring from my current job but not work. I want to start a security company here in South Texas. It's close enough to the metroplexes and the border to ensure plenty of business. It will also keep me closer to home." His rueful look communicated more than the words. "Plain as the nose on my face. Like you, though, it took me a while to figure it out."

Glad as Paige was to hear the news, she couldn't resist ribbing him. "It's nice to have something in common, even if it's dithering about important decisions."

His laugh assured her she hadn't overstepped. That their relationship wasn't as tenuous as she'd believed. The way his arms wrapped around her, alien as it felt, also comforted. The closer she got, the mystique surrounding her father faded. Perhaps it explained why Ed's aura had pulled at her. The desire to know the man underneath the façade. Except with both her dad and Gus, their inner person was solid and real. Ed had become lost in his different roles.

Her resolve to provide a strong foundation for her siblings and Heidi revved up her pulse like a go-fast motor. This dance with her dad wasn't exactly closure, but it had helped to clear the fog she'd been in about him and their relationship.

When the song ended, she gave him a heartfelt hug. He held her to him and seemed reluctant to let go. It was her turn. "I love you too, Daddy."

He took her hands and squeezed. "My beautiful firstborn. Thank you for the dance." An eyebrow arched as he glanced over her shoulder. "Your husband has come to claim you, so I'll step aside." A smile ghosted his lips, as he said loud enough for Gus to hear, "But you let me know if he's not doing right. I'll call somebody's army to straighten him out."

Laughing, he shook hands with Gus and moved away,

just as the twins appeared. They wore black jeans and lightweight jackets with boots. She'd insisted Carlos get a brown jacket to match his tan boots. Miguel, of course, chose black. Untrimmed curls fell to their shoulders, looking more like messy bird nests than hair. Heidi stood like a porcelain doll between them, though her skirt had green streaks as if she'd taken a tumble or two on the stadium grass.

They angled in on either side of Gus, vying for his attention. He stepped back to see both of them. "Hey, guys."

They wiggled all over themselves like puppies. Paige held in an eye roll. "We just wanted you to know ..." Carlos began.

"We want to do what you do," Miguel finished.

Gus asked politely, "Okay. What do I do?"

"You're a police officer. Yeah, that's what we want to do, uh, be."

"No, I want to be a detective," Miguel protested.

Carlos turned on his twin. "We both have to be police officers."

Gus held a palm up. "First off, you can't just decide you're going to be a police officer—or a detective. You have to pass tests. Have you guys checked the requirements?" Paige hid a smile at the mix of exasperation and skepticism. At least they were thinking about their future. She pressed her hand against Gus's jacket.

Gus used his no-nonsense voice. "Need I remind you Paige and I just got married? Now's not the time for a serious discussion about your careers. I promise, though, we'll get together soon, and I'll answer all your questions. I'll ask some too, so be ready. Got it?"

"Got it." Carlos tittered with excitement, and Miguel nodded like a bobble toy. Heidi pulled on their hands, and the three of them scampered to the dance floor.

She gave in to the eye roll and leaned into Gus. "You know we've got our hands full, don't you?"

"Nothing we can't handle together," Gus murmured. "Much as I'm enjoying this, I'm looking forward to 'just us.'" He kissed her ear.

"Me, too." She bent her head, smiling. Across the room, Rick caught her eye and motioned her to him.

"Husband," she said playfully. "I, uh, need to speak with your brother."

"Yes, wife," he answered back with a grin. "I'll be right here waitin' on you."

TAVO WATCHED as Paige floated to where his brother stood. As their heads bent together, he sighed happily. She was a keeper. And now she was his. His toes curled in anticipation.

"You think he's in love, Jess?" Rory asked. His friends moved toward him, deliberately blocking his view of Paige.

"If sappy looks count, he's a goner." Jesse clapped Tavo on the shoulder. The sensitive one. He sucked in a breath, stifling the urge to yowl.

To cover his discomfort, he said, "If I recall, and I'm never wrong, you two were the worst ever. Besides, there's nothing wrong with admiring my girl."

After a round of snorts and protests, Rory said, "That's so outrageous, I'm speechless."

Jesse lifted a brow. "If only."

"What we came to tell you, *Chief*, "Rory emphasized his nickname, "Is Jess and I got you a wedding present."

"Something just for you ..." When Jesse gave that flashy smile, it usually signaled mischief.

"Since you're the original Big Foot—or Big Body—we knew

a regular bed wouldn't work for you," Rory explained. "So we took it upon ourselves to find the largest mattress we could. You know, so you'll be comfortable ... have plenty of room."

"And not squash Paige." Jesse looked quite virtuous.

"I bet she's pretty lonesome, though, sleeping in that giant bed all by herself." Rory's brows waggled.

"It's a done deal, Chief. We installed it days ago. Well, I installed it." Jesse pointed to himself. "Ro, here, was completely useless."

"I helped him get it in the house. No easy feat, I assure you. Jess insisted on setting it up by himself. Wouldn't have it any other way."

"It was faster than giving you dot-to-dot instructions." Jesse turned to Tavo. "Paige gave Rick a list of things to pack, so your clothes and toothbrush are already there too."

His things were already at Paige's house? A new bed? This wedding had happened so fast, he hadn't considered the details. Apparently, Paige had. She had a knack for dotting i's and crossing t's. His heart wanted to thump right out of his chest, and a suspicious film covered his eyes. Drat these emotions. For lack of a better response, he clamped the two of them—his best buds—in a bear hug. "Thanks, guys."

Rory pulled away when his eye caught Vi. Tavo had heard she was in a wheelchair these days. Something about a difficult pregnancy. Only his cute little wife wasn't anywhere near her wheelchair. She was chatting and gesturing with Silas and Nat on the opposite side of the room. A growl issued from his throat.

"I'm sure she's fine, dude." Tavo wanted everyone to be as happy as he was.

Rory's long-suffering look was comical. "She will be as soon as I get some rope and tie her in the chair." He stalked off.

Tavo glanced at Jesse who only shrugged. "He adores her."

Claude and Ochee sauntered up. They also wore jeans and boots, and Ochee sported a cowboy hat. "Thought you'd want an update about Clarkston."

Tavo wanted to forget the superstar ever existed. "Make it short."

"Not much to tell," Claude said. "But I'm glad I was there. You called it, bud." His gaze rippled with sympathy. "Thank God, I walked in when I did. Clarkston was on the verge of losing it. No way Paige could handle him."

Tavo's hands fisted at his sides. It was the first he'd heard about the events leading up to Paige's swim in the ocean. "Thanks for interfering. I'd have knocked him to the moon." Small wonder she had seemed so fragile. He'd chalked it up to her near-drowning, but that had only been part of it. She'd already told him about Ed's actions before the rip current. Now, it seemed, there was more.

"Yeah, sounds like God protected you as well, else you'd have a massive lawsuit on your hands."

"As it is," Ochee pulled Tavo's dark thoughts away. "Ed immediately lawyered up. Dunno if he'll face actual prison time. More likely, a slap on the wrist. Celebrities get away with above-the-law behavior."

"Oh, yeah, he's flush with dough. Enough to pay off whoever." Claude adjusted the brim of his cowboy hat. "We put a bad enough taste in his mouth about our fair state, though. I doubt he'll return."

Tavo heartily hoped not. He'd discuss it with Paige later and get the whole story. Encourage her to talk to Pastor Mike, if needed. To all outward appearances, she'd put it behind her, but bad stuff had a way of hiding. Paige was resilient, but as her husband, protecting her was paramount. Her well-being was his responsibility. Another happy sigh escaped.

Ochee and Claude immediately stepped back when the

Chief of Police joined their small circle. He favored them with a smirk. "You two need to find a pretty girl to dance with."

Ochee made to leave, but Claude merely shifted. "I don't dance."

Tavo's dad gave him a steely look. "You do now." Ochee grabbed Claude's arm and led him away over protest.

"Aw, go easy on him, Dad. He might wanna work for you someday. The department will be better for it. He's got great instincts."

Chagrin shone in Dad's granite features so fleetingly Tavo almost missed it. "He'll be fine. But we need to talk, and your wedding seems a good time. Fresh start and all."

Tavo held up a hand. "Before you get started, I'm dying to know—How did you get in on this?" He left the rest unsaid. Paige had a legion of fans, but Dad had never been one of them.

"A very determined woman asked for my blessing so sweetly, I couldn't say no."

Tavo scrubbed a hand over his jaw, not sure what to say. Words, no matter how reasonable or sweet, rarely swayed his father. But Tavo would be the first to admit his new wife could be ... persuasive.

"When I asked her why she wanted it, she looked me straight in the eye and said, 'Because I love your son with all my heart.'" Dad cleared his throat, though his eyes were suspiciously wet. "Took a lot of guts to say that."

"Bet she was shaking in her boots," Tavo murmured. His heart rocked to an unnamed melody.

"She was. But my crusty old soul loved her for asking. I saw firsthand how much she loves you. And since I've known for a long time how you feel, I gave my blessing with no reservations."

Tavo sensed a weepy display of affection would undo both of them. "Took you long enough."

Dad pursed his lips, then laughed heartily, easing the emotion pulsating around them. Once they got past the mirth, he said soberly, "You know I wanted you to have a different career path."

Oh, here it comes. "Seems to me you were pretty set on me singing for my supper." Tavo confronted it head-on.

"I was. A voice like yours doesn't come along often, and I wanted you to make the most of it." He held a hand up when Tavo started to speak. "It wasn't a bad idea. But I can see now it wasn't God's idea.

"Son, I should have picked up on what made you tick much sooner. I'm glad you stood your ground about that too. You're an excellent police officer. You carry authority well, and I find no fault in your decision-making skills." His eyes had taken on an earnestness that melted any resistance on Tavo's part.

"I enjoy singing, Dad, but it's not my passion." He looked down. "Valiant's my passion. All I've ever wanted to do is follow in your footsteps." The last phrase came out in a whisper.

"It's a hard job, bud. But you're not pushing at a closed door anymore. If my years of experience count for anything, I'll share what I know. If it's within my grasp, I'll get you the training for how God's leading you.

"I'm not going to live forever. Thinking more about retirement these days." His eyes scanned the room and focused on Heidi. "Spending more time with your mom and Heidi, and whoever else comes along"—His brows lifted infinitesimally—"sounds mighty appealing.

"It's a comfort to know you and Rick are fine men." He took Tavo's arm, and they embraced. Tears slid down Tavo's cheeks at his father's words. Mopping his face, Tavo turned and found Paige standing next to him.

He leaned down. "A couple of big yakky birds told me I'm staying with you tonight."

A pretty pink stain spread across her cheeks. "It's why people get married, Gus. Two people becoming one. And, as much as I love you, I'm not living at your dad's." When she flashed her only-for-him smile, his knees went swimmy.

He wrapped his arms around her waist and hugged her tightly. "Agreed. I'm lovin' what happens when you make up your mind."

"I was hoping you'd sing since it's our wedding."

"What do you want me to sing, doll?"

"Whatever you want. The ones you sang ... recently will be fine."

The night he poured his heart out onstage and said he wanted to marry her. "The night everything went wrong?"

She took his hand, entwining her fingers through his. "Not everything. That was when I knew my love for you was still alive."

"That night also let loose a string of disasters." He ran a hand through his hair. "Mercy. How did we survive the last few weeks?"

She shook her head. "What kept me going was the desire to hear your golden voice again."

"So you planned a wedding and a reception so I would sing to you?" he teased.

Her hand tightened on his. "I planned to marry you either way."

He leaned down, so his lips brushed hers. "Just so you know, I'll sing to you for the rest of your life." He kissed her again. She was possibly the sweetest thing he'd ever tasted.

Slowly, they made their way to the stage, greeting family and friends. Plenty of time to reflect on love's crooked path.

God had taken Tavo's simple desire for reconciliation and accomplished more than he could ask or think. Beside him, one of Paige's helpers welcomed everyone to the wedding dinner. Tavo stared around the room mesmerized. God had turned the worst mistake of his life into an ongoing blessing. He watched his fairy-child twirl around with Carlos and Miguel. Mending the relationship with his mom never occurred to him, but God not only exposed the hidden reef, he'd also knocked it into submission. Reconciliation had spilled over for Paige too, with her dad.

Lush acceptance flowed from spirit to spirit, inviting everyone to partake. It hung in the air, a lovely wild plant, poised for growth.

After a brief conference with Rick, Tavo swallowed and took the mic. Paige stood with her parents, positively vibrating with joy. His confidence soared to the point he no longer needed to summon his stage persona. He nodded to Rick. Taking his cue, his brother let the opening strains of music undulate into every nook and cranny of the transcendent venue.

A reverent hush fell over the group as he gazed upward. *Thank You, Lord.* He looked tenderly at the woman he'd never stopped loving. "Every song I sing is for you, Paige. You're the love of my life." A chuckle rose from his chest. "It's been a minute since we fell in love ... but you've been worth the wait."

Something new crept into the timbre of his voice as he sang. Its velvety caress captured hearts as it grew and rolled like a mighty wave through the reception hall.

The love of God. Warm. Inviting. Eternal.

AUTHOR'S NOTE

I hope you enjoyed Tavo and Paige's story. At times, they'd cooperate with me. More often than not, though, they'd act difficult. I was always the last one to know their thoughts. But they persevered, and their ending was quite satisfying. Despite their wild fluctuations throughout the story, I never lost faith they were much better together. Can't you see their love growing sweeter as they live useful, happy lives? Their big hearts make them an irresistible force that will draw the lost and hurting to Christ.

As the story closed, I deliberately left a thread or two open. The twins could use more page time, and I'm not sure Pastor Mike's story is finished. If you'd like to see what's next, go to my website at marypatjohns.com and sign up for my monthly newsletter. It has all my book news, giveaways, and lots of other goodies.

Please consider leaving a review on Amazon if you enjoyed *Waitin' On Paige*. Two or three sentences and the star rating helps tremendously. It's also a way of telling an author *thank you*.

ACKNOWLEDGMENTS

I'm very thankful for Linda Fulkerson, publisher of Scrivenings Press. She does a fabulous job of being there for her authors and provides the tools we need to succeed as writers. She also listens to my vision for book covers and surpasses my expectations. I'm also thankful for Regina Merrick and Heidi Glick, my content and line editors. My writing shines because of your expertise. And Gwen Gage, my longtime crit partner—your help in getting "the top button buttoned right" with my rough drafts is indispensable.

My family is so supportive, I don't know where to start. My ever-patient husband listens to my half-formed ideas, picks up the slack whenever I have a deadline, and loves me through all of it. My children actually enjoy hearing about the writing and marketing process and are always asking me what's next. And my grandchildren, just by being themselves, help me remember there is life beyond the writing world.

And to my Lord. You promised to supply everything I needed to finish this book. That strong assurance helped me cross the finish line with joy. The words may have come from my hand, but it's your story in every sense that matters.

ABOUT THE AUTHOR

Mary Pat Johns' writing career began once she retired from teaching speech and writing. She has written devotions for an online publication, had short stories published by *Chicken Soup for the Soul*, and wrote a column for the *Victoria Advocate*, a local newspaper.

Countin' On Jesse, her first novel, debuted in 2023, and books 2 & 3 of the Valiant series, *Lovin' On Red* and *Glitter and the Grouch*, released in 2024. God put it in her heart to tell stories of brave veterans and their reintegration into civilian life after suffering the traumas of war.

She writes Christian romance because when we see life through the hope of Christ's sacrifice, we find that happily ever after is God's idea.

ALSO BY MARY PAT JOHNS

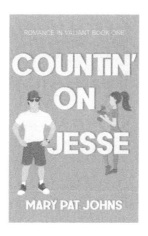

Romance in Valiant—Book One

Accountant Brenna McKinley only wants what's best for Peeps, the wildly popular gym in Valiant, Texas. But when money goes missing, and she's the obvious suspect, will she be able to clear her name or face criminal charges? Keeping her dream job matters, but falling in love with her boss isn't part of the plan. Neither is the creepy guy stalking her.

Young veteran Jesse Jacobs manages and co-owns Peeps. He needs help to gain accreditation for the exercise facility, and his new accountant is all in. But is she who she seems? Too bad he's falling for her like a man with no parachute. When the pressure builds, PTSD renders him moody and volatile, risking everything he loves.

Get your copy here:

https://scrivenings.link/countinonjesse

Romance in Valiant—Book Two

Rory is a wildly successful contractor with all the right connections. He has everything, except the woman who sees past his missing foot. If only the tiny redhead he's insanely attracted to would go on a date with him, it could work, but Vi refuses.

Licensed massage therapist Vi Summers needs her childhood home remodeled, and Rory Spence is the perfect man for the job. Only he's the last person she wants to work with. Despite Rory's reputation as a flirt, his tender attention to getting her house right helps Vi see into his heart. Too bad her past mistakes prevent a future relationship.

Drawn together like magnets, they navigate trouble with illegal squatters, family expectations, and fire. Will they finally be honest with each other, or will their secrets tear them apart?

Get your copy here:

https://scrivenings.link/lovinonred

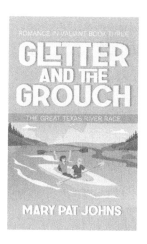

Romance in Valiant—Book Three

Silas and Nat don't get along, but they can't leave each other alone either. When a prank goes terribly wrong at their workplace, they are faced with an impossible choice.

Either they compete in a canoe race to prove they can work together or forfeit their futures at Peeps. Quitting isn't the norm for either of them, but their boss isn't giving an inch. He assures them they can accomplish anything they set their minds to, even if it's 3 days and 260 miles of river.

There's only one catch—they'll have to be in the same boat.

Will they reach deep inside to find out what they're made of? Or will they succumb to the physical rigors of the event and the machinations of Nat's controlling ex?

Get your copy here:

https://scrivenings.link/glitterandthegrouch

Stay up-to-date on your favorite books and authors with our free e-newsletters.

ScriveningsPress.com

Made in the USA
Middletown, DE
13 June 2025